A PIRATE'S LIFE FOR RI

SERIES BY NELLIE H. STEELE

Cate Kensie Mysteries

Shadow Slayers Stories

Lily & Cassie by the Sea Mysteries

Pearl Party Mysteries

Middle Age is Murder Cozy Mysteries

Duchess of Blackmoore Mysteries

Maggie Edwards Adventures

Clif & Ri on the Sea Adventures

Shelving Magic

A PIRATE'S LIFE FOR RI

A HIGH SEAS PIRATE ADVENTURE

CLIF & RI ON THE SEA
BOOK TWO

NELLIE H. STEELE

CHAPTER 1

The tip of the sword grazed Henrietta's chin as she stared down the length of it. Her breath came in ragged gasps as she bit the side of her cheek in frustration. She would lose this battle unless something changed quickly.

She licked her lips, her eyes darting to the side. A giant swell approached off the starboard side of the ship. It would smack into the ship in seconds, pitching the vessel sideways. If she timed it right, she could use the rocking ship as a diversion and escape.

Her fingers curled around her own sword and she fingered the gun tucked into her belt with the other hand. She flicked her gaze to her opponent as she counted the seconds.

The giant wave slammed into the ship's side with a boom. As the craft rolled, she parried, ducking under the sword, knocking her feathered cap from her head, and twisting uphill on the deck. She darted a few steps away, her opponent quick to recover and chase her.

Henrietta climbed the steps two at a time toward the deck

housing the ship's wheel. She slipped and slid across the wet floorboards to the opposite railing. With her sword at the ready, she spun to face her opponent.

He took no mercy on her, his sword crashing down against hers with a force that brought her to her knees. She gritted her teeth as the metal blades screeched, sliding against each other.

"You cannot win," he hissed.

She groaned as the pressure against her blade increased. "Watch me," she spat back, using the force of her entire body to throw him off. She slashed the blade in the air, driving her opponent back a few steps as she swung the sword, smacking it against his blade time and time again.

He darted backward, fending off her blows with flicks of his wrist. His tricorn hat tumbled from his head, crashing onto the deck. She pinned him against the railing, but he easily shoved her away from him.

"My turn," he said with a vicious grin. He parried and raised his sword, driving her backward with a similar maneuver. When he'd pinned her against the railing, he held his sword to her neck again. "Give up. You can't win."

"Never!" she shouted. She struggled against him, trying to find the leverage to push him away from her. Her feet slipped on the wet decking.

He arched an eyebrow at her and lowered his sword, taking a step backward with a sigh. She flung the sword up, holding it to his chin, and arched an eyebrow.

He rolled his eyes at her and flicked it away with his fingertip. She raised it again, anger pinching her features.

"Do you wish me to say you've won?"

"Yes," she said with her chin raised high.

His chest rose and fell as he heaved a sigh. "Fine, Ri. You've won. Are you happy now?"

She raised her chin even higher as she lowered her sword and gave her brother a curt nod. "Infinitely."

"You will not be if you are ever faced with a fight against someone other than your own brother, you know."

"Perhaps I will not lose," she said, shoving her sword into its sheath.

Clifton retrieved his hat from the floor, dusting it off before settling it onto his head. He arched an eyebrow over his dark eyes. "You will."

Henrietta set her lips in a thin line, displeasure apparent on her delicate features. "Why must you taunt me?"

"I am not taunting you, I am teaching you."

"You are showing off. Using your considerable skills with a sword to belittle me."

He lifted his chin and raised a finger in the air. "Ah, I see. And you think the other pirates will not use their considerable skills against you in a heated battle?"

Henrietta cocked her head at him as they descended the stairs to the main deck. "I thought your skills to be legendary. Was I mistaken?"

He offered her an amused glance. "Yes, they are legendary, though all other pirates' skills will be quite good."

"Are you saying mine are not?"

"I am saying yours could use some polish, Ri."

Henrietta snatched her hat from the deck, striking his arm with it before she donned it.

He leaned away, raising his arm to defend himself. "I am only trying to help!"

Henrietta drew her sword and raised it in a challenge. "Let us try again."

"There is no need to–"

Henrietta waved the sword in his face, silencing any further discussion. She arched her dark eyebrows and stared at him in a silent challenge.

"Ri, I–"

She raised the sword to his chin, grazing his beard.

"Henrietta," he warned in a low voice.

"Are you too cowardly?" she questioned. "Afraid you may lose?"

He cast his eyes down, giving his head a shake as he squashed his lips together. With one swift motion, he swung his arm up, knocking her sword to the side. She stumbled as the blow took her off-guard, tumbling a few steps forward. Clif did not wait for her to recover, ramming into her side as he pulled a knife hidden in his boot. He slid the tip under her chin, poking the flesh and threatening to pierce it as he pinned her against his cabin door.

"Ah!" she cried out as he smashed against her.

"I will not lose," he said.

"You've cheated!"

"Do you not expect no-good scoundrels like pirates to cheat, Ri?"

"You've overpowered me because you are bigger!"

"Every pirate on these seas is bigger than you, sister. You are a woman, whether you prefer to acknowledge it or not. You are weaker."

"I am not weak!" she cried, squeezing her eyes shut as a tear rolled down her cheek.

He kept her pinned, his strong arms preventing her from escaping. "Physically, you are. You do not have that advantage."

"Then I shall never win," she lamented, her voice wistful.

"Untrue."

She opened her eyes, sliding them sideways to glance at him. "How?"

He raised his eyebrows at her, the knife still threatening at her throat. "You cannot overpower them, Ri, no matter how good of a swordswoman you are. You must be smarter than them. And that I know you can be."

Henrietta's chest heaved as she considered his words. She cocked her head at him and raised her eyes to his, arching her eyebrows.

She ceased her struggle against him, no longer wishing to shove him off. Instead, she allowed him to lean into her before she slipped to the deck below. She slid between his stretched legs and scrambled to her feet as he fell into the cabin door. He spun to face her, but she'd already raised her gun.

With an arched eyebrow, she cocked the gun and said, "I win."

A sideways grin crossed his face as he raised his arms in defeat. "This time you have, yes."

She held the gun at arm's length a moment longer before she lowered it, flicking her eyebrows upward as she stowed it in her belt.

"I knew you could do it," Clif added as he sheathed his sword.

She cocked her head at him as another wave smashed into the side of *The Henton*. They spread their legs in a wide stance as they rode out the massive hit.

Henrietta took a steadying step as the ship rolled with the swelling ocean. "Did you? Yet, rather than tell me, you forced me to endure that ridiculous sword fight."

"You must learn, Ri," he answered, removing his hat and shaking water from it.

She grimaced at him. "I think you just like to lord over me that you are the better pirate."

He arched an eyebrow, grinning at her as he backed to the cabin door and swung it open, motioning for her to enter. "I shall take advantage while I still can."

Henrietta ducked into the room, pulling her hat from her head and studying it in the dim lantern's light. She frowned down at the sodden headpiece.

"What is it?" Clif asked, striding to the desk and collapsing into the chair.

"My feather," Henrietta said, the grimace still on her lips. "It is as limp as a drunken sailor."

He flicked a gaze at the soppy black feather poking from her tricorn hat. "I told you not to get the feathered cap."

She snapped her eyes upward, an unimpressed expression on her features. "Yes, I know. But I prefer it."

"Well, then if you insist upon having a feather in your cap, you must accept that it will be a sodden one when you have been smashed by a wave."

"I wouldn't have been if you hadn't insisted on that ridiculous battle." She plopped into the hammock on the far side of the room with a pout.

Clif eyed her before returning to his charts. "You know, Ri, I only challenge you so that you are safe when it comes to a real battle."

Henrietta sat up straighter, her legs dangling over the fabric. "Do you foresee one in the future?"

"Yes, of course. *Neptune's Servant* saw many battles in her day. Before I sank her in favor of *The Henton*."

"*The Henton* has yet to see one," Henrietta lamented, tossing herself back into the hammock with a sigh.

"Do not be too eager," he warned as his compass slid from one side of the desk to the other as the ship rocked again.

Henrietta flicked her dark eyes toward him, reaching out to catch the metal item before it hit the floor. "Awaiting action months after setting sail is hardly overeager."

She climbed from the hammock and dumped the navigation tool on the desk before she strode across the floor, pacing from one side of the cabin to the other.

"Sit down, Ri, relax," he said, his eyes never leaving his map.

She stuck her hands on her hips with a sigh. "Relax, Ri. Sit down, Ri. Practice for battle, Ri. Always waiting, but never achieving anything. When you asked me to join you on *The Henton*, I expected excitement! I had more excitement as mistress of Whispering Manor, guarding our treasure than as a pirate on the high seas."

"You exaggerate."

Henrietta slammed her hands down on the desk's wooden top. "I do not."

She leaned forward toward him, her features set. "I want all the excitement you promised I'd have as a pirate."

He lifted his eyes from the map in front of him, gazing up at her. "Are you certain?"

"Yes," she said without skipping a beat. "You bragged to me about sea battles. Blustered on about swinging across to raid another ship. Boasted about blowing holes into things. So far, the only casualty of my time as co-captain has been my feather." She flung her hand at the broken plume.

Clif arched an eyebrow at her, a devilish grin crossing his face. "I can give you excitement. And I guarantee we'll see at least one battle if not two."

Henrietta straightened, crossing her arms over her chest and raising her chin. "You guarantee?"

"I do," he answered, smoothing the map onto the desk and nodding.

Henrietta resumed her pacing, the heels of her boots slapping against the wooden floorboards as she stalked back and forth. "Forgive me, dear brother, for doubting you when you already promised so much yet delivered so little."

A concerned expression contorted his features. "Delivered so little?"

He leapt from his seat and stepped into Henrietta's path,

blocking her from moving forward. "Every day, we sail about and see sights you've never seen before in your life. We have engaged in sword battles, gun battles, and we've swum with sharks. We've sailed the Caribbean for months, enjoying life to its fullest. And yet you claim I've delivered so little?"

She stared at her brother for a moment before she flung her hands up, sinking into a squat. "I want *real* battles, Clif. Try to understand. I feel as though I am at home with Mother and Father. You are putting on a show for me. I am under the pretense of being a pirate. I sail about on your ship being protected from all manners of harm and strife."

"I thought we were having a nice time."

"It's not a nice time I'm after! I want excitement. Adventure. I want to be a *real* pirate, Clif. I don't want to pretend to be one!"

"You may regret your request when the ship is rocked by a cannonball courtesy of Her Majesty's Navy."

"So be it. At least I shall know I lived."

He arched an eyebrow at her, his hands on his hips as he considered her statement.

"Are you quite certain? I feel responsible for you, you know?"

"That's just it! I don't want you to feel responsible. Do you feel responsible for the others on this ship?"

"Yes, of course, I am their captain." He cocked his head at her. "Well, co-captain, but still, their lives are in my hands."

"And do you treat them with kid gloves? Do you slink about the seas avoiding conflict?"

He stalked away from her, returning to his map. "You know better than that, Ri. I did not amass a fortune by slinking away from battle."

"Yet now you do."

He tugged his lips to the side at her words. "Perhaps I have been a little less adventurous of late."

"You don't say," she answered as she plopped into the hammock again.

"I want to be sure you're ready."

"I am more than ready. My first battle will likely be terrifying. I am not a fool. I realize full well what I seek. But I cannot become battle-hardened by not ever seeing a battle."

Clifton drew in a deep breath and collapsed into the desk's chair. The flame of the lantern flickered, casting long shadows across his chiseled features, hidden under the scruffy beard.

He tugged open a drawer of the desk and pulled a silver flask from within, unscrewing the cap. He pressed the metal to his lips, flinging the container upward to down some of the alcoholic beverage.

He breathed out a sigh as he held the container toward Henrietta, wiping at his chin with his other hand. She waved it away.

He raised his eyebrows at her. "You want to be a pirate. Rum comes with the territory. Drink up."

"You're ridiculous," she said, swiping the flask from his hands and drinking from it.

She thrust it back in his direction. "There, happy?"

"Very," he answered with a grin as he accepted it, recapping it and setting it on the desk. He reached into the drawer again and withdrew a large leather tome.

Papers stuck from within at odd angles and writings, sketches, and notations filled the pages. He slapped it against the desk and pulled it open.

Henrietta stood from the hammock and wandered over, craning her neck to study the book. "What is that?"

"My idea book."

She glanced from the book to him, her expression quizzical.

He flipped to the page he sought, tapping the illustration at the center of the yellowed paper.

Henrietta studied it. "What is it?"

"Guaranteed adventure," he said with a gleam of mischief in his eye.

CHAPTER 2

*H*enrietta rubbed at her chin as she studied the illustration on the page. She arched an eyebrow and flicked a gaze at her brother. "A broken-down structure like that is a guaranteed adventure?"

Clif nodded without a word.

She straightened and crossed her arms staring down at the drawing. The large doorway framed by pillars appeared to crumble on the edges. Squiggled lines poked from its blocks.

Henrietta wrinkled her nose. "How?"

With a coy smirk, Clifton flipped the page.

Henrietta read the words at the top aloud. "Cuidad de Diamantés. What does it mean?"

"City of Diamonds."

"City of Diamonds?" Henrietta repeated.

Clifton flicked his eyebrows up, smirking at her. "Diamonds, Ri. Large, goose egg-sized diamonds. Diamond-encrusted chalices. Diamond jewelry. Diamonds so large you can only carry one per hand, just lying in wait for the crew brave enough to seek them out."

He closed his hands into fists, waving them at her.

Henrietta arched an eyebrow at him. "And you happen to know where this City of Diamonds is, do you?"

"No," Clif admitted. "I only have a few clues. Odd references. Stories I've picked up in my travels."

"Then how do you propose we find it? And what makes you so sure someone hasn't beaten us to it?"

Clif stood and wandered around the cabin. Henrietta plopped into his desk chair to study the drawn image in his journal.

"If someone had beaten us to it, we'd have heard about it. I am well-connected."

Henrietta perused the page, flipping to another and staring at the scrawling. "Black Jack was well-known. Clifton is not."

He ceased his pacing, shooting her a glance over his shoulder. "I still have my connections, I assure you, Ri."

She glanced up through her eyelashes. "All right, I believe you. No one has found the City of Diamonds. Then how do you propose we find it? And why have you not sought it out already?"

He grinned at her, spreading his arms from one end of the desk to the other and leaning his weight against it. "I have not sought it out before because I lacked the ability to find it."

"And now? You have stumbled upon new information that will allow us to navigate to it?"

Clif straightened and crossed his arms, shaking his head. "No. I have no new information."

Henrietta slammed the book shut, her lips forming a frown. "Then where is my guaranteed adventure? Are we to sail the seas in search of it? Is that the adventure?"

"No," he answered. "Of course not. Where's the fun in

that? You may crave adventure. I desire treasure. And fame." He pulled his lips to one side in a sideways smirk.

Henrietta rose to her feet, matching his stance. "And again I ask: how do you propose we find this adventure, treasure, and fame?"

"Simple."

"I fail to see how. You have amassed a book's worth of clues," Henrietta answered, picking up the leather-bound volume and waving it in the air, "and, by your own admission, still cannot find it."

"Yes, but one thing has changed."

She arched her eyebrow at him again, prodding for a response.

His lips curled into an amused grin. "I have you now as a co-captain."

Henrietta let the book flop from her hands onto the desk. "You jest."

"I do not."

She rolled her eyes and stalked away toward the rear of the room, her arms crossed. "You do. You ridicule me. First with the mock battle and now with this."

"I am being quite genuine, Ri, I assure you."

"You are not. You have first-hand knowledge of these waters. You have collected the clues. Why would you suggest me as a co-captain will make you any more likely to find this lost city if not in jest?"

Clif skirted the desk and closed the distance between them, spinning her around to face him. "Because I could not piece the clues together, but you can. You are far more clever than I."

Henrietta cocked her head, refusing to make eye contact with him. "You are correct on the last count."

He squeezed her arms. "I am correct on all counts. With your acumen and my savvy, we are an unstoppable team."

Henrietta raised her eyebrows, flicking her pouty gaze up to her brother's dark eyes. She studied him for a moment, finding no untruth in his words. "Unstoppable?"

He smirked, squeezing her shoulders again before stalking around the room. "The City of Diamonds is but one of many conquests. No more raiding ships for treasure. We shall only do that for fun!"

He waved a finger in the air. "No, we shall pursue prizes no one else can pursue."

He flipped his book open and pointed to a cryptic drawing. "We shall solve all the puzzles."

He danced across the room in a fake sword-fighting, thrusting his imaginary sword forward to stab his invisible victim. "Vanquish all the foes."

"And grow rich until we retire in our old age to enjoy our spoils." He collapsed into the hammock, setting it swinging back and forth in a lazy dance.

Henrietta raised her chin and stuck her hands on her hips. "And we shall have an adventure."

"And you shall have twenty hats, all with feathers. You may change them out every time a wave strikes you and wilts your plume."

Henrietta bit her lower lip as she considered the prospect. "All right. I'm game. What must we do?"

Clif kicked his feet as he flung himself out of the hammock. "You must study."

He grabbed the journal from the desk and shoved it into her hands. "Read all there is to know about the City of Diamonds from my notes."

He collapsed into the chair behind the desk, pulling a map toward him.

"And what will you do?" she inquired.

"I shall plot a course. No more dallying in the Caribbean."

"Plot a course for where? I doubt I will have any answers

even by this evening from this unintelligible scrawl you call notes."

"We shall go to Tortuga and there we can ask the blind beggar more about the legend."

Henrietta wrinkled her nose. "Blind beggar?"

Clifton traced his finger along the paper. "Yes. He supposedly has seen a map to the city."

"And why did he not find it? Where is the map?"

"Torn to pieces," he answered, his eyes not leaving the map, "and his eyes gouged out."

Henrietta's eyes widened at the statement. "What?"

He flicked a devilish gaze upward at her. "You asked for danger. I am providing it to the fullest. Men have sought Cuidad de Diamantés and paid a horrible price."

She suppressed a shiver, a frown on her lips. "Let us hope we do not."

"Indeed. I rather like my eyes."

Henrietta tugged one side of her lips back in a frown and shook her head at him. "I am pleased your sense of humor remains intact, Clif. If we find ourselves destitute, you could perform at a traveling comedy show."

"Always have a backup plan, Ri." He dipped a quill into the ink and scrawled something on a scrap of paper. "Might you call for Johnson on your way?"

Henrietta flopped into the hammock. "On my way where?"

Clif raised his eyebrows. "Oh, I thought you were heading out for some sunshine on the deck."

"No, I have studying to do. I cannot fritter away my time with such trivialities."

"Hmmm," Clif grumbled. "You do not wish to stretch your legs? Ponder your task ahead. Take one last breath of sea air before you buckle down to your work?"

Henrietta crossed her legs at the ankles and turned the

corners of her mouth downward as she shook her head.

"Are you certain?"

She sat up straighter, the hammock swaying under her. "Are you attempting to get me to do your work for you?"

He leaned back in his chair. It creaked under his weight as he puckered his lips and tented his fingers. "No, I simply imagined if you happened to be on deck where Mr. Johnson is, you could mention to him that I am seeking him to discuss our course."

"Yet, I will not be on deck as I am busy beginning my project." Henrietta settled back into the hammock again and flipped the book open.

Clifton puckered his lips and narrowed his eyes at her. "You have several days to complete your study, Ri. No need to rush."

She lifted her eyes to him, sliding them closed to slits. "You really want me to go find Mr. Johnson for you, don't you?"

He shook his head, his lips forming an upside-down smile. "As captain, I thought you may enjoy ordering him to the cabin."

"Co-captain, as you oft remind me. And I have already given Mr. Johnson orders. It is hardly the first time I shall order sailors about on this ship. Go and find him and order him here yourself as co-captain."

"Yes. A role I am quite used to fulfilling. Just figured I would give you a go."

"I don't want a go," Henrietta said as she slouched lower and paged through the journal, stopping a few times to study an illustration or a notation.

Clif wrinkled his nose and bit his lower lip, heaving a sigh. He gripped the arms of the chair and pushed himself up with a groan.

He circled the desk past the swinging hammock.

"Oh, Clif," Henrietta said, waving a finger in the air, "before you go find Johnson, may I trouble you for the quill and some paper?"

Clifton's eyebrows shot upward as he stared down at her. "You wish me to fetch you items for note-taking?"

She flicked a gaze to him, lifting a shoulder into a shrug. "While you're up."

"Perhaps you should sit at the desk whilst you work. The quill and paper are at the ready."

Henrietta returned her gaze to the book, studying another illustration of an odd-looking temple. "No, I am quite comfortable here in the hammock."

He huffed a sigh and stepped back to the desk, snatching a quill and paper from it. With a bow, he offered them to her on his upturned hands. "Are you certain you would not like me to stand holding the ink for you, m'lady?"

"No, that won't be necessary," she said, shooing him away as she flipped to the page he'd shown her earlier.

He stood and narrowed his eyes at her as she swung lazily in the hammock, her eyes scanning the pages. He strode from the room in search of his first mate, finding him on the main deck.

"Captain," the rugged man greeted him. "What orders?"

"Make course for Tortuga," Clif said. "One night in port, no more. Tell the men to keep their wits, we sail the following morning at sunrise."

Mr. Johnson raised his eyebrows, running a hand through his thick, dark curls. "I smell a plan, sir."

Clifton grinned at him. "I have one, yes."

"Information on a large bounty?" the man questioned as they strolled the length of the docks.

"Something like that."

"Do you plan to be this coy when we sail off for it?" Johnson inquired, his hands clasped behind his back.

They climbed to the deck above. "No, I do not. We seek Cuidad de Diamantés."

Mr. Johnson ceased his forward motion, grinding to a halt at the words. He snapped his gaze up to Clif's face, studying it, searching to determine if he spoke in jest. "Captain…"

Clif wiggled his eyebrows as he leaned against the railing. "Yes, Johnson?"

"Surely, you are not serious? Many a sailor has been lost in the pursuit of such fabled stories as the City of Diamonds."

"And what a glorious claim to our fame when we find it!"

"But, Captain, no one has found it. It's a myth. A legend."

Clif crossed his arms, eyeing the blue horizon. "One man has information."

Mr. Johnson wrinkled his nose and shook his head. "That man is a drunkard with a vivid imagination. Nothing more. He tells his tales for a donation and uses it to fill himself with drink."

"It exists, Johnson, we just need to find it."

Mr. Johnson stared at the azure sky filled with fluffy white clouds as he formed his response.

"Have I ever steered you wrong in the past?"

"No, sir," the man admitted.

Clif firmed his jaw and nodded at him. "Then get us on course to Tortuga. One night only. And then we move on to retrieve an item crucial to the search."

Clif trotted down the stairs as Mr. Johnson called over the railing, "Have we any idea where this item may be, sir?"

Clif shot him a glance over his shoulder and grinned. "Hideaway Bay."

CHAPTER 3

$\mathcal{H}$enrietta crossed her arms and cocked her hip, staring at her brother. He stared back, lounging with his feet on his desk and his chair rocking underneath him on two legs.

"Are you joking?"

Clif flung out his arms. "Why is everyone always asking me that?"

"Hideaway Bay? We must make port in Hideaway Bay?"

"It is where we stored our treasure."

Henrietta flung her arms out to the sides, her hands slapping her thighs. "A treasure we left behind when we faked our own deaths!"

"And a piece of which we now need and must retrieve." He let the front legs of the chair smack down onto the floor with a thud. "I thought you craved adventure."

"Adventure, yes. This isn't adventure, it is stupidity."

Clif frowned at her, his lips wrinkling. "It is not."

Her eyebrows shot up, and she paced the floor of the cabin. "Isn't it? What do you propose we do? Dock *The*

Henton in port and stroll into town for an ale before heading to the house and asking if we might have a look around?"

Clif snorted a laugh. "Of course not."

Henrietta spun to face him, an eyebrow arched as she sought his plan.

"We'll have to be pirates, Ri," he answered.

"Explain your meaning."

Clif rolled his eyes and rose from his seat, pacing the floor. "We shall lower anchor in the hidden cove, row to shore, sneak into the house, steal back the portion of the treasure needed to seek the City of Diamonds, and sail away. Simple." He crossed his arms and stared at her.

Henrietta's head wobbled as she threw out her arms again. "Oh, yes, quite simple. We must simply break into the house while making certain no one identifies us."

"The house should be empty."

"How do you know?"

"Carolina hasn't sold it yet."

Henrietta flopped into the hammock, considering the statement. "Why not?"

Clif shrugged as he returned to his desk chair and sipped the ale from his stein. "I haven't a clue. Perhaps she took our supposed deaths harder than we expected."

Henrietta shot him a glance. "That may be true in your case. I doubt it is true in mine. Which is what befuddles me. Why hold on to Whispering Manor of all places?" She turned pensive, biting her lower lip as she focused on her boots.

"That's not true. Carolina looked up to you."

Henrietta let out a sharp laugh. "Ha! She detested me. Though she always had a soft spot for you. Perhaps she held on to the house since you owned it last."

"My sources tell me she's living there."

Henrietta snapped her gaze to her brother, her eyebrows squashing together. "What?"

He shrugged as he sipped at the stein again.

Henrietta leapt from her seat, parading around the room. "Why would she take up residence in *my* home?"

"It isn't your home any longer, Ri. Henrietta Blanchard is dead."

Henrietta balled her fists at her sides. "And my little sister has moved into my role!"

"Did you expect Whispering Manor to sit idle for years, devoid of a mistress because none could follow in your footsteps?"

"No, though I did not expect Carolina to be the next mistress. Her tastes are quite different from mine. Whatever would she want the house for? Surely she'd find it too large or ostentatious."

"Perhaps she feels close to you there."

Henrietta spun on her heel with a roll of her eyes and continued her pacing.

"You misjudge her, Ri. She idolized you as much as you claim she idolized me."

"Untrue."

"You're wrong. Carolina admired the strong woman you were...are. If she saw you now, she would be quite impressed."

Henrietta offered a grunt in response as she chewed her thumbnail. "So, whilst we break into our sister's home to rob it, we run the risk of being spotted by her."

"No, she is away."

Henrietta stopped and stared at him, her arms falling to her sides. "How do you know all of this?"

He leaned back in his chair, kicking his feet up again. "I have my sources."

Henrietta flicked her eyebrows upward and crossed her arms again. "Let us hope they are correct, and we do not come face to face with our strict little sister, lest she turn us into the law."

Clif let his arm fall to the chair's wooden arm. "She isn't *that* bad, Ri. Do you forget she wanted to sail on my pirate ship?"

"She wanted to sail on your ship. She did not realize you were a pirate."

"Still, while she may not be as adventurous as you, she is far more outgoing than you realize."

Henrietta sank into the hammock, resting her elbows against her thighs. "Are we speaking of the same Carolina? The bookworm who rarely left her room?"

"Yes, we are speaking of the same Carolina," Clif answered with a roll of his eyes. "That Carolina who was quite studious, I agree, married a researcher and is currently traveling on an expedition with him."

"I am surprised he wrangled her from her room and down the aisle. Did she marry with a book in her hands?"

"That I do not know," Clif said as he rose to his feet. "What matters is that the house is empty, making it easy for us to sneak inside and retrieve what we need."

"Let us hope no one catches us knowing the house is empty."

Clif perched on the corner of the desk, one leg dangling over the front edge. "I have the perfect cover for that."

"You always do, brother."

He grinned at her and wiggled his eyebrows. "I told you I'm quite a good pirate."

"And what is this fool-proof plan?"

"Simple. There is a story running around Hideaway Bay, and I plan to capitalize on it. It should come in handy should we ever need to return for any more of our special items."

Henrietta's eyebrows squashed together as she glanced up at him. "Story?"

He offered her a mischievous grin, a gleam in his dark

eyes. "It's turning into a bit of a legend, really. Quite impressive given the small amount of time that has passed. But I am not surprised."

Henrietta flung her hands out to the sides. "Well, are you going to reveal the legend or continue to play coy?"

He frowned at her and wrinkled his nose. "I was quite enjoying playing coy."

He launched from the desk, pacing the floor of the cabin. "But I shall tell you. I think you shall enjoy the story. You see, since your tragic death, a rumor persists that Whispering Manor is haunted."

She guffawed at the story, her eyes floating to the ceiling. "Haunted? How ridiculous. By whom? Is it the ghost of my dead husband who drove me to my death? Or perhaps some other specter that caused me to throw myself over the widow's walk?"

Clif spun to face her, arching an eyebrow. "No, Ri. The house is haunted by none other than–" He paused, jabbing a finger toward her. "You."

"Me?" she cried. "I am the ghost roaming Whispering Manor?"

"That is the word about town. The locals swear you appear there, roaming the house, or turning up on the widow's walk, constantly searching for The Captain even after your death."

Henrietta stood and stalked to the window overlooking the rear of the ship. She stared at the calm seas in their wake. "How absolutely preposterous. What an outrageous tale. To think if I should actually be dead, I would roam the house in search of William is beyond belief."

"Your hopeful widow act made an impression. You should be pleased, Ri. Your performance proved so truthful, people believe even in death that you cannot rest as you search for your husband."

"Ridiculous drivel," Henrietta said with a shake of her head. "Although I suppose at least I am still being talked about."

She spun to face him, finding his eyes upon her and a grin on his face. "I thought that prospect of becoming a local legend may please you."

"It does after some thought, though, I fail to see how this helps us."

Clif held up a finger before retreating to a trunk across the space. He kicked it open with his foot and reached inside, drawing out a white dress. "The tale says you wander the house in a white dress."

Henrietta arched an eyebrow at the white fabric he waved at her, flicking her gaze up to him for further explanation.

Clif let his arms fall, the white fabric sweeping across the floor as his shoulders slumped and the grin left his face. "Really, Ri?"

"I fail to see what this legend has to do with burglarizing my former home."

"It's quite simple. You will don the dress and sneak into the house while I fetch the item, and then we'll return to the beach. Anyone who sees you will assume you are merely a ghost. The legend will grow stronger and we will not be caught." He grinned again, waving the gauzy fabric at her.

"Are you mad?" she inquired, crossing her arms.

"No."

"You propose that I wear that dress to sneak into Carolina's home whilst you steal back whatever it is you say we need. That is your brilliant plan."

"It is quite a brilliant plan. It will work. And if you'd like you could even put on quite the show and wander the widow's walk. Anyone spotting you will eat it up, Ri. They will assume you to be a ghost, and race to tell all their friends they have spotted the specter of Henrietta Blanchard. No one will investigate a presence. No one will suspect anything is amiss."

She cocked her head at the dress. "I suppose my acting skills are still exceptional. I can, without a doubt, pull it off."

"So, you have no objections?"

She lifted her chin, her arms still crossed over her chest. "Other than the plan being too easy, no."

He tossed the dress into the trunk and kicked it shut, waving his fists in the air. "Excellent. Then I shall retrieve the golden staff we need for the venture whilst you distract any curious onlookers. Your first taste of true adventure, Ri."

"Barely a sip of adventure if you ask me. When do I get to blow holes into things?"

"Patience, sister. Once word spreads of the treasure we seek, someone will try to beat us to it. And you may have the pleasure of blowing a hole into the side of his ship."

"Or hers," Henrietta said, her eyebrow arched.

"His," Clif answered with a sharp nod. "You're the only female pirate sailing these waters to my knowledge."

Henrietta crossed her arms, the corners of her mouth lifting into a grin. "I rather enjoy that fact."

"I figured you would," Clif said as a knock sounded at the door. "Yes?"

"We have arrived in port, sir. We are securing the ship now," Johnson's voice called in.

"Excellent," Clif answered before returning his gaze to his sister across the room. "Ready to hear a fantastical tale?"

"I thought you'd never ask," Henrietta said. She retrieved her hat, with the feather dried as best as she could manage, and donned it. "Let's go."

The pair emerged from the cabin as the port city of Tortuga slid into view. Men worked to anchor the ship near the dock. A gangplank extended to the wooden pathway below.

Clif approached the wooden board, bowing and signaling for Henrietta to precede him. She nodded at him, her feather bobbing in her cap as she mounted the steep descent, leaning backward to steady herself.

She hopped onto the floating dock below and spun to await Clif's arrival. He leapt from the gangplank onto the dock next to her. She staggered back a step to stay upright.

"And where do we find this blind beggar?" she questioned as they strolled toward the small seaside town.

"He is usually somewhere near the pub."

Henrietta arched an eyebrow. "Typical."

A few women eyed them as they marched toward the drinking establishment, giggling and grinning at Clif as they passed.

Henrietta offered them a look of disdain as she huffed at the display. "My, aren't we popular."

"It's likely my dashing good looks that draws them," Clif said.

"Undoubtedly."

Clif glanced sideways at her. "Really, Ri. I cannot believe you would comment given the looks you receive."

Henrietta set her jaw and crossed her arms. "I receive looks because I am a female sailor, not because they hope to share my bed for a fee."

"Untrue. You receive them because you are a female sailor with whom very many men would like to share a bed."

"Too bad for them. I am quite enjoying my freedom and have no desire to relinquish it." They arrived at the pub and Henrietta scanned the area, her legs in a wide stance. "Now, where is this blind beggar with all the answers?"

"I did not say he had all the answers, only a story to tell." Clif glanced around the area, his nose wrinkling. "He is usually just here by the door. Where is he?"

"Perhaps he's moved on."

"I doubt it," Clif answered, spinning to search the area.

A woman sidled up to him, scantily clad with a painted face. "Is it me you're searching for, captain?" She slid her arm up his, resting it on his shoulder as she offered him a coy smirk.

"No, it is not," Henrietta answered.

The woman slid her gaze to Henrietta, letting her eyes travel up and down the length of her. "What's it to you? You his wife?"

Henrietta arched an eyebrow and cocked her head. "Hardly. I am his sister. We have urgent business, none of which concerns you."

She grabbed Clif's hand and tugged him forward.

The woman threw her shoulders back, her lips turning into a frown. "Just a moment, we haven't finished our discussion."

She grasped hold of his shoulder and tugged him back toward her.

"You are quite finished," Henrietta said, yanking Clif's arm again. He stumbled forward a step toward his sister.

The woman's frown deepened and she wrinkled her nose. She grasped his arm and pulled him back. "We're finished when he says we are."

Henrietta crossed her arms and scowled at the woman. "Clif, tell her you are finished, and let's get on with our business."

Clif flicked his eyebrows up and studied the woman. "Perhaps you may be able to help us."

The frown on the woman's face turned into a smile and she ran her hand up his lapel. "Of course, I can help you, love." She shot a knowing smirk at Henrietta.

Henrietta sighed as she placed her hands on her hips.

"There is usually a man here," Clif said, pointing toward the tavern door. "Might you know where he is?"

The woman flicked her eyebrows up at him as she leaned closer to him. "Man? The only man I can see is you, love."

"Oh, for heaven's sake," Henrietta groaned, "must I be subjected to more of this, Clif?"

"I appreciate the sentiment," Clif answered, grasping her hand as it caressed his face, "however, I must find the blind beggar."

"Old Bill?" the woman asked. "Aw, he can't do anything for you. Not like I can."

"We do not require *those* services," Henrietta claimed. "Give up, woman, and leave us."

"Pipe down, wench, we're busy."

Clifton winced as he shot a glance toward Henrietta. She pulled her top lip up into an angry sneer as she thrust her fists at her sides. "That does it!"

She took one step forward, pulling her right fist backward, and swung at the woman. The woman stumbled backward, skirting around Clif and hiding behind him. She peered from behind his shoulder as she clung to him.

"You crazy minx," she shouted.

Clif caught Henrietta as she side-stepped around him, chasing after the woman. "Easy, Ri."

The woman danced around, keeping Clif between her and Henrietta. "She ought to be locked up! She's crazy."

Henrietta balled her hands into fists as she glared at the woman. "Yes, I am. And now my crazy sights are set on you!"

CHAPTER 4

*H*enrietta lunged for the woman again, her fingers reaching for her. She grasped hold of her hair and tugged on it.

The woman screeched as her head twisted sideways. "Ow! Get away from me you crazed banshee."

"I'll show you a crazed banshee, you tart." Henrietta grabbed hold of the woman's shoulders and slapped her across the face. "When you are told to be gone, leave as you were instructed."

"Help me!" the woman shouted at Clif. "She's mad!"

Clif eyed the angry exchange with an arched eyebrow. "Ri, be reasonable."

"I am being perfectly reasonable," Henrietta shouted back as she spun the woman around and shoved her forward. "She has no information about the beggar, and she is a nuisance. I am dealing with her accordingly."

The woman shot a pleading glance at Clif who shrugged. "My sister has a point," he called after her. "Have a pleasant evening."

Henrietta continued to march the woman back toward

the brothel she'd originated from, using the tip of her sword to keep her moving. As they approached the establishment, a grizzled man with an eye patch wandered from the open front door.

"What's this?" he asked. "What's going on here?"

"This crazed devil has stopped me from doing my business."

The man eyed Henrietta's sword poking toward the woman's back.

Henrietta cocked her head, the plume in her hat wobbling. "Your harlot interrupted important business and was asked to leave several times."

The man arched the eyebrow over his remaining eye as he flicked his gaze to Henrietta. "You're a woman!"

"Yes, I am, how perceptive of you."

He studied her up and down. "Whatever are you doing here dressed like that?"

"I am the captain of *The Henton*," Henrietta answered. "What am I doing here is none of your business."

"Captain of *The Henton*?" the man questioned.

Henrietta bobbed her head up and down, the feather in her cap quavering again.

The man and woman exchanged a glance before they both burst into laughter.

Henrietta's muscles stiffened as she straightened her posture and curled her fingers into fists.

"Captain of a pirate ship?" the woman choked. "You? You are crazy."

"I am not!" Henrietta insisted. "I am the captain of that ship and you'd do well to remember it."

"Come now, darling," the man said, "you're no captain. But if you're looking for work, you'd do quite well with that face."

Henrietta's full lips formed a frown and she squeezed her

fists closed tighter. "When I am finished with you, your face will not do so well."

She tugged her arm back and started to swing it forward when a strong hand clamped down on her bicep.

"No need to pummel the poor man, Ri. He couldn't possibly have the wits to understand a female pirate captain."

The man arched an eyebrow as Clif lowered Henrietta's arm to her side and stepped between them. "Captain Jack," he murmured. "My apologies. I did not realize this is your wench."

Henrietta stamped her foot on the ground as she tried to shove her way around Clif.

Clif held her at bay, stretching his arms to his sides to prevent her from moving. "She is not my wench, but rather my captain."

The color drained from the man's face and his eyes widened. "Captain? Her?"

"She captains *The Henton*, yes. And I signed on to her crew after my misfortune with *Neptune's Servant*."

Henrietta cocked her head and crossed her arms over her chest as she settled into a self-assured stance. She offered the man an arrogant stare.

"A female pirate captain?" he questioned.

"Yes, a female pirate captain. And quite a good one. We plan to go after a bounty few seek. And on that note, do you happen to know where the blind beggar is that usually sits over yonder?" Clif motioned back toward the pub.

"Old Bill?" the man asked, his eyes flitting back and forth between Clif and Henrietta.

"Yes, Old Bill as you call him," Henrietta snapped. "We have urgent business with him."

The man adjusted his eyepatch and thumbed into the building behind him. "He's inside, enjoying the company of one of my girls."

"Thank you," Henrietta said, her voice still dripping with agitation. She shoved past Clif and between the man and woman, knocking them both back a step as she strode toward the brothel.

"Hey! Wait just a minute! You can't go in there!" the man shouted.

Clif offered them a half-bow as he strode after her. "You may want to let her conduct her business and be on her way. It's far easier than arguing with her."

He rushed after her as she stormed through the open door and pounded up the stairs.

"Ri, wait!" Clif shouted as he rushed up behind her. "You may want to let me handle this."

Henrietta continued her storming up the stairs. "Why? I am perfectly capable of fetching this blind beggar."

Clif arched an eyebrow at her. "It's a brothel, Ri, you may prefer–"

"Nothing I haven't seen before. Besides, I have been offered a job by the establishment's owner. Perhaps I should inspect the working conditions in the event pirating does not work out for me."

Clif wrinkled his nose as she continued to trudge up the steps. Scantily-clad women darted around the upstairs.

Henrietta poked her head into one room before she continued down the hall. She flung another door open and glanced inside, retreating and crossing to another. She twisted the doorknob and pushed on the door. It did not budge.

"Locked," Clif said. "Perhaps he is inside. We may wait for him in the–"

His words were cut off by the raising of Henrietta's leg. She swung forward and kicked the barrier down with one sharp movement.

Clif nodded as he followed his sister inside. "Or we could kick the door down."

A man with sunken eye sockets lay on his back in the single bed in the room. A woman lay next to him. She shrieked as Henrietta trudged into the space, grasping at the sheet to cover her.

Henrietta waved her fingers at the girl, shooing her away. "Your services are no longer required."

"Just a moment–" the woman shouted at her.

Henrietta flicked a narrowed-eye gaze at the woman, her jaws set and her glare stony. She arched one eyebrow.

"I'd listen to her," Clif said.

The girl fled from the room with the sheet still wrapped around her.

"You could have been nicer, you know," he said to his sister.

Henrietta rolled her eyes, offering her still icy stare to her brother. He held his hands up in defeat, motioning toward the eyeless man who tugged on his trousers. Henrietta pushed past Clif to stand in front of him.

"Who are you?" the sightless man asked.

"The Captain of *The Henton*," she snapped, her arms crossed over her chest as she hovered over his slight frame still perched on the edge of the bed.

The man's eyebrows raised and his face twisted into an amused grin. A belly laugh emerged from him, and he slapped his thighs as he chuckled.

Henrietta's eyebrows shot skyward, and her posture stiffened. "Just what do you think you are laughing at?"

The man continued his whooping, his mouth hanging open in a wide grin showcasing his rotted teeth.

Henrietta's eyes widened as he continued his show. "I asked you a question, old man."

"A female ship captain." He snickered as he rubbed his

hand over the few hairs remaining on his head. "That'd be the day."

She wrinkled her nose, scowling at him as he stuck her hands on her hips. "You filthy–"

"That's sufficient," Clif said as he approached them. "Listen, old chap, she speaks the truth and you'd do well not to rile her."

The man sobered, his forehead wrinkling. "Who is that?"

The corners of Clif's mouth tugged upward in a devilish grin.

"Speak again, son, you sound familiar to me."

"I bloody well should," Clif answered him. "We've spoken on many occasions before."

The man's brows scrunched together tighter and he shook his head. "No, it can't be."

Clif wiggled his eyebrows and shot a grin at his sister. She rolled her eyes at the game.

"You're dead!" the man shouted. He pushed himself backward, scrambling back across the bed until he fell off the other side. He landed hard on his backside, his legs flying over his head.

He rolled onto his side, desperately trying to scramble to his feet and dash out the door.

Clif hurried toward the door, flinging it shut and blocking it with his body before the man could scurry away. Henrietta dove across the bed and grasped his trousers, tugging him backward as he stood.

He plopped onto the dirty mattress with a groan.

"You're not going anywhere," Henrietta informed him. "We have urgent business with you."

The man shook his head, an expression of anguish on his features. "No, no, it can't be."

Clif strode toward him. "But it is, old friend."

"Black Jack is dead!" he shouted.

"That's what we all thought," the establishment's owner said as he flung the door open. "But I assure you, old man, he stands in front of us, alive and well."

"Very well," Clif said with a grin.

"Get out," Henrietta told the owner. "We have business with the blind man."

The man lifted his grizzled chin and set his jaw. He waved a hand in front of him, his fingers curling toward his palm. "Ain't nobody does business under my roof without paying for it."

"Like fun!" Henrietta shouted. "I will not pay a brothel owner to have a word with a client."

The man narrowed his eyes, his hands falling to his hips. "Then you won't be having no words with him."

Henrietta rolled her eyes and crossed her arms. "Get out."

"You get out. It's my place of business," he spat back.

"We shall gladly oblige," Clif said. He grabbed the blind man by his bicep and lifted him to his feet. "But we shall take Blind Bill with us."

"Now, just a minute," the owner answered, barring the door. "No one removes a client of the Doyle brothel without their express permission."

"I didn't hear him complaining," Clif answered as he took a step forward, dragging the blind man with him.

"And I didn't hear him agreeing," the owner said with a sneer. "Now, if you don't mind, I'll be taking my payment."

He thrust his hand out, palm up, his eyes narrowed at Clif.

"I've got your payment right here," Henrietta said.

"Smart girl, I knew you'd see reas–" The man's words stopped short as he spun to collect his money from Henrietta. Instead, he met the tip of her sword.

He leapt back a step, raising his arms in the air.

"I wouldn't test her," Clif warned him. "She can be quite deadly. Especially when perturbed."

The owner's lips curled with fear as he stared down the length of the blade.

"Surely, Mr. Doyle," Henrietta said, "there is some arrangement we can come to that is satisfactory to both parties."

The man's breathing turned ragged as he backed to the door. "Sorry, Bill, you're on your own with these two."

He spun on his heel and flung the broken door open before dashing through it.

Henrietta slid the blade into its sheath. She shot Clif a glance and raised one eyebrow. "And you said I'd never win with the sword."

Clif shrugged as he snatched the man's shirt and jacket from the bedpost and shoved him forward through the door. "Come on, old Bill, I'll even buy you a pint."

"I don't want a pint from a ghost," the man shouted.

Henrietta followed them through the splintered doorway and down the stairs. Clif led the sightless man into the night air, parading him down the dirt street toward the pub.

"Here are your things. You may like to don them before we enter the pub."

"How can you be Jack?" the man questioned as he tugged his shirt over his head.

"That has already been explained," Henrietta sniped. "Are you deaf and blind? He did not die." She punctuated the last four words by slapping the back of her hand against her other palm.

"Your ship sank! Everyone knew!"

Clif waved his hand in the air. "Yes, yes, the ship sank. But I am quite alive. I assure you it is me."

The man's features pinched as he considered the statements. "Jack? Is it really you?"

"Yes, it's me, Bill," he said, placing his hands on the man's shoulders and squeezing. "Now, how about that drink? "

"I daresay I'm going to need it after that news."

Clif smirked at him, flicking his gaze to Henrietta as he steered the man into the pub.

Music filled the room, played by a fiddler, and nearly drowned out by chatter and laughter and the occasional heated disagreement between drunken men. A few of the patrons stumbled around returning with a fresh brew or on their way to retrieve another.

One sleepy-eyed man staggered nearer to them, a full stein in his thick hand. He arched an eyebrow as he studied Henrietta. One side of his lips lifted into a half-smirk, half-sneer as he stared up and down the length of her.

His beer sloshed onto her boots as he leaned forward and sniffed her. "Care for a little fun?"

She glanced down at the ale spattered across her black leather boots before she raised her icy gaze to him. "Yes, I do."

A ridiculous grin crossed the man's face as he leaned backward, stumbling a step away from her. She reached for her sword, wrapping her fingers around the hilt.

CHAPTER 5

nother set of fingers encircled her wrist. "Will you stop threatening everyone with your sword?"

She glanced at Clif, her jaw unhinged. "I will when everyone stops insulting me."

"Stay your blade, sister, and deal with it another way."

She shoved the blade back into its sheath with a huff. "Fine." She approached the unsteady man, a coy smile playing on her lips. "May I?"

She waved a finger at his drink. He arched an eyebrow, still grinning at her, and handed the stein over.

She smiled again as she accepted it. With one quick flick of her wrist, she tossed the mugful of liquid into his face, shoving him backward. He floundered for a moment before he fell onto his rear. Raucous laughter rose from the other patrons as Henrietta tossed the stein at his feet and dusted her hands.

"Excellent work, Ri. See how creatively you can solve your problems?"

She shot him a sideways glance. "Let's just get going with this, please. This has *not* been the adventure you promised."

Clif offered her a nod, pushing the blind man further into the crowded tavern and shouting to the bartender, "Three rounds and the use of your back room!"

The man nodded, filling three steins and setting them on the bar. Henrietta collected them with a wink as the man stared after them, dumbfounded, most likely from recognizing the deceased pirate who pushed the blind man through the bar.

She balanced the three beers in her hands as she darted after Clif, pushing through a wooden door and into a hallway. Clif steered the man into a large room with a few round, wooden tables scattered about.

He guided the man over to one and eased him into a chair, placing one of the steins in his hand. He took a long sip of the ale before he lowered the mug, wiping at his mouth with the back of his hand.

A few drops of the ale dripped from his chin as he opened his mouth into a toothy grin. "Well, Jack, I'll be damned. I thought you dead!"

Clif took a sip of his beer before grinning at him. "Everyone did. That was rather the point."

"And now?"

"Now, I have big plans. I cannot remain hidden forever."

The man grew serious, a concerned expression shooting across his features. "You know Redbeard's son still sails these waters, don't you?"

Clif arched an eyebrow. "Yes, a problem I plan to deal with soon. But before then there is something I need from you."

"Oh?"

"My sister sails with me now. She craves adventure. I aim to provide it. So we are seeking the Cuidad de Diamantés."

The man's eyebrows lifted, pulling at the closed eye sockets below them. "No, you mustn't."

"What I mustn't do and what I will do are not the same, Bill. I need the information you have again. Ri will be able to piece together the clues, I'm certain."

"No, Jack. It's too dangerous."

"Danger is my middle name," Clif said after downing another sip of his beer.

"Not like this. It's a fool's errand. It can't be found. And even if it can be, it's guarded by nightmarish beasts that will rip you to pieces and eat you alive."

Henrietta arched an eyebrow at him and scoffed. "Nightmarish beasts? Do you jest, sir?"

Clif screwed up his face, shooting her a glance and shaking his head.

"No, dear lady, I do not. I only wish to save you and Jack from certain death."

Henrietta rolled her eyes at the statement. "We shall be fine. Please proceed with your tale."

"No," he said, shaking his head, "no, you cannot do it."

Clif pulled a chair nearer to the man and straddled it. "Come on, old friend, you've recounted the tale for me before. Tell it again for Ri."

The man's lower lip trembled for a moment before he firmed his jaw and shook his head.

Henrietta sighed and stamped her foot. "Really, Clif, this is a waste of time."

"It's not," Bill informed her. "I've seen pieces of the map leading to it. I've spoken to the tribesmen who insist anyone who gets too close to the hidden entrance will be killed. And anyone who enters... well, they won't return even if they make it that far."

"You've spoken with them?" Henrietta questioned. "But you will not tell us their tale."

"Would you tell us for say fifty pieces of gold?" Clif asked.

Henrietta shot him an unimpressed glance.

"No," Bill said. "No amount is worth being responsible for your deaths."

"No amount, eh?" Henrietta asked, cocking her hip and setting her hand on it. "I suppose, then, you wouldn't be interested in one hundred and twenty pieces of gold. Too bad, that could have bought you a warm bed and many nights of drinking."

She heaved a large sigh and spun on her heel. "Come on, Clif," she called over her shoulder, "he's not interested."

She took two steps toward the door when the man's voice stopped her. "Now wait just a minute."

Her lips curled into a smile, and she raised her eyebrows before spinning on her heel to face him. "Whatever for?"

"I could be persuaded," Bill answered, lifting his chin in the air, "for one hundred and fifty pieces of gold *and* a cut of the haul."

Henrietta let out a sharp laugh. "Ha! No. Let's go, Clif. We are wasting our time."

Clif's eyebrows shot up and he signaled for her to stay and tone down her refusals. She offered him an icy stare, crossing her arms over her chest. She waved a hand in the air, motioning for him to proceed.

"You know, Bill," Clif started, leaning forward and balancing his hands on his knees, "you've told me the story for only an ale. So, the price seems rather steep."

"But I'm not just offering the tale this time," the blind man said.

Clif arched an eyebrow, flicking his gaze to Henrietta.

"And what exactly are you offering?" Henrietta questioned.

"A piece of the map," Bill answered, an amused grin on his face.

"A piece of the map?" Clif inquired, scoffing as he spoke the words.

"Aye, that's right. Worth quite a bit as far as I see. So, I want one hundred and fifty pieces of gold and–" The man puckered his lips as he considered his offer. "Twenty-five percent of the haul."

"You're out of your skull," Henrietta said. "You oughtn't be named blind Bill, but rather, mad Bill because you're crazy."

"You won't find it without my map piece. It has the legend bit. You'll need it. I'd say that's worth far more than the pittance I've requested."

"Look, Bill," Clif began.

"We are risking life and limb," Henrietta interrupted. "You'll not take anything from the haul. I'll concede the one hundred and fifty pieces of gold."

Clif shot her a glance, flinging a hand in the air. Henrietta waved his questioning stance away as she shook her head.

"You won't be risking anything without my information and my piece of the map. One hundred pieces of gold and twenty-five percent. Final offer."

Henrietta cocked her head. "Final offer, is it? Two hundred pieces of gold and no take of the haul. My final offer."

Clif opened his mouth to speak when Bill beat him to it.

"One hundred pieces of gold and twenty percent," the man said, rising to his feet.

Clif sucked in a breath ready to make a statement.

"One hundred and twenty pieces of gold and one diamond," Henrietta countered taking a step toward him.

"One hundred and ten pieces of gold and ten percent," the man said inching closer to her.

"One hundred pieces of gold and two fistfuls of diamonds," Henrietta said, her hands on her hips as they stood nose to nose.

Clif screwed up his face as the exchange between the two continued.

"Deal," the blind man said. He thrust his hand out.

Henrietta accepted it, pumping it up and down before she spun to face Clif. "Clif," she said, cocking her head in the blind man's direction, "pay the man."

He wrinkled his nose at her as she spun back to face Bill, her palm out to receive her end of the deal. "Hand over the map piece."

"Just a moment, dearie. I ain't got my payment yet. And besides, I don't keep it on me. For safety's sake."

Henrietta's jaw dropped open and she scoffed. "Don't keep it on you? You jest. You do not have it!"

"I have it, all right!" Bill shouted, his face reddening at the accusation. "In a safe place."

"And where is that, pray tell? The brothel."

"Certainly not! Would be a rather stupid place to have put it."

Henrietta cocked a hip and set her jaw. "Then where? At the local bank under lock and key?"

"In my own hiding spot. But I'll need your help to retrieve it. I ain't saying nothing until I get my gold though."

"Come now, Bill," Clif said, finally entering the conversation, "we're old friends. Surely, you know I'm good for it."

"I ain't saying you're not, Jack, but I want to be paid before I take you to it."

Clif sighed, licking his lips. "The thing is, I haven't got it on me."

Henrietta's shoulders slumped and she let her hands fall to her sides. She huffed at her brother. "Honestly, Clif."

With a shake of her head, she dug into the pocket of her trousers and pulled out a pouch. She wiggled it open and dumped the gold onto the nearby table. The coins clattered across the wood, gleaming under the candlelight that lit the room.

Clif's jaw unhinged at the massive pile that fell from the pouch. Henrietta slid pieces from the pile, stacking them in piles of ten as she counted out the sum. She whipped a handkerchief from her pocket and laid it out, transferring the coins to the center before she pulled up the corners and tied them in a neat bow.

She grabbed the blind man's hand and pulled it upward, laying the makeshift purse in his palm. "Here you are."

She slid the rest of the coins back into the leather pouch. "Now, lead the way."

"Mind if I count it?" the man asked.

Henrietta shoved the leather purse into her pocket. "Yes, I do. If we are short, which I am certain we are not, we shall settle up after we've received the map. You have the first installment of your payment. Now take us to the map piece."

"She did not shortchange you, old friend," Clif assured him.

The man jangled the coins in his hand, squeezing the pouch and bouncing it in his hand. "Feels right," he said, sliding it into his trouser pocket. "We can't go now. Someone may see us. It has to be in the dead of night."

Henrietta heaved a sigh and shook her head. "Fine. We shall meet at the front of the pub in an hour. Clif will stay with you until then."

Clif shot her an incredulous glance. Henrietta shrugged at him. "He's your friend and someone must keep an eye on him."

She strode toward the door.

"Where are you going?" he asked her.

"I have to see a man about a thing," she called over her shoulder before she disappeared through the door.

Clif stared after her as she sashayed from the room,

confusion etched into his features. A hand clapped on his shoulder and he twisted to find his blind friend next to him. "Odd sort, your sister."

Clif directed his gaze back to the open door. "She is a unique individual, that is for certain."

"What do you say about buying an old friend a drink to pass the time?"

Clif's eyebrows shot up and he grinned though the man couldn't see it. "I'd say with the load my sister just paid you, you ought to buy me the drink."

Bill burst into laughter, his yellowed teeth gleaming in the candlelight as his body shook. "Come on. I'll buy the first beer and you can tell me all about this unique individual that is your sister."

"Deal," Clif agreed, wrapping an arm around the man's thin shoulders and leading him from the room.

* * *

Henrietta strode across the tavern, ignoring the few whistles and catcalls she received. It took all in her not to roll her eyes at the ridiculous behavior men exhibited. Particularly, when they'd imbibed even a small amount of alcohol.

Truthfully, it turned her stomach. Drunk men were stupid men. She set her jaw as she recalled her circumstances. Widowed at twenty-five by a drunkard. The man, supposedly a revered sea captain, had gambled away every penny of his fortune and left her destitute.

On top of that, his reckless pursuit of more treasure to be squandered at the poker table had gotten him killed.

Henrietta slammed through the door and into the night air. Was she any better? She recklessly pursued treasure and adventure. Though she did not leave a spouse behind that she'd promised to provide for.

45

She licked her lips as she glanced up and down the dirt street in front. A few drunks milled around outside. One of them retched, clinging to the railing framing the bar's porch. He righted himself, spittle dribbling into his thick, grisly beard. His sleepy eyes struggled to stay open before he stumbled toward her.

He swiped his hand across his wet lips and studied Henrietta up and down. When his eyes reached her face, he raised his eyebrows. A belch escaped his lips and he chuckled.

She set her jaw in disgust and shook her head as she tried to push past him.

"Where you going, darling? I could use some entertainment," he said as he reached for her.

She side-stepped him and he stumbled forward, collapsing onto the porch. "Stay away from me, old man."

She skirted past him, stepping onto the dusty dirt. He grumbled, reaching for her and catching her ankle.

Henrietta tugged against his grip, losing her balance and slamming to the ground. Air escaped her lips as she smacked against the dirt.

"That's just plain rude," the man claimed, his voice gruff. "And I don't tolerate rudeness from women."

She kicked her foot, trying to free it, but his grasp remained firm. He lunged toward her, flipping her onto her back. His fat belly pressed against her thighs as he slithered on top of her.

"Now, I'll need to teach you a lesson," he said.

Henrietta squirmed underneath him as he reached down toward her trousers. Straddling her, he tugged at his belt to loosen it.

CHAPTER 6

*A*nger coursed through her. She recalled two similar instances when a man assumed he could take what he wanted from her. In both instances, Clif had stopped him. In the second, he had stopped him from harming another woman ever. She still recalled the sight of his blood soaking his shirt after the fatal shot had been accidentally fired.

She wrapped her fingers around her pistol and slid it upward, freeing it from its holder. She clenched her jaw as she shifted the weapon in her hands. "I said leave me alone."

She lifted her arm and swung the pistol toward him, striking him on the temple. He cried out as the butt of the weapon cracked his skull, wavering on his knees but not falling over.

His nose wrinkled, and his eyes lit with anger as he refocused on Henrietta. He stretched his fingers out as his gaze fell to her neck. He reached toward it. "You little bi–"

Henrietta swung again, hitting him a second time. This hit knocked him sideways. He fell to his hands and knees beside her.

She did not hesitate to strike him again before scrambling

to her feet. He writhed in the dirt as he tried to push himself to kneel again. Henrietta put her foot on his shoulder and shoved him into a heap, glaring down her nose at him.

"Don't ever lay a finger on me again." She shoved the pistol into her holster and stalked toward the alley abutting the pub.

Before she made it two steps, another individual accosted her. This one, however, was no threat. A thin waif of a girl hurried toward her. Her dirty nightgown slipped off one shoulder, revealing pale, bruised skin. With wide eyes, she stumbled backward, frail fingers clutching at Henrietta's sleeve.

Henrietta shook her off as she continued her determined march to the alley. "No, I do not wish to pay for any services. Do not even attempt to convince me."

"Please," the girl said.

"I said no. Now, be gone. I will not be badgered by your lot."

"No, please," the girl said again, tightening her grip on Henrietta's arm. "I do not wish to sell myself to you."

Henrietta glanced down at the pale fingers wrapped around her forearm before she stared into the girl's light eyes. A bruise graced her alabaster complexion, marring her cheek. Dark, puffy bags hung under her eyes.

Henrietta swallowed hard and flicked her gaze back to the girl after glancing at the alley. "Then what?"

"Take me with you."

Henrietta scoffed at the statement and took a step away. "Go back to the brothel."

"No, please," the woman begged, grasping Henrietta's arm again. Tears filled her haunted eyes and she pulled her lips back into a desperate wince.

"I cannot help you. Now, I am late. I must–"

"Please, I cannot go back there." A sob escaped her lips and a few tears spilled onto her cheeks.

"And I told you I cannot help."

The girl refused to let go of Henrietta's sleeve, tugging at the fabric with her white fingers. "Please. You are a sea captain unlike any other. No one else can help me. Only you can."

Henrietta rolled her eyes and set her jaw. "I am already late, and I can do nothing for you."

The girl dropped to her knees as tears streamed down her pale cheeks. She clasped her hands together under her chin. "Please. I beg of you. I cannot go back there. I cannot continue. You are a female sea captain. You have made your own way. Please I beg of you help another woman to do the same. I throw myself on your mercy and plead for your help."

Henrietta arched an eyebrow at the dramatic display as her hands fell to the belt around her hips. She huffed out a sigh as she stared down at the girl's tear-stained cheeks and her frail body. Her thin flesh stretched over the collarbones that protruded under her neck. Her tiny, bony wrists held up her skeleton-like hands. She'd likely blow off the ship with one good gust of wind.

Henrietta sucked in a breath as she chewed the inside of her cheek. Clif had freed her from a life she detested. Should she deny that to another woman roped into a life she'd likely never imagined?

She chewed her lower lip a moment as the girl's light eyes stared up at her, pleading. She flicked her own dark eyes down to the waif's face. "I shall return in several weeks. I may be in a position to help you then. I cannot help you now."

"No, please!" the girl shrieked as Henrietta took a step away from her. "No! I cannot wait weeks. I–"

Another voice interrupted her pleading sobs. "*There* you are, wench."

The brothel's owner stormed toward them, his chin tucked to his chest and his eyes narrowed at the young woman. She swallowed hard, her eyes widening as she rose to her feet, shuffling away from him.

"No, Isaac, no." The girl held her trembling hands out in front of her.

He poked a finger at her as he continued to close the gap between them. "You ran out on a client. A very important client."

"No, please," she sobbed, fresh tears flowing down her cheeks.

Henrietta took a step away from the dramatic scene, intending to leave them to their business.

"That's the second time." Isaac grabbed her by the arm and dragged her like a rag doll toward him. Her legs gave out as she crumpled at his side. "Get up, whore."

"No, please. He's too rough. He'll kill me. He's already beaten me once. He'll do it again."

"I don't care what he's done. He picked you and paid for you. And you'll do as you're told."

Henrietta glanced back at the pair. The skinny girl hung listlessly as the man shook her roughly.

"Get up!" he shouted at her.

"No," she sobbed, collapsing to her knees.

Isaac's features hardened as he stared down at her. He firmed his jaw, speaking through clenched teeth. "What did you say?"

"No," she breathed out again.

Isaac raised his hand and slapped her hard, knocking her from her knees into a slack form in the dirt. She lay in a heap, the only movement coming from her heaving chest as sobs wracked her.

"Get up!" Isaac screamed.

The girl pushed herself up to her hands and knees, struggling to pull herself to stand. She rubbed at her cheek where he had struck her as she balanced on one hand.

"Stop sniveling, you stupid whore." He kicked her backside, sending her sprawling into the dirt again. She gasped out a choking cry as she smacked into the ground.

Henrietta chewed the inside of her lower lip as she attempted to force herself away from the scene and to the meeting she'd secured. She took one step away when the girl wailed again. It drew her attention back.

Isaac hauled her upward mercilessly, giving her another shake before he began to drag her along with him. Henrietta shook her head, squeezing her eyes shut. She implored herself not to get involved.

With a sigh, she resigned herself to the notion that she could not walk away. Her fingers wrapped around the hilt of her sword and she lifted it from its sheath as she stalked forward.

"Unhand her," she said, raising the blade to shoulder height.

The man ignored her, tugging his prisoner behind him as he continued toward the brothel.

"I said unhand her," she called again.

"Or what?" Isaac asked, spinning to face Henrietta. His eyebrows shot up and he chuckled. "Oh-ho, what have we here? Playing pirate again?"

Henrietta gritted her teeth and inched the blade closer to him. "I'm not playing anything. Now I told you to unhand her. Or I will take action."

The man let out a belly laugh, throwing his head back. He let the girl drop to the ground as he grew serious. "You wouldn't dare."

"Wouldn't I?"

He lowered his chin, glowering at her. "Big brother Black Jack isn't here to ensure your safety, so no, I'd say you wouldn't."

Henrietta cocked her head. "Actually, he's my younger brother. And I don't need him to ensure my safety. I do just fine on my own, thank you."

She eased her left hand back to her hip, wrapping her fingers around her gun. "Now, let the woman go."

The girl scrambled to her feet and raced toward Henrietta, hiding behind her.

"See, I can't do that. I own her."

"Says who?" Henrietta spat.

"Says me. And the man who sold her to me."

Henrietta narrowed her eyes at Isaac, cocking her head. "Someone sold her to you?"

The man snorted before spitting on the ground and clutching his belt. He bobbed his chin up and down. "That's right. She's my property."

Henrietta huffed in annoyance at the statement. "Women are not property."

"This woman is."

"Who sold her to you? How did he have the right?"

"None of your business."

Henrietta raised the sword closer to his chin. "I said who sold her and how did he have the right?"

The man twisted his neck, cracking the bones as he glared at her. "Her father."

Henrietta wrinkled her nose, her lips lifting with disgust. "Her father sold her to you? Her own father sold his daughter to a brothel owner?"

"That's right," the man said, jiggling his pants up and down. "Now lower your sword and allow me to collect my property."

Henrietta thrust the sword under his chin again as he

tried to step around her. "I don't believe you. What kind of father sells his own daughter to a brothel?"

"A broke one," the man claimed.

Tiny fingers closed around Henrietta's arm. "It's true," the girl squeaked. "My father sold me. For twenty pieces of gold."

The man flicked his eyebrows up, a smirk forming on his lips. "There. You heard it from the whore herself. Now lower your sword and let me collect my property."

He took a step around her again as she let the sword fall. The fingers tightened on her arm. "No, please."

"Stop your blubbering. And don't think admitting the truth earlier is going to help you. If Ronnick doesn't beat you senseless, I will for this little stunt."

Henrietta squeezed her eyes closed as the girl used her as a shield to hide from her employer. She licked her lips and raised her sword yet again. "Stop."

Isaac scoffed and shook his head, an amused expression flitting across his features but diminishing quickly. He sneered at her. "I'm growing weary of this game. If you want to play pirate do it on someone else's time. Now get out of my way and allow me to collect my property before I teach both you and her a lesson."

"I am not playing. Lay a finger on her and I will gut you right here on the street."

The statement elicited a belly laugh from the man. "You haven't got the courage to gut a man, darling. Why do you insist on playing this game?"

"Do not refer to me as your darling, I am not. And do not test my patience. I bent my will to men for far too long. I assure you I have the willpower to end your life."

The man's jaw flexed as he considered her threat. "Pay me for her and you can have the wench."

"Or I could kill you and take her."

"You don't want to do that."

"Don't I? Explain to me why not. Why should I not end the life of a man who treats women as his property, uses them for his own gain, and is generally despicable?"

"I can be useful. Perhaps you should call your brother, Jack, and run this reckless decision past him. I'm certain he will agree ending my life would be a mistake."

Henrietta's nostrils flared in irritation. "I do not need my brother's permission or blessing to make decisions."

"Whether or not you do, ending my life would be foolish and reckless. Particularly when I have offered a suitable solution."

Behind her, the waif of a girl trembled, clutching her arm tightly. Henrietta bit her lower lip. "Fine. Twenty gold pieces. I–"

"No," Isaac said, clasping his hands behind his back, "one hundred gold pieces."

Henrietta's jaw dropped open and she furrowed her brow. "One hundred gold pieces? Are you mad? You paid twenty for her."

"She's worth far more to me as a whore. I've got to make up for lost income."

"Lost income?" Henrietta questioned. She chewed the inside of her cheek as she shook her head. "Thirty gold pieces."

"Eighty."

"Forty," she countered.

"Seventy-five."

"Fifty, final offer."

The man arched an eyebrow at her. "Sixty, no less. Meet my demand or the girl comes back with me."

"No, please," the girl cried, squeezing Henrietta's arm.

Henrietta's nose wrinkled at the bold statement. "Ten gold pieces."

Isaac sneered at her. "Are you deaf? I just said I won't go

below sixty. Perhaps it's because you're a woman and you're too stupid to understand. You see, darling, ten is less than sixty."

Henrietta cocked her head and flicked her gaze to the sky, feigning a confused look. "Oh, right. How silly of me. I owe you something more to make up for the missing fifty."

Isaac arched an eyebrow. "And what would that be, darling?"

"This." She whipped the pistol from within its holster and fired.

CHAPTER 7

The man screamed in pain as the bullet pierced his shin. He fell to the ground, blood spattering across the dirt. "You bitch!"

She shoved the pistol back into the leather holder and tugged the purse from her pocket. She counted out ten coins and tossed them in the dirt next to him. "Consider us even. The girl is mine." She took a step forward, looming over him and staring down her nose at him. "Agreed?"

"No, we're not agreed," he spat out as he continued to writhe in pain.

Henrietta stowed her sword in its sheath, lifted her foot and pressed the heel of her boot into the wound. The man screamed in agony. "Are you certain? I could put a bullet in your other leg if you feel you are still owed something."

"You crazy harlot! You're going to pay for this."

"Mmm, I doubt that."

"I'll get you for this!" he shouted as Henrietta strode away from him.

The young woman hurried behind her as she sashayed toward the alley. "Thank you!"

"Do not thank me. Your life may be no easier now," Henrietta answered, her hand resting on the hilt of her sword.

"I shall do whatever you ask. I am indebted to you."

Henrietta spun to face her. "Yes, you are. And you shall work off your debt. You will swab the decks. You will scout from the crow's nest. You will learn every nail and board on my ship until you can locate them blindfolded. You will become a sailor. Do you understand?"

The girl's head bobbed up and down. "Yes."

"And you will *not* fraternize with the other sailors. Do you understand that? If you are caught performing any of your former duties with the men, I shall cast you into the sea myself."

"I understand, Captain. I don't want no parts of that life or those... duties."

"I do not want any," Henrietta corrected.

The girl wrinkled her nose.

"If you are to be a member of my crew, you shall speak properly. We are pirates, not simpletons."

The girl straightened her posture, rolling her shoulders back. "Yes, Captain. I do not want any parts of my old life."

Henrietta offered her a curt nod before eyeing her up and down. "We shall have to find you clothes. You cannot wear that filthy nightgown."

"I shall burn it myself, Captain," the girl said. "I should very much like clothes like yours. Trousers and the like."

"Yes, trousers are a requirement for the work you shall do." She waved a finger at the girl. "But you shall not have a hat with a feather."

The girl nodded again. "Yes, Captain. No feather."

"What is your name, girl?" Henrietta asked as she took another few steps toward the alley.

"Abigail. Abigail Turner. Abby."

"All right, Miss Turner. We shall fetch your clothes when we board *The Henton*. Now, wait here, do not move, and do not eavesdrop."

Henrietta pressed Abby against the tavern's side, hidden in a shadow before she proceeded down the narrow alley.

A figure loomed at the end, cast in darkness and hidden from the moonlight. "I almost left, lassie," his Scottish accent said as she approached.

"My apologies, the delay was unavoidable."

He tugged at his graying beard as he studied her in the moonlight. He jutted his chin toward Abby. "Thought you preferred to keep your business private."

Henrietta twisted to glance at the young woman, her white nightgown a beacon against the tavern's dark wooden side. "Never mind my associate. What of our deal?"

"I can provide you with what you asked. Got the perfect one in mind. I need payment, though. Tonight."

"About that," Henrietta began, her fingers tightening around her sword's hilt, "I have the money. Most of it. But I–
"

"Most of it?" I need all of it, lassie."

"I can provide the remaining sum when I am next in port."

The man shook his head. "No, that won't do. Deal's off." He strode toward her, aiming to skirt around her.

"Just a moment," Henrietta said, side-stepping to block him from leaving. She freed the purse from her pocket and waved it in the air. "I've got almost everything. Something came up earlier this evening, and I had to use some of the funds. But I will have the rest when I return. I'll even provide you with an extra ten percent for the trouble."

The man rubbed a thumb against his lips as he considered the new offer. He motioned for her to hand him the pouch. After tugging it open, he glanced at the coins inside and wrinkled his nose. "Make it fifteen percent and we have a deal."

Henrietta puckered her lips as she flicked her gaze to the side. "Fine. The remainder plus fifteen percent."

A grin grew on the man's grizzled face as he waved the purse in the air. "A pleasure doing business with you, lassie." He bowed to her before he stepped around her and strode down the alley, disappearing into the pub.

Henrietta stood for a moment, sucking in a breath as she pondered the latest deal when a shout sounded behind her. She whipped around to face the front of the pub. Abby leaned around the corner, staring at something beyond Henrietta's vision.

She hurried toward the other street, skidding to a stop near Abby. "What's going on?"

"Isaac's found help. And they do not appear to be happy."

Henrietta studied the posse of six men, two of which tugged Isaac upward, cradling him between them.

"The wench shot me!" he screamed. "Find her!"

"Time to go," Henrietta said, adjusting her hat on her head and grasping Abby's arm.

Abby nodded as Henrietta led her along. "When we get to the ship, I–"

Her words were cut off as two men stood in their path. "Here they are," one man said, narrowing his eyes at the two women.

Henrietta raised her chin. "Stand aside."

"No. You've got stolen property in your possession, and you shot Isaac. Now it's time to make you pay." He slammed a closed fist into his other palm, then cracked his knuckles.

Henrietta ripped her sword from its sheath and held it out in front of her. The man's yellowed teeth gleamed in the ethereal moonlight that glowed down as he chuckled at her weapon.

Two more men closed in around her, encircling them. Abby pressed her back against Henrietta's as a fourth man approached. Henrietta pulled the pistol from its holster and aimed it at one of the men.

She twisted her neck, and whispered to Abby, "There is a knife in my boot."

Abby squatted and drew the short knife from within the holder in Henrietta's boot, thrusting it out in front of her.

"You can't kill all of us at once, sweetheart," another man said with a sharp laugh.

Henrietta's eyes darted around as she considered if she could take at least one of them out. The unloaded pistol did her no good except as a threat. Could she remove one of them with her sword? Likely, yes. Though that left three and she'd never beat all of them. She hadn't even beaten Clif earlier one-on-one.

Her mind scrambled for a solution. With the young woman in tow, a sudden dash for the bar's interior was not an option. The girl would become ensnared in their trap, and she'd have lost the woman she'd just fought to free.

"Maybe not, but I can kill at least one of you and I'm confident my newfound friend can at least maim another. Which two should it be?" she questioned, waving the sword and the gun at them.

"Kill the bitch!" Isaac shouted from across the way where he hobbled on one leg as he clutched at the man holding him up.

"With pleasure," one of his posse growled before they took a step toward Henrietta.

"What is going on here?" a new voice inquired. The sound of a sword sliding from its sheath sliced through the night air. "Move away from my sister."

"These men hope to end my life," Henrietta said to Clif.

"Then I shall end theirs," Clif answered, approaching the group as he tugged his pistol from his belt.

One of the men held his hands up as he backed a few steps away. Clif backed the man at the tip of his sword several more steps away.

"No!" Isaac shouted from across the street. "No! She shot me and stole my whore! She must pay!"

One of the posse lunged toward Henrietta and Abby. Henrietta swung her sword toward him as Clif stepped forward, pressing his shoulder against Henrietta's.

Clif raised an eyebrow as he swung the gun to aim at one man, his sword at another. "One of you lays a hand on either of them and I will end you. Make no mistake, I am not green, I can end all of you and I will."

"It ain't worth it," one man said, spinning on a heel and racing away.

"Get back there! I want that girl back!" Isaac shouted.

"Let's get out of here, Isaac. I ain't messing with Black Jack." Another man sped into the night, leaving only two aggressors, Isaac, and his crutch.

"No!"

"Come on, Isaac. Let's get that bullet out."

Isaac's face turned into a mask of anger and he balled a fist, waving it in the air. "You'll pay for this! All of you! I'll get you for this!"

The other man dragged him away, still screaming into the night at them as his posse retreated.

Clif shook his head as he slid his sword into its sheath, stowed his gun, and spun to face Henrietta. "What the bloody hell was that about, Ri?"

Henrietta slid her sword away. "A minor disagreement."

Clif's eyebrows shot up. "Minor? Those men were ready to kill you both! And who, by the way, is this?"

Henrietta stuffed the gun into her holster. "Our newest crew member. Abby Turner."

Clif stared at the woman in the dirty nightgown. She shifted the knife from one hand to the other before Henrietta held out her palm for it. "Here you are, Captain."

"Thank you. We shall have to secure weapons for you," Henrietta said as she slid the knife into her boot.

"Captain?" Clif said, his eyebrows shooting high and his hands on his hips. "I'm going to need a little more explanation than that, Ri."

Henrietta forced out a sigh as she puckered her lips. "Miss Turner has endured abuse at the hands of her employer and wished to leave. She was sold to the brothel by her father. I paid for her release. She is now a member of *The Henton's* crew."

Clif raised his eyebrows again as Abby offered him a wave. "You paid for her release? Then why did Isaac claim you stole her?"

"I did not pay what he wished."

He crossed his arms over his chest. "What price did he ask?"

"No lower than sixty gold pieces."

"Sixty?" Clif fluttered his eyelids at the price. "And what did you pay him?"

"Ten."

He flicked a gaze to the moon, confusion fluttering across his features. "Ten?"

Henrietta held a finger in the air. "Oh, and the bullet I put in his leg."

Clif's shoulders fell back between his shoulder blades. "Ri, honestly. I cannot believe–"

"I shall stop you there, brother," she said, holding a hand in the air. "I will not stand by and allow this woman who begged for my help to be thrust into a life she did not choose.

Furthermore, I will not be taken for a fool merely because of my gender nor by a gutter-crawling half-breed like Isaac."

"You cannot continue picking fights with every person you meet, Ri!"

Henrietta stuck her hands on her hips and stared at him. "Are we not pirates? Is that not our trade? Or are only you permitted to pick fights?"

Clif pressed his lips together in a thin line and shook his head. "Pick as many fights as you'd like, sister. Just be sure they are fights you can win." His lips curled into a devilish grin and he winked at her.

"Honestly, Clif," she said with a roll of her eyes. "Where is Bill? Shall we proceed?"

"In the pub, I shall retrieve him. I only came out when I heard the shouting in the event that you needed my assistance."

Henrietta arched an eyebrow. "I did not, really. But it did rather come in handy."

"Of course, you didn't. I don't know what I was thinking. Just a moment. Try not to shoot anyone while I'm gone." He held a finger up as he slipped back into the tavern.

He emerged a moment later with Bill in tow. "All right, old friend. Time to retrieve that map piece."

CHAPTER 8

The blind man rubbed his hands together in front of him. "We shall need several things. First, we must ensure we are alone."

"We are," Henrietta said.

Bill wrinkled his nose and his forehead, cocking his head to the side. "No, there is another."

"Me, sir," Abby answered. She snaked an arm behind her back, clasping the other.

"Who is it?"

"One of our crew. It makes no matter. Tell us what we need to retrieve," Henrietta said.

"The deal was you and Jack. Not various members of your crew!" Bill said.

Henrietta cocked a hip and puckered her lips in annoyance. "It's not various members. It is one. And it is due to a special circumstance. She cannot be left behind. How did you know anyway?"

"I could smell her," the man said, lifting his chin.

"In any case, Bill," Clif said, clapping the man's shoulder, "we may proceed with her."

The man tugged the corners of his mouth into a frown. "I suppose it won't hurt. We'll need a lantern and a shovel. And be sure no one is following us."

"All right, I shall arrange it. Wait here," Clif said. He shot a glance at Henrietta. "And don't shoot anyone."

"Shoot anyone?" Bill questioned as Clif strode down the street toward the docks. "Have you shot someone?"

"Yes, I have," Henrietta admitted. "I shot Isaac."

"In heaven's name, why?"

"Because he deserved it. And if you don't take us to that map, I'll shoot you, too."

The man scrunched his face and swallowed hard. "Never fear, it's there."

"For one hundred gold pieces, it had better be." Henrietta spun to scan the street, crossing her arms over her chest as she tapped a foot on the ground, impatiently awaiting her brother's return.

A bobbing lantern closed the gap between them moments later as Clif returned with a shovel slung over his shoulder.

Abby stepped forward with outstretched arms. "I'll carry it, sir."

Clif arched an eyebrow and glanced at Henrietta. She flicked her gaze to the girl, then back to Clif with a nod. "Give it to her. She shall carry the shovel and dig the hole."

Clif swung the shovel off his shoulder and passed it to Abby. She winced as the handle smacked against one of her bruises. Clif arched an eyebrow at Henrietta as they set off, following Bill through the town's streets.

Henrietta lifted a shoulder at her brother. He narrowed his eyes at her as Abby trailed behind them. Leaning closer, he flicked his eyes over his shoulder at the girl. "Are you sure about…" He bobbed his head toward her.

Henrietta glanced over her shoulder, then back at Clif as they strode along the dirt road. "Yes."

Clif eyed the girl again before he whispered to Henrietta again. "We have no reason to trust her."

"We have every reason to trust her," Henrietta argued.

"Such as?"

"We have saved her life. She will remain loyal."

Clif's boots scuffed along the increasingly rocky path. He arched an eyebrow at the statement. "You seem positive."

"I am."

Clif scrunched his face, kicking a stone out of his path. "Ri, not to argue, but you're not the best judge of character."

"When have I proven to be a bad judge of character?"

Clif shot her a sideways glance.

"Don't answer," she said before he could. "I must learn to trust my instincts in order to survive in this world. I realize I have made some... questionable choices involving my romantic life, however, this is business."

Clif held his hands up in defeat. "I shall say no more about it."

Henrietta offered him a tight-lipped smile as the small town faded behind them.

"Although where do you plan to put her on the ship?" Clif questioned, flinging his arms in the air.

"I thought you were saying no more about it?"

"It's a valid question, Ri. Surely we cannot put her below decks with the men."

"I hadn't planned on it."

"Then where?" Clif shot her a wide-eyed glance. "The captain's quarters are a bit cramped at the moment."

"I hadn't planned on that either. I agree with you. The captain's quarters are hardly appropriate."

"So, where do you plan on putting her?" he questioned again as they trudged up a sharp grade near a large stone protruding into the night sky.

"The storage area."

"Where we keep the bucket and mop for swabbing the decks?"

Henrietta nodded and shot him a sideways glance. "She's not much bigger than it. She should fit quite nicely."

"Comical, Ri, perhaps you can join me on my comedy tour."

"It provides her privacy and keeps her away from the other sailors."

Bill stopped as his hand swept over the stone. He felt around until his fingers wrapped around the edge, then he followed it upward to the pointed tip.

"And you intend for her to work?"

"I promise I will, sir," Abby said as she caught up to them. "Swab the decks, keep watch from the crow's nest, and learn every nail and board in the ship. Just like the Captain told me. I shall be the second-best sailor on the *Henton*."

Clif furrowed his dark eyebrows. "Second-best?"

"Of course, sir. Second best only to the Captain, sir." Abby swung the shovel from her shoulder, letting it clatter to the ground as she snapped her arm up into a crisp salute at Henrietta.

"Clever girl," Henrietta said, curling the edges of her lips into a grin. She flicked her gaze to Bill, who continued to flit his hand over the stone. "Are we there?"

"Not yet. But this is the starting point," he answered, spinning around and pressing his back against the stone. He raised a finger in the air. "Thirty paces from the arrow stone."

Henrietta, Clif, and Abby eyed him as he stepped forward, placing his right heel against the toes of his left foot. He continued the process for thirty paces. They followed him into the field, wading through the high grass.

He came to a stop, his arms outstretched as he brought his feet together.

"Is it here?" Henrietta asked. "Do we dig here?"

Bill shook his head and twisted a quarter turn to his right. "Forty-five paces."

Henrietta lifted her eyebrows at the man as he stomped forward with one foot in front of the other. Clif puckered his lips, following behind. Abby brought up the rear.

"You believe him, don't you?" Henrietta whispered.

Several paces ahead of them, Bill snapped his head to the side. "I'm not lying!"

"It just seems rather convoluted," Henrietta called.

"Well, I do not want it found!" he answered as he continued his deliberate march forward.

He stopped and balled his hands into fists, his eyebrows pinching together. He sank to his knees, feeling around on the ground. His fingers smacked into a large stone and his lips curled up at the corners.

He rose to his feet, dusting his hands off.

"Dig at the stone, Bill?" Clif asked.

"No," he answered. He spun again and pointed a finger in front of him. "There is a cave yonder. Hard to see. Should be fifty paces away."

Clif squinted into the darkness in the direction Bill pointed. "There's nothing there, friend."

"It's there," Bill said, his smile broadening. "You can't see it. That's what makes it such a good hiding place."

Henrietta arched an eyebrow at her brother as they continued to follow the blind man into the night. As they ambled forward, a large stone wall rose into the sky. It appeared solid from a distance. Even as they approached it closer, they could see no opening.

Bill strode toward it, his arms outstretched until his fingers banged into the stone. He bounced back a step before he pressed his hand forward again, running it along the rough stone's edge. After a moment, his hand disappeared into the stone.

"A hidden cave," Henrietta said with a satisfied grin as she relieved Clif of the lantern. "Reminds me of something."

Clif wiggled his eyebrows at her. "And you didn't believe him."

"I stand corrected." Henrietta answered, holding her hands up as Bill twisted sideways and slipped into a black hole.

She strutted forward and slid into the difficult-to-find hole where Bill had disappeared. Clif motioned for Abby to precede him, following her into the cave after a glance around.

Henrietta's meager light bobbled in front of them, bouncing off the stone on either side. The passage narrowed, requiring them to inch through sideways before it spilled into a large chamber.

"We're here," Bill announced as he stepped into the round chamber. "We dig against the far wall."

Henrietta nodded and glanced behind her at Abby. She thumbed toward the stone on the opposite side. "Get to it, Miss Turner."

Abby nodded and hurried across the sandy soil, thrusting the shovel into the earth and tossing it aside. Henrietta held the light overhead as Abby worked, sweat beading on her brow as she toiled to remove dirt from the hole.

"How far down is it buried?" Henrietta questioned as Abby, out of breath, swiped her forearm across her forehead.

"Deep enough to be safe," Bill assured her.

"I shall keep going," Abby said after sucking in a deep breath.

"You may rest for a moment if you'd like," Henrietta told her.

She leaned against the shovel and licked her lips before she shook her head. "No. I shall dig until we find it."

She firmed her lower lip and thrust the shovel into the hole again. Henrietta puckered her lips as Abby lifted shovelful after shovelful of dirt and dumped them on an ever-growing pile in the middle of the chamber.

Sweat soaked the back of her thin nightgown as she continued to work.

Henrietta held a hand up. "All right, stop."

Abby knit her brows but stepped back from the oval-shaped hole she'd dug. "I'm sorry, Captain…" she began.

"There is no apology needed. However, you need to rest a moment." Henrietta flicked a finger to the opposite wall. "Sit down and collect your strength."

"I can keep digging–"

"I ordered you to sit down. Sit down," Henrietta answered, snatching the shovel from her hands.

Abby flicked her hand up to her forehead in a crisp salute. "Aye, aye, Captain!"

Clif scrunched his nose at the girl's overzealous behavior as she strode across the cave and collapsed in a heap against the wall. Henrietta handed the lantern off to Clif and slammed the shovel into the earth. She lifted it and flung the dirt over onto the pile.

"We're already deep into the earth, Bill," Clif said as his sister tossed more dirt from the hole. "How deep is it?"

"Deep, I tell you. It must be kept safe!"

"Safe isn't the word for this, old man," Henrietta gasped as she drove the shovel into the dirt again and lifted more soil out.

She pulled six more shovelfuls out before the shovel smacked into something hard as she stabbed it into the deep hole. A tremor shot through her arm. She snapped her gaze up to Clif, a surprised expression on her features.

A smile formed as she tapped against the object again. She tossed the shovel aside and bent over the hole, stretching into it to uncover the object. Clif dropped to his knees, setting the lantern at the edge and joining her.

They brushed away the sandy earth, uncovering a dark wooden box. Henrietta raised her eyebrows as she grinned at Clif. They scraped dirt away from the sides, and Clif wrangled it out from the hole, and set it on the ground in the middle of the chamber.

"Did you find it?" Bill asked, his eyebrows raising.

"That we did, old friend." Clif shot a devilish grin at his sister. He rubbed his hands together as he tugged the latch open. It squeaked before it smacked against the lid.

Abby climbed to her feet, her jaw unhinging as she rose to her tiptoes to peer over the box's lid as Clif swung it open.

Henrietta's eyes went wide at the contents and she offered Clif a giddy smile. A fist-sized diamond sat atop a folded parchment. She snatched it from within, eyeing it in the flickering flame from the lantern.

"And there's more where that came from," Bill said as she blew out a breath.

Clif pulled the map piece from inside the box and unfolded it, his brows pinching as he stared at it.

A gurgling gasp filled the air. Clif's and Henrietta's gazes snapped in the direction of the tunnel leading outside.

The smile faded from Bill's face. "What's happening?"

Henrietta rose to her feet, the diamond dropping to the earth as she unsheathed her sword. Clif shot to standing, pulling his pistol from his holster.

"I'll be taking that stone and that map piece," the grizzled man said. His dirty fingers wrapped around the pale skin of Abby's neck while the other waved a pistol toward them.

CHAPTER 9

"I don't think so," Clif answered.

Henrietta narrowed her eyes at the man. She recognized him as one of Isaac's posse. "You'll have to kill us for it."

"Or her," the man answered.

Abby winced as he tugged against her. A tear rolled down her cheek. "I'm sorry, Captain," she choked out.

Henrietta squeezed her lips together and shook her head. She'd saved the woman hours ago and offered her a chance at freedom only for her to be caught by the same men and threatened again.

"Kill her and you die, too," Clif warned.

"I can shoot her," he said, waving his gun at Henrietta, then kill her. He tightened his grip on Abby and jiggled her. "Don't think you want that, do you, Jack?"

"It will cost you your life."

"Yeah, it may. But your precious sister'll be gone, too."

Henrietta narrowed her eyes as she inched sideways before taking a step toward him. "Is your aim that good?"

"Good enough," he answered. "Stay where you are!"

He swung the pistol to follow Henrietta's movement. With his attention distracted, Clif rushed toward him. Abby stopped tugging at his grip on her neck and elbowed him in the gut. He doubled over, releasing his grip on her. She stumbled away from him as he staggered back a step, the pistol wavering in the air.

The gun fired in a brilliant flash. A deafening blast echoed throughout the chamber.

A cry escaped Henrietta's lips as Clif rammed his shoulder into the man, slamming him against the wall.

Air escaped the man's lungs as he crumpled to the ground below. Clif pummeled him with his fists until blood sprayed from his nose and tricked down from his lips. The man, bloodied and bruised, fell into an unconscious heap.

"Clif!" Henrietta called.

Clif snapped his gaze to her. "Ri? Are you shot?"

Henrietta knelt on the ground across the chamber. She twisted to face him, her features pinched.

Clif handed his gun to Abby. "Keep it trained on him."

She nodded as he hurried away from her toward Henrietta. "What is it? Are you hurt?"

She shook her head, her lips squeezed tightly together. "No, it's Bill."

Clif dropped to his knees next to the man sprawled in the dirt. Henrietta clutched his hand in hers as blood bloomed across his shirt.

Bill gasped in ragged breaths. Clif stared down at the blood-soaked shirt for a moment before he tore it open. Blood oozed from a wound in his stomach.

Abby rushed over, hovering over them with the lantern. "Stomach wound."

"He won't make it," Clif breathed. He raised his voice, patting Bill's shoulder. "Easy, old friend. Try to relax."

Bill groaned, his lower lip quivering as he sucked in a

breath. Abby squinted down at him, the lantern's light bouncing around as she leaned closer.

Henrietta gasped in a breath. "He needs help."

"Won't do any good," Clif answered. "Stitching is not what he needs."

Henrietta furrowed her brow, snapping her gaze to the woman hovering next to her.

Abby shook her head and nudged her way between them, dropping to her knees. "The bullet is still in there. That's the problem. We need to get it out and then press hard against his wound until he can be stitched."

Clif shook his head. "It's a gut wound. I've seen them before. And seen men die from them."

"Yes," Abby answered. "If they are in the wrong spot, yes. But this is to the side. Saw a man in the brothel with a scar in almost the same place. He's living just fine."

She leaned over him and tugged open his mouth, running her finger around inside. She pulled it out and studied it in the dim lantern light before wiping it on her nightgown and shoving him on his side.

"What are you doing?" Henrietta asked as Abby gnashed her teeth and tried to push at him again.

"He has no blood in his mouth, so the wound may not be fatal. Help me roll him over and we'll check if the bullet came out."

Clif grabbed hold of Bill's arm and together they rolled him onto his side. He groaned in pain as he moved.

Abby tugged his shirt up and pointed to his unblemished back. "No wound. You see? The bullet remains inside. We must remove it."

Bill choked on air before coughing a few times as they settled him back to the ground. "Find the city," he gasped.

"Easy, Bill."

Bill thrashed his head back and forth and puffed another few breaths. "Find it."

"We will, but not before we save your life," Henrietta promised. "We still owe you two fistfuls of diamonds and I'll be damned if I don't pay you."

A chuckle escaped his lips, turning into a sharp cough.

"Put pressure against his wound," Abby instructed. "It would be better if we had a cloth to press against it." Her gaze darted around the darkened chamber. She rose and raced to the unconscious man across the cavern. "Help!"

Henrietta hurried toward her as Clif shoved his hands against Bill's stomach. Together, the two women wrangled a vest from their former attacker.

Abby sprinted across to Bill and handed the garment to Clif. "We should remove the bullet here, then carry him to the ship to be stitched."

"Johnson is an excellent stitcher," Clif answered, "though it may be best to leave him handle the bullet as well."

Abby shook her head as she pushed Clif's hands away. "No, moving him with the bullet in his wound may be worse."

"How do you know?" Henrietta inquired as she retrieved the diamond and map piece, shoving both into her pockets.

"My father was a doctor before he turned to the drink. I've seen many a man with wounds and the bullet can do more damage inside than not."

"Good to know," Henrietta said, sinking to her knees next to the woman. "What must we do?"

"Give him the cloth to bite on," Abby said. "I'm sorry, sir, this will hurt."

Clif wadded the vest and shoved it into Bill's mouth as Abby stuck her finger into his wound. Bill's muffled, yet agonized screams echoed off the stone walls as Abby bit her lower lip and continued to wiggle her finger inside his abdomen.

"Hold him down," Abby instructed as he flailed, trying to strike her.

Clif shoved his shoulders back to the ground as Henrietta laid across his legs.

Abby pressed her lips together, her eyes flicked upward. "Almost… a few more seconds."

The shrieking stopped and Bill's limbs went limp as he slipped into an unconscious state.

A bead of sweat formed on her brow as she clenched her teeth and wrinkled her nose. She squeezed her eyes shut and retracted her finger. A round lead bullet thudded against the ground as she raked a hand across her forehead.

"Got it." She sat back on her haunches and blew out a breath. "Remove the cloth from his mouth and press it against his wound."

She raced across the chamber again and loosened the other man's belt buckle, whipping the belt from around his waist. She returned to Bill and slipped it around his waist. "We'll tighten this around him to hold the cloth on while we carry him."

They cinched the belt around his wound, tugging it snuggly against his skin to keep the cloth tight to the wound. Carefully they began to lift him to his feet.

"Did you get the map piece?" Clif asked Henrietta as they straddled him between them.

"I did, yes."

"Good, Bill will kill us if we left it here."

"No chance, brother," Henrietta said with a hard breath as she adjusted the man's arm around her shoulder.

Across the chamber the other man groaned as he awoke.

"Time to leave," Clif said.

"Hurry," Henrietta gasped as they shambled across the chamber.

Abby retrieved the pistol she'd held earlier and pulled back the hammer. She aimed at the man as he rolled onto his back, his forehead pinching before his eyes snapped open. His gaze flitted around before he recalled the events from moments ago.

He growled as he tried to push himself to stand.

"Not so fast," Abby said, pointing the pistol at him.

"What are you going to do? Shoot me?" He flashed her a grin, his gold tooth gleaming in the flickering light.

"Yes," she answered. She lowered the pistol toward his leg and fired, stumbling back a step from the recoil. The gunshot echoed off the walls. Abby's ears rang from the shot.

The man cried out as the bullet struck him. He toppled over to the dirt, grasping at his bloody leg. Abby darted after Clif and Henrietta as they labored to drag Bill along with them in the narrow passageway.

"Did you shoot him?" Henrietta questioned. A bead of sweat rolled down her hairline, dripping from the edge of her jaw.

"Yes, of course," Abby confirmed as she handed the pistol back to Clif and waved Henrietta away from Bill. "I'll take him, Captain."

Clif shoved the pistol into his holster, his brow crinkling at her statement. "What do you mean 'of course?'"

Abby swung Bill's arm over her shoulder as Henrietta shimmied to position herself to lift his legs when they cleared the narrowest part of the passageway. "I mean I shot him. In the leg. We couldn't have him following us."

Clif shot Henrietta a glance as they labored to pull Bill closer toward the open air.

"Quite right," Henrietta said.

"I cannot believe you shot him!" Clif exclaimed as the

night air tickled their cheeks while they struggled the final few steps.

"He was a filthy sod. A regular at Isaac's. Liked to rough up us girls," Abby answered as they stepped under the starry canopy. "It felt quite good, actually."

Henrietta raked the back of her hand across her forehead before nodding at Abby. "Good for you. Let's get him to the ship and have Johnson patch him up."

"And then what?" Clif inquired.

Henrietta tugged the diamond from her pocket and waved it in the air. The massive rock caught the moon's light, scattering it across the ground in a rainbow. "And then we sail."

"With Bill?"

"We cannot leave him here," Henrietta argued.

Clif pressed his lips together, hefting the unconscious man higher before they stepped forward. "Why don't you just invite the entire island?"

"That would be ridiculous, Clif," Henrietta said with a sly grin as they marched back toward the docks.

They reached the outskirts of town, hurrying through the streets toward the tavern. Loud voices reached their ears as they rounded the corner. The tavern came into view, lit up brightly against the night sky.

Torches burned, their flames shooting toward the stars. Angry voices grumbled and shouted.

Henrietta stopped walking, surveying the scene. She twisted and spoke over her shoulder, her eyes remaining trained on the crowd. "We should avoid this."

"I'd agree. It appears to be trouble," Clif answered. "Though circling around will take us past the brothel."

"Then we circle around that, too," Henrietta replied.

"There is a back alley we can use to avoid them," Abby whispered.

Henrietta adjusted her grip on Bill's legs. "Lead the way."

Abby motioned with her head toward their right. They slipped between two buildings. A foul stench met their nostrils as they reached the end. A wooden fence pressed them against the back wall of the smithy's shop behind them.

Henrietta swallowed hard, choking back the bile rising in her throat. "What is that smell?"

"The pigs," Abby answered as they side-stepped their way past the building.

"It's awful," Henrietta groaned.

"You live on a ship," Abby retorted. "You cannot tell me the smell is much better."

Henrietta choked out a cough. "I can and I will."

"I cannot imagine the smell below decks being worse than this," Clif added.

"Oh, it's getting worse," Henrietta said with her nose wrinkling.

They continued lumbering to the building's corner.

Abby jutted her chin out toward the last few slats of the fence. "The pigs are at the end of this fence."

They emerged from the narrow passage. The alley next to the tavern stretched toward the angry mob.

"We'll just need to squeeze behind it at the tavern," Abby whispered before a shout sounded behind them.

They twisted to eye the crowd. A burly man swung his torch toward the alley. "I found them!"

"Uh-oh," Clif said, his eyes going wide. "We'd better start squeezing."

"They're heading behind the pub! Circle around and cut them off!"

"Damn it," Henrietta cursed. "Now what?"

"This way," Abby said, tugging them in another direction.

Henrietta pulled back against her. "Which way? We cannot go back the way we came!"

"No, of course not."

"Then where?" Henrietta's eyes scanned the surroundings.

Men marched toward them down the alley, guns waving in the air. Light bloomed around the corner of the tavern's opposite side. Henrietta sucked in a breath as they closed in around them.

"This way!" Abby insisted, tugging Bill and the others toward a post and rail fence in front of them.

Henrietta held back, her eyes wide. "Into the… pigsty?"

"Yes, into the pigsty! It's the only way." Abby dropped Bill's arm and climbed through the fence, reaching for him. "Give him here while you climb through."

Bill moaned as he started to awaken.

Clif leaned him against Abby as he darted over the fence. "Lift his legs over, Ri."

Henrietta nodded as the group continued to close the distance between them. With a shout, she flung the nearly conscious man's limbs over the fence. Abby and Clif stumbled back a step into the mud but remained upright.

"Hurry, Captain!" Abby shouted as they began to cross the pigsty, a moaning Bill draped between her and Clif's shoulders.

Henrietta swung a leg over the lower rail and squatted, sliding her back under the top board. She lifted her other leg, pulling it through as she steadied herself against the post.

Her leg caught, a piece of her trouser fabric becoming stuck on a shard of wood. Henrietta yanked on the pant leg, trying to free it while balancing on one leg.

She wobbled on her ankle as she reached for the caught fabric and worked to free it.

"Ri! Hurry!" Clif shouted.

Henrietta flicked a wide-eyed gaze at the angry crowd approaching. Her breath caught in her throat and she wrenched at the pant leg in a desperate attempt to free herself. A groan escaped her lips as the fabric tore but not enough to free her.

She swayed on her one foot. Her lips pulled back in a grimace and she let out a frustrated cry. Tears welled in her eyes.

"Ri! Get down!" Clif shouted.

Henrietta gasped in a breath, snapping her head in the direction of the mob as she tried to squat down. A loud bang ricocheted off the buildings around them. Heat seared her cheek as a bullet grazed past her.

CHAPTER 10

Henrietta's jaw dropped open as warmth gushed down her cheek. She reached toward it, pressing her fingertips gently against her flesh. She gasped as they stung her skin, pulling her shaky hand away.

The moonlight reflected the blood smudging them. She glanced at the man still pointing the pistol at her. Luckily, the bullet only grazed her cheek.

She tugged at the pant leg again, desperate to free herself, keeping her eyes trained on her attacker.

Another gunshot resounded in the air. She jumped, all her muscles tensing. A second later, the man who had shot at her stumbled backward, clutching his shoulder. The weapon flew from his hands, clattering onto the ground as he cried out in pain.

Henrietta whipped her head behind her. Smoke curled from the end of Clif's pistol. He shoved it into his belt and hurried toward her. She returned to teasing the fabric from the jagged piece of lumber.

"Hurry, Ri. They're closing in and I can't hold them all off."

Henrietta yanked at the fabric. It shredded, tearing down the length of it to the hem. With the force tethering her leg to the wood gone, she wobbled before stumbling back a few steps.

Her arms flailed before she flopped backward. Mud splattered around her as she sank into the smelly substance.

"Ugh!" Henrietta cried, her lips forming a disgusted grimace. She shimmied back and forth trying to free herself from the muck.

She pushed against the ground with her hands, sinking further into the sludge.

"Hurry!" Abby's voice called from across the pen.

"Come on, Ri! Quit mucking about in that mud." Clif stuck his tongue between his teeth, an amused grin on his face.

"Help me up," she snapped, yanking her hand out of the thick mud and reaching for him. Mud flung from her fingers onto his face.

The grin faded as he wiped the dirt away from his cheek and reached for his sister's hand, tugging her from the sludge.

They hurried toward Abby as another bullet blazed past them. Henrietta ducked her head as she ran alongside Clif.

"You really know how to make enemies, Ri."

"Oh, like you didn't make many as Black Jack."

"None that chased me from Tortuga with torches and pitchforks."

"They've got a bit more than that," Henrietta said as they reached Abby.

Clif flung Bill's arm over his shoulder. Henrietta grabbed his feet and together they carried him across the rest of the pen.

"Thank goodness," Henrietta exclaimed as they reached the end. "This end has a gate."

She dropped Bill's legs as she chucked open the gate. Bill moaned again as she lifted his legs. He went stiff before he began kicking and screaming.

"Easy, Bill," Clif said as the men chasing them scrambled over the fence while others attempted to skirt around the pen. "We're nearly there."

"No! No!" Bill shouted.

Henrietta grabbed hold of his feet, steadying them. "Quiet, old man. We're saving your life."

Bill let out another low moan as they continued through the gate.

"Wait!" Abby shouted as they cleared it.

"What?" Clif hissed.

"We need to close it." Abby struggled to stretch back and swung the gate shut, latching it.

They continued along the way, winding around the grassy knoll at the edge of town before they rounded toward the docks.

A few of the mob made their way toward *The Henton*.

"Oh, bollocks!" Henrietta shouted as they continued toward the docks. "They're here, too."

"Of course they are. Can you ladies carry him the rest of the way between you?"

"Clif!" Henrietta exclaimed as she dropped Bill's feet. "Are you mad?"

Clif swung the man's arm off his shoulder and shoved him toward Henrietta. "I'll be fine. Take him."

The woman adjusted his weight between them. Bill's head lolled toward his chest as he drifted in and out of consciousness. A string of drool dripped to the dirt below. His feet dragged behind them, scraping against the ground and sending a cloud of dust billowing into the air.

They raced to the floating dock. Bill's feet thumped

against each board as they hurried toward the ship. Henrietta glanced over her shoulder.

Clif stood behind them, his sword drawn as three men approached. He waved it in the air, strafing it back and forth.

"Give us the girl," one of the three yelled, pulling a knife from his belt.

"Mmm, no," Clif answered. "She's paid for. She is ours."

"That's not what Isaac said," another shouted, thrusting his sword toward Clif.

Clif knocked the sword aside as the man stumbled forward. "You've been drinking far too much to win, Angus."

Clif swung at him again with his sword, knocking the blade from the other man's hand before he delivered a left hook. The stunned man's eyes crossed before he stumbled a step, spinning from the blow. Clif kicked him in the rear, sending him splashing into the ocean below.

Another man shrieked, racing forward and slamming into Clif's shoulder. Clif threw him off, waving the sword toward him. They danced back and forth, thrusting and parrying as the dock floated under them.

Clif drove him backward, their swords clashing against each other. The second man joined in the fight. Clif switched his attention toward the other man, their swords clanging as he tried to drive him away from their ship.

He shifted his attention back and forth between the two men, trying to keep them both at bay. They began to drive him back toward the edge of the dock.

He inched closer to the edge, wobbling as he attempted to stay upright and on the floating wood. One of the men lunged at him. Clif side-stepped, sending the man spilling over the edge into the water.

He grinned as the man splashed into the ocean. As he twisted to face his remaining opponent, he found himself at the tip of the man's sword.

"Drop your weapon, Jack. You're defeated."

Clif lifted his chin, swallowing hard as he lowered his arm, his sword still clutched in his fingers.

"Drop the sword," the man growled again, his lips twisting with disdain. "You're beaten."

"I don't think so," a new voice answered as a sword slipped under the man's chin and pressed against his neck. "Move and you're a dead man."

The man's eyes slid shut as he dropped his sword arm to his side.

A grin spread across Clif's face, and he raised his sword in the air. "You know," he answered, "I have a reputation for leaving one man alive. So I suppose that shall be you."

The man stepped back a step away from them, his hands raised in defeat.

"Though that does not mean I will let you stand on the docks as we slip away," Clif added. He raised his sword and inched the man backward toward the edge of the dock. "Off you go!"

Clif poked him in the belly until he stepped backward, plunging into the ocean. He spun to face Henrietta, offering her a bow. "Thank you, Ri. I was nearly captured."

Henrietta smirked at him as she sheathed her sword. "I have no doubt you could have wiggled your way out of that sticky situation. However, a little help never hurt."

He cocked his head and grinned at her. "Did you take Bill to Johnson?"

"I did and we are ready to set sail. Johnson recalled the crew when the trouble began brewing in town."

"Excellent." Clif glanced over his shoulder at the growing crowd that thundered toward them. "I suppose we should go."

"Unless you prefer a challenge?"

"I propose we save the challenges for the City of Diamonds."

"Then, shall we?" Henrietta inquired, sweeping her hand toward the ship.

"After you, my dear sister," Clif said with a bow.

She grinned at him as they set off toward the ship. They climbed aboard, pulling the plank up. Clif strode across the deck, asking one of the sailors on deck about Johnson.

"Below deck, sir, tending to the wounded man."

Abby hurried across the deck boards toward them, her nightgown stained with blood. She skidded to a halt in front of them, snapping her arm up in a salute at Henrietta. "Blind Bill is nearly stitched, Captain. What orders?"

Clif opened his mouth to answer but Henrietta beat him to it.

"Send Mr. Johnson up and finish up with Bill, then report to my quarters," Henrietta answered.

Clif arched an eyebrow at his sister's commands.

Henrietta glanced at him as Abby saluted and sprinted across the deck and disappeared down the stairs. "What?"

"Nothing, *Captain*," he answered with a salute.

"We are both Captains," Henrietta argued as they waited for Mr. Johnson to appear. "And I should learn to give orders and run a ship."

Clif crinkled his brow at the statement but the arrival of Johnson interrupted any further discussion.

Johnson wiped his blood-stained hands on a rag. "He'll live. Damn good thing that lass pulled the bullet out when she did."

"Good," Clif answered with a nod. "Weigh anchor and set course for Hideaway Bay."

"Now, sir?"

Clif glanced at the crowd that had reached the floating dock. The angry mob stormed toward them. He turned the corners of his mouth down and nodded. "Yes, I'd say the sooner the better."

"Aye, aye, Captain!" Johnson exclaimed before he barked orders at the sailors.

Preparations began, and the anchor and sails were raised. The boat slipped away from the dock. The angry mob reached the edge as the distance between the floating boards and the ship grew.

"Coward! We'll be waiting when you return!" one of them shouted.

Johnson raised his eyebrows at the sentiment, flicking his eyes to Clif.

"Don't worry, Mr. Johnson," Clif said, clapping him on the shoulder, "once we find the City of Diamonds, we shall be welcome everywhere. Inform me when we approach the Bay."

After a salute from Johnson, Clif and Henrietta strode toward the captain's quarters, letting themselves inside.

Clif collapsed into the chair behind the desk, tugging his belt from around him and tossing it onto the desk. His sword and gun clattered against the wood as he slouched in the chair and kicked his feet up. "You made quite a number of enemies."

Henrietta removed the diamond and map piece from her pocket, tossing them onto the desk before retrieving the notebook from her hammock. "The job of a pirate."

She flipped it open and removed her notes, spreading them across the desk before she unfolded the map. The lantern flickered as the ship rocked to and fro when it hit open waters.

She snatched it by the holder and dangled it over the map piece, narrowing her eyes at it. She puckered her lips as she traced her finger along the elements before referencing the notes.

"Anything?" Clif asked, his fingers interlaced behind his head.

Henrietta flung her arms in the air. "This is impossible. The few vague references and this partial map are of no help to us."

"What's this? Ri defeated? And I thought there was nothing you couldn't do."

Henrietta shot him an unimpressed glance as she set the lantern down near the scrap of parchment and studied it again.

Clif's nose crinkled as she leaned over the desk, tracing a mark on the parchment. He flared his nostrils, glancing around the dimly lit room.

Henrietta slid a sheet of her notes closer and compared the information to the map.

Clif removed his feet from the desk, leaning forward with his eyes narrowed. He glanced under the desk before craning his neck to sniff under his arm.

"What are you doing?" Henrietta asked.

"What is that smell?" he asked.

Henrietta sniffed in the air. "What smell?"

"That horrid smell. It smells like–" His nose unwrinkled and his shoulders slid down his back as he set his lips.

Henrietta straightened and stared down at him. "What?"

"It's you."

"Me?" she cried.

Clif stood and poked a finger at her. "Yes, you! You fell into the muck in the pigsty and you stink. Ugh!"

He pinched his nose shut with his fingers. "Take those off," he said in a nasally tone.

Henrietta scowled at him, crossing her arms over her chest. "I do not smell."

He waved a hand in the air, flicking it away from him. "No, you don't. You stink. It's foul. Oh, Ri!"

"You're a pirate. You live on a ship, and you can't take the smell of a bit of mud from a pig."

"No, it's awful. Please, I beg of you, change those clothes. You cannot sleep in here tonight if you do not."

"You jest! This is my cabin as much as it is yours! You cannot kick me out."

He stuck his hand on his hips and raised his eyebrows as he circled behind the hammock away from her. "I can and I will."

A knock sounded at the door, interrupting their conversation. Henrietta flicked her gaze over her shoulder at it. "Come!"

The door creaked open and Abby stepped inside. She eased the door closed behind her and snapped her arm up into a crisp salute as she stiffened her posture.

"Reporting, Captain. Bill is resting. I am here to retrieve the clothing. And ask where I shall sleep. Or I could ask Mr. Johnson."

Henrietta crossed the room to a trunk and tossed it open. She tugged a set of trousers, a shirt, a vest, and boots from within. The lid snapped shut as the ship rolled on the waves.

Abby stumbled backward before catching her balance.

"You need your sea legs," Henrietta said as she handed the clothing off to her new crewman.

"Yes, Captain. I am certain I shall have them soon. I was only on the sea once before when my father took me to Tortuga. But I did not become sick even once. Of course, the ship was not this large."

"I believe these boots will fit."

"They are most appreciated, Captain. And I shall speak with Mr. Johnson about my assignment and sleeping arrangements."

"Report to Mr. Johnson tomorrow morning at first light for your assignment. You will sleep across the deck in the storage room. There is a door on the starboard side. Set up a hammock inside."

"Yes, Captain!" Abby said with another crisp salute.

She spun and grabbed the doorknob.

"Just a moment," Clif said.

Abby spun backward and cocked her head at Clif. She flicked a nervous gaze to Henrietta, swallowing hard. "Yes?"

"Settle a matter for us before you go." Clif crossed his arms over his chest as he wandered around the hammock. "Does Captain Blanchard smell?"

Henrietta clicked her tongue and rolled her eyes.

Abby's eyes widened and she flicked a gaze to Henrietta, pressing her lips together.

"Go on," Clif encouraged with a wave of his hand. "Give her a sniff."

Abby's lower lip bobbed up and down for a few moments before any noise came out. "Uhhh…"

"Go ahead, Miss Turner," Henrietta answered, signaling her to come closer. "Sniff away."

Abby pressed her lips together and leaned closer to Henrietta. She flared her nostrils and inhaled deeply. Her lips tugged downward at the corners as she straightened. She pulled them into a thin line, her eyes narrowing as she forced a smile onto her face.

"Well?" Clif inquired.

"Nothing," she answered.

Henrietta arched her eyebrows high and glanced at Clif. He cocked his head at her. "Give her another, longer smell."

"Really, sir, I did not…"

"Another," Clif said, pointing to his sister.

Abby shot a pleading glance at Henrietta who waved a hand in the air.

"Go ahead."

Abby crinkled her forehead as her lower lip quivered. She leaned forward, giving a tentative sniff.

"No, a good, long whiff," Clif instructed.

Abby swallowed hard, puckering her lips and inhaling deeply. A gagging cough escaped her lips halfway through her inhale.

"A-ha! I knew it! I knew it!" Clif shouted. "She stinks. The pigsty tainted her."

"I fell into the mud. What do you expect? It cannot be that bad. Surely at the brothel, you have smelled worse stenches than this," Henrietta said, turning her attention to Abby.

"Not many so bad as that, Captain," Abby said, her eyes lowering to the floor.

Henrietta flung her arms out to the side. "Fine. I shall change." She poked a finger at Abby. "Your first assignment will be to launder my clothes."

She disappeared behind a changing screen stuffed into the corner with a change of clothes, flinging the dirty ones across the floor as she stripped down and pulled on a new set.

Abby scurried to retrieve them as Henrietta stepped out from behind the screen, still fiddling with her belt. "There, happy now?"

"Infinitely," Clif said with a bow to her before he spun to Abby. "Do not worry about washing them, simply burn them."

Abby sucked in a breath and nodded.

"You shall do no such thing! Wash them," Henrietta retorted.

Abby's eyes went wide and she shook her head before changing it to a nod at Henrietta.

Clif set his jaw, his eyes burning into his sister. "Burn them. I would suggest tossing them overboard, but I fear for the ocean life."

"Clean them," Henrietta said, her eyebrow arched as she stared at her brother.

Abby's lips formed words that did not come out. She flicked her gaze back and forth between the siblings.

"Burn," Clif said, his eyes narrowing as he accentuated the word.

"Clean," Henrietta answered, setting her hands on her hips as she stared him down.

Abby flung an arm between them. "I shall attempt to clean them and if the stench remains, I shall burn them."

Henrietta slid her gaze sideways as the ship rolled again. "You will make an excellent sailor, Turner."

Abby raised her chin and balled the clothes under her arm before offering another salute. "Good night, Captain."

"Good night, Miss Turner."

The girl stepped from the room with both sets of clothing balanced in her arms, leaving them alone.

"Quite a smart girl," Henrietta said.

"Very savvy," Clif answered. "Now, about your progress to find the City of Diamonds."

A violent rocking of the ship interrupted their conversation. Henrietta stumbled back a few steps, struggling to stay upright as Clif pitched forward, bending at the waist as he fought against the pull of the ship.

"Now what?" Henrietta questioned as she grasped at the wall to stay upright.

A massive boom thundered, shaking the ship.

Clif stumbled to the door and flung it open. Crewmen scrambled back and forth across the deck, shouting to one another.

He stepped out of the cabin and glanced backward to the ship's wheel in search of Johnson. The man scurried down the stairs to the main deck.

"Captain! Captain!" he shouted as he hurried across the deck.

"Johnson? What the hell is going on?"

"We're under fire."

"From what?"

Johnson dragged Clif toward the railing and thrust his arm behind them. Another ship closed the gap between them. Clif's eyes bulged as a cannonball shot toward them.

CHAPTER 11

The round iron ball splashed into the ocean on their port side. Water splashed over the side of the ship as Henrietta stepped to the railing.

"Ugh," she groaned as she removed her hat and shook the water from it. "Damn it. Another feather ruined!"

"Never mind the feather, Ri. We have an issue." Clif held his hand out. "Spyglass."

Johnson tugged it from his belt and passed it to Clif. He extended it and studied the ship. His nose crinkled as he handed the spyglass to Henrietta and pointed.

Henrietta squeezed one eye shut and stared through the spyglass. "Are they a threat?"

"Definitely," Clif answered. "That is Whitemane Webb."

Johnson's eyes grew wide. "No, not Whitemane."

"Unfortunately, yes. We must make a stand."

"Captain!" Johnson shouted.

"We cannot outrun *The Pillager*. She is faster."

"She is also better equipped! Captain, this is a losing battle."

Clif rubbed his lower lip. "We have no choice. We cannot outrun them. We must outfight them."

Clif stepped away from the railing, striding to the stairs leading up to the helm. "Captain! We are outgunned."

"Then we must be smarter than them and make the best use of the weapons we have."

Another cannonball sailed toward them, splashing into the ocean on their starboard side.

"He likely will not miss many more times," Clif said as he took the steps two at a time.

Henrietta followed behind him with Johnson hurrying after them.

"Let out the sheets," Clif said as he grabbed the spyglass back from Henrietta and trained it on the horizon in front of them.

Johnson bellowed the order. "I assume we will try to outrun them."

"Negative, Johnson. But we need time to plan."

Clif swung the spyglass backward and studied the approaching ship. With four more cannons and twenty more men aboard, they could easily be overtaken.

"We should make a stand," Henrietta said, her hands on her hips.

"Yes, we must. But if we do not plan well, we shall be easily overtaken."

"What's your plan?"

Clif pressed his lips together as he scanned the horizon again.

"Clif?" Henrietta prodded.

"We cannot win outright. We cannot outrun them. But we can attempt to disable the ship and skedaddle."

"I'd prefer to stay and fight," Henrietta said.

"We would lose. Our men are brave, yet we are outnumbered and outgunned. We must save the fight for another day when we have the advantage. There are no islands near behind which we can duck and hide."

Henrietta narrowed her eyes as she stared at the approaching ship. "If we are both outnumbered and outgunned, how would we ever have the advantage?"

"Simple. If we have surprise on our side. In this case, we do not. He has us on the run and it will take an excellent plan and a pinch of luck to get us out of this."

"Clif!" Henrietta screamed, her finger pointed behind them.

Clif grabbed hold of her and pulled her down toward the deck boards. A cannonball slammed into their stern. The ship rocked from the impact, shuddering under them.

"Damn it!" Clif said, rising to stand. He raced to the railing and stared over it toward the water. A head popped out of the hole now blown into the ship's rear. "Patch that hole, sailor!"

"Yes, Captain!" the man called before ducking back inside.

Clif spun and stalked toward Johnson. "Mr. Johnson, have the men on the port side only load all cannons and be prepared to fire them. When they are ready report to me. Tell them to hurry."

"Aye, sir," Johnson said with a salute. He barked a few orders out, sending a man scrambling down below decks with the message.

Henrietta glanced around at the barren sea, then over her shoulder at the fast-approaching ship. "What is your plan?"

"Simple. When the cannons are ready, we shall fire."

"Fire?" Henrietta questioned. "The port side cannons will do us no good. Perhaps if you stuck a cannon out of the hole he just blew in our stern we would have a fighting chance of hitting him."

"I plan to turn the ship before we fire, Ri," Clif answered.

"You'd better start turning," Henrietta replied.

"No," Clif said, "he'll anticipate our move and prepare for a battle."

"Will it not be?"

The ship rocked on the sea as Clif glanced at the fast-approaching enemy ship. "No. I plan to strike him with a critical blow and sail away as quickly as possible."

"Critical blow?" Henrietta shouted. "How do you plan to strike a critical blow with cannons facing the wrong direction!"

Clif handed her the spyglass and pointed toward the other ship. She squeezed one eye closed as she stared through it.

"See the front of his ship? Right below the mermaid?"

"Yes?" Henrietta answered.

"I plan to blow a hole right through it. It should be enough to slow him while we make a getaway."

Henrietta squashed the spyglass closed and stared at her brother with wide eyes. "Are you quite mad? You have yet to explain to me how you will blow a hole through his ship *with guns facing the wrong way!*"

"I already told you, we will turn."

Henrietta's eyebrows scrunched. "By the time we turn, he will be upon us."

"Not if we do it quickly."

Johnson's face blanched at the statement. "Oh, no."

"Oh, yes," Clif answered with a nod.

"No, no, Captain, please," Johnson begged.

"Will someone please explain to me what is going on?" Henrietta huffed.

"He plans to–" Johnson scrubbed his face with his hand and swallowed hard. "A clubhaul."

"A clubhaul? What are you saying?"

"A clubhaul. My signature move," Clif said with a raise of his eyebrows. "Simple and effective."

"Also dangerous," Johnson argued, "and untested in this ship. *Neptune's Servant* was smaller and more agile. You could tip us, Captain. *The Henton* may not recover as deftly. Please. This is foolish."

"What choice have we?" Clif questioned. "Show me a valid alternative with better odds of success and I shall use it."

He stared at the man, his eyebrows lifted as he waited for an answer. Johnson's features pinched and he shook his head.

"As I suspected. Clubhaul, it is," Clif said, poking a finger in the air.

Henrietta flung her arms in the air. "What on earth is a clubhaul? Will someone please explain to me?"

A pale Johnson swallowed hard again, his features still wrinkled with worry. "We swing hard toward port, then drop the anchor. The weight will snap the ship back, twisting us sideways."

"At which time we fire the cannons, raise the anchor, let the sheets out full, and glide away," Clif added, his fingers fluttering in the air.

"If we are not capsized by the force that will be exerted on the ship."

"We will not capsize, Johnson," Clif assured him.

A sailor raced up the steps and saluted to them. "Cannons are loaded and ready."

Johnson shot a pleading glance at Henrietta. "Please talk sense into him. This is a foolish plan."

Henrietta studied the man before directing her gaze over her shoulder at the ship approaching.

With a deep inhale, she twisted back to face Clif. "I trust him. Clubhaul it is."

"Oh, heaven help us," Johnson said.

"Prepare the crew, Johnson. We shall put into port at Hideaway Bay by daybreak."

"If we are not putting into port at the bottom of the ocean first!"

Clif offered a devilish grin at his first mate. "We will survive this. I have no intention of dying today, Mr. Johnson."

Henrietta clapped a hand on the first mate's shoulder. "Neither do I. Though I do crave a bit of adventure and this should do."

"Ohhhh," Mr. Johnson groaned as he removed his hat and ran his fingers through his unruly hair. He huffed out a worried breath before he began to shout orders to the crew.

They dashed to their stations, preparing for the tricky maneuver. Another cannonball shot from the boat behind them, narrowly missing their stern and splashing into the water.

"Shall I give the order, Captain?" Mr. Johnson asked.

"Not yet."

"But, Captain–" he began.

"Hold, Mr. Johnson. We must time this perfectly."

"Captain, he is nearly on top of us!" Mr. Johnson shouted, waving his arms in the air.

"Hold!" Clif said, lowering his chin to his chest as he stared at the ship approaching them.

Henrietta crossed her arms over her chest, arching an eyebrow before flicking her gaze from the other ship to her brother.

Clif raised a finger in the air, the corners of his mouth turning upward as he waited, counting the seconds before he swept his hand downward. "Now!" he shouted.

"Hard to port!" Johnson shouted.

The helmsman spun the wheel at breakneck speeds until it turned no more. "Hard over!"

"Drop anchor!" Johnson shouted. He firmed his jaw, adding through clenched teeth, "Hold tight, and pray."

The rattling of the chain resounded through the air as the anchor dropped into the water. The weight tugged the ship sharply sideways. Clif grabbed Henrietta's arm as she stumbled back a step from the shuddering tug that whipped the ship into a near-perfect quarter turn.

The ship tipped, rolling toward the ocean. The mast leaned toward the undulating waves, threatening to kiss them.

Henrietta grasped tightly onto Clif's arm as he stood firm on the deck. For a moment, she worried Mr. Johnson would prove correct and they would capsize. She swallowed hard as the horizon disappeared, her view becoming nothing but dark sky.

Mr. Johnson squeezed his eyes closed, his hands clasped together as they tilted, coming dangerously close to tipping over. The ship groaned before she began to right herself.

The moment the horizon appeared in their vision again, Clif uttered one word. "Fire."

"FIRE! FIRE! FIRE!" Johnson shouted.

Cannons blasted as the approaching ship started a slow turn to engage in battle. Cannonballs roared from within *The Henton*'s belly. They sailed toward their target.

"Lift anchor and reset course," Clif answered, his eyes trained on the other ship.

Johnson shouted the orders as the first cannonball splashed into the water. Clif wrinkled his nose at the miss. The next cannonball found its mark, smashing across the bow of the ship and blowing a chunk of the mermaid into the water. Another blasted into the ship's side, blowing a hole into its hull.

Yet another found its mark, crashing through the railing of the ship and clunking onto the main deck.

Whitemane shouted orders to his crew who scrambled to stop the turn of the ship and ready cannons to fire.

The Henton's helmsman swung the wheel hard to starboard as the crew below decks hauled the anchor up. The ship continued along the same course. Clif chewed the inside of his lower lip as he waited for the ship to turn.

"Captain, they are preparing to fire upon us. We may not escape it. We are not turning fast enough."

"Turn, damn it," Clif muttered.

"Drop the other anchor then pull it up immediately," Henrietta said.

"What?" Mr. Johnson exclaimed before shaking his head.

"Drop the other anchor," Henrietta repeated. "Do it now before they fire."

Clif furrowed his brow, his eyes sliding sideways as he considered the move. "Do it."

Johnson heaved out a frazzled sigh before issuing the order. The crew dropped the port side anchor, snapping the ship again to the opposite side. They hauled it up as the ship continued its turn, putting distance between it and *The Pillager.*

Henrietta stared back at the other ship as it struggled to turn and pursue them. "We did it."

"He will not catch us now. We can slip away."

"But he caught us before," Henrietta said, her brow furrowing.

"His ship turns too slowly, it will cost him time. Plus with the damage we inflicted, he's lost some of his speed."

"So, we may make our escape."

Clif offered a sly salute to his sister. "Good thinking on dropping the opposite anchor, Ri. You are becoming an excellent sailor."

Henrietta raised her chin at the compliment.

Clif glanced around her to his first mate. "Now, Mr. Johnson, we continue on to Hideaway Bay. Awaken us when we have arrived."

Johnson saluted before clasping his hands behind his back. "Aye, aye, Captain!" He spun to shout orders to the other sailors as Clif and Henrietta descended the stairs and ducked into their cabin.

"Now," Clif said as he settled into the chair at the desk, "you were telling me your progress with the search."

Henrietta strode toward the desk, collecting the papers, journal, and map piece that had toppled to the floor in their wild effort to escape the other pirate ship.

She set them on the desk and leaned forward, placing her palms on the edges. Her lips curled into a smirk. "I think I know where we will find the next clue."

CHAPTER 12

Being dead was more interesting than being alive. Memories of a more turbulent time raced through Henrietta's mind as she peered through the spyglass before handing it off to her brother.

The ship rocked on the gentle waters as they approached the seaside town of Hideaway Bay. Streaks of red limned the buildings in a rosy glow as the sun set behind it and darkness crept over the eastern sky.

Henrietta leaned against the railing as she stared at her former home. "Appears deserted."

"I told you Carolina is away," Clif said as he glanced through the spyglass. "Still, we should wait for the cover of complete darkness before we attempt to enter."

Henrietta spun and pressed her back against the railing, her arms crossed over her chest.

"Do you miss it?" Clif asked her as he squashed the spyglass into its retracted form.

"Life at Whispering Manor?" Henrietta questioned.

Clif nodded at her as he balanced his elbow against the railing.

"Not in the slightest."

He raised his eyebrows at her. "Really? You find life on *The Henton* more appealing than being mistress of a grand home?"

"Infinitely. I am loathed to even don a dress and return to pretend to haunt the home."

"Come on, Ri," Clif said with a devilish grin as the light around them continued to dim. "I believed you would enjoy the role of the frightening apparition."

"I far prefer my role as Captain and all the freedom it allows me. Though if I manage to alarm the townsfolk in this sleepy burg, so be it."

"I never realized how much you disliked life in Hideaway Bay."

Henrietta cast her eyes down at her toes. "I did not dislike life in Hideaway Bay. I did not mind life in Hideaway Bay after we reconciled, and I established my freedom."

"Would you have preferred not to leave?"

Henrietta arched an eyebrow as she considered the question. "No, I prefer to move forward. And this life allowed me to do so."

"Are you quite happy then?"

"Yes," Henrietta said, the corners of her mouth turning upward, before she flicked her gaze to Clif, "I am."

Clif flicked his eyebrows up and down and grinned at her. "Good. Well, I suppose we should get to our plan so we can be on our way to begin our search for the next component."

"Perhaps you could play the role of the ghostly grieving widow," Henrietta said, cocking her head at her brother.

Clif guffawed, drumming his hands against the railing. "Me? Are you mad?"

"I am not. You seem positively tickled by this plan. Perhaps you would prefer to don the dress and wave it about in the wind whilst I retrieve the staff."

"You wouldn't know where it is. I can find it faster."

"I am certain I will manage. I would find it rather amusing to see you waving your arms about from the widow's walk."

Clif arched an eyebrow and wrinkled his nose. "Surely, you jest."

"I do not."

He slapped his hand against the railing again as he twisted to face her. "Sorry, sister, I have no desire to imitate a fair lady such as yourself. In fact, I am quite certain I would never match the finesse and gusto with which you could haunt your former home."

Henrietta pressed her lips together and narrowed her eyes, shaking her head at him. "Fine. And I quite agree, your ability to play the ghostly widow is likely far, far below mine."

"Without a doubt," Clif said with a grin. He offered his arm and she accepted. They strolled down the stairs and into the cabin. Clif bowed to Henrietta. "I shall see you when you are ready to row across and visit the old homestead."

Henrietta bobbed her head up and down at him as she pulled the dress from inside the trunk. Abby slipped past Clif before he pulled the door closed behind him.

"I came as soon as Johnson told me, Captain," Abby said with a crisp salute. "He said it was a special mission."

"Indeed," Henrietta said as she waved the dress in the air. "I will need a bit of assistance."

Abby cocked her head at the fabric swishing in the air. "Oh! Are you going ashore for dinner?"

"No," Henrietta answered as she tossed the dress to Abby. "I am going to haunt a house."

She slipped off her belt and tossed it over the screen before she tugged her shirt from her pants.

"Haunt a house?" Abby answered, her blonde eyebrows smashing together as she unfurled the fabric.

"Yes. Did you see the large seaside dwelling off the port side?"

Abby nodded as she readied the dress for Henrietta to step into after she slipped off her trousers.

"It is my former home."

The girl's eyes went wide. "Captain! You owned that home?"

Henrietta rolled her eyes as she tossed the trousers over the top of the screen and stepped into the dress. "No, I did not own it because the laws do not allow it. Ridiculous, however, I did live there."

"As a child?" Abby inquired, skirting around Henrietta to begin fastening the dress in the back.

"No, as a married woman."

"I did not realize you are married, Captain."

"I am not," Henrietta answered, sliding her arms into the dress and pulling it up around her shoulders. "I was married. My husband died at sea."

"Oh, how tragic. Was he, too, a pirate?"

"No, he was a legitimate sea captain. Or so I thought," Henrietta explained. "He died in search of a treasure after gambling away most of our money. Fortunately, for me, Clif purchased the home and I remained in it."

"That was very kind of him," Abby said as she worked to close the dress.

Henrietta snapped her head to glance over her shoulder, annoyed by the comment. "I provided a service in return, so only half kind."

"Of course, Captain," Abby said, her head bowed.

Henrietta pressed her lips together and gave a slight shake of her head. "It was kind, you are correct. Clif has always taken care of me. It is because of him I escaped from that life and am able to make my own way on the sea."

"Which is what I wish to do," Abby answered as she finished with the fastening and adjusted the dress.

Henrietta spun to face her. "And I aim to provide you and other women with the same opportunity. If all goes to plan, we shall be able to do just that."

"With your trip to the mainland, you mean?"

Henrietta fussed with the frills on the dress's bust as she shook her head. "No. Something quite different. As soon as I have finalized it, I shall share it with you."

Abby grinned at her and nodded. "I am so pleased you accepted me onto your crew, Captain. I promise to work hard and learn all I can. I have some knowledge of nautical knots and I am learning all the parts of the ship."

"Good," Henrietta said. "Do not allow the men to deter you from your goal or intimidate you."

Abby raised her chin high. "I will not. I plan to become a great sailor and serve you always. You shall be a shining example of bravery to me."

"Go seek out Mr. Johnson and ask him to teach you the sail riggings."

Abby offered a crisp salute. "Yes, Captain!" She scurried from the room in search of the ship's first mate.

Henrietta glanced down at the material around her. It swayed and glided across the floorboards as she moved. She wrinkled her nose at the fabric and tugged at the lace collar around her neck. *It may as well be a noose.* She'd left this life behind and she wanted no part of it now.

Still, a job needed to be done. And she would do it. Even if it sent shivers up her spine to don the clothing of her old lifestyle. She sucked in a deep breath as anxiety coursed through her. She feared becoming stuck in these clothes, becoming stuck in that life again.

Henrietta shook her head. Clif would not abandon her. She would return to the ship and her pirate lifestyle as soon as they retrieved the golden staff. And, with any luck, she'd have frightened a few townsfolk, leaving a lasting impression of Henrietta Blanchard on the town.

The corner of her mouth ticked upward into a smirk. Yes, she would be brave and she would take this in stride.

With a dip of her head in silent agreement with her affirmation, she strode from the cabin and into the night air.

Clif leaned against the railing, gazing up at the stars. He straightened as she stepped out, floating across the deck in the light fabric. He raised an eyebrow at her as she lifted her chin.

"Well, am I frightening?"

"Ghastly," Clif answered with a mischievous grin. "Shivers run down my spine at the sight of you."

Henrietta smirked at him. "Well, let us go. I have no desire to remain trussed up in these clothes for longer than I need to be."

"Really?" Clif inquired as he waved her to the open railing.

She lifted her skirts and climbed into the skiff before settling onto a hard wooden seat and letting the fabric fall around her. "Yes, really," she answered. "It is most uncomfortable."

"Who would have ever thought my sister would prefer trousers," Clif answered as he settled next to her and the crew lowered them to the water.

The boat hit the water and the crew plopped the oars into the calm sea and rowed them to the shore. Clif scooped Henrietta into his arms before splashing into the water and striding to the shore. He set her on dry land where her dress would not become wet.

"Thank you," she answered. "And this is why I prefer

trousers. I am not quite so helpless then."

"Helpless is not a word I would ever use to describe you, Ri."

She grinned at him as they approached the house, hiding behind the pine trees near it. Moonlight filtered around them as they hid in the shadows. "A smart answer, brother."

They peered from behind a large conifer trunk at the darkened home. "I do not see anyone," Clif whispered.

"Neither do I."

"Come on. I shall jimmy the lock on the front door. You go to the widow's walk while I access the passage. With any luck, Carolina has left us a candle handy with which we can navigate."

Henrietta rolled her eyes as they stepped from within the canopy of the trees and hurried across the open space toward the house. "Knowing Carolina, she has a striker laying next to it to be used the moment she returns."

"Really, Ri," Clif said as they climbed the porch steps, "you ought not be so hard on her."

Henrietta glanced over her shoulder, scanning their surroundings. "Old habits."

Clif bent to one knee in front of the door, sliding a tool into the lock. "Give me light."

Henrietta struck a striker and lit a piece of parchment, shining it near the door lock. Clif wrangled the thin metal back and forth with a grunt as he twisted the doorknob.

The paper burned down to nothing, singeing Henrietta's fingertips. She dropped it as smoke curled from the burnt edges, shaking her hand in the air as she issued a curse. "Ouch!"

"Light another," Clif said.

Henrietta lit another paper aflame and held it toward the lock. "Try to be faster this time. I do not wish to burn my fingers again. Nor do I think we can easily explain why I, as a ghost, must break through the front door of the house I haunt."

With a flick of his wrist, the door creaked inward on its hinges. Clif rose and bowed, swinging his arm inside. "After you, my dear specter sister."

"Do not dally whilst retrieving the staff," Henrietta chided as she lifted her skirts and stepped over the threshold of her former home.

Dark silence met them as they stepped inside. Henrietta lifted her chin, her eyes raising up the wide staircase framed by two angels carrying lanterns.

"Oh, goody, Carolina left a candle," Clif called from the library.

"Surprise, surprise." Henrietta stepped to her left and lit the wick.

Clif held the tiny flickering flame under his chin and grinned at Henrietta. "Try to have fun, Ri."

"Try not to dally, Clif," she retorted as she spun on her heel and stalked from the room. The stairs creaked as she mounted them.

The footsteps receded and the floor above Clif creaked as Henrietta climbed to her ghostly perch. With a glance over his shoulder, Clif eased his sister's novels from the bookcase and held the flame closer.

Six brass reels glowed at the rear of the shelf. Clif spun the dials, spelling HENTON. The locking mechanism disengaged and the shelf popped forward. A smirk crossed his lips and, with one final glance over his shoulder, he tugged the shelf open and disappeared behind it into the secret passage.

The candle's flame flickered as he hurried down the corridor hewn from the rock below the house toward the blocked-off sea cave. The passage turned from manmade to natural before spilling into a large cave.

Clif raised the candle high over his head as he scanned

the trunks scattered throughout the room. His lips pulled back into a grin as he eyed the treasure he'd collected over his years as the infamous pirate, Black Jack. Now he searched for a new treasure. But a piece of his former collection would help him.

Before securing it, he filled several pouches with gold and jewels. After securing them to his belt, he wandered across the cavern and lifted the lid of a chest with his foot. Gold gleamed back under the orange candlelight.

He set the candle on the floor as he knelt in front of the chest. His fingers glided over the bejeweled chalices before shoving them aside and reaching deeper into the chest.

He withdrew a large golden rod. A pair of wings rose from the top of the lavishly decorated staff surrounding an egg-sized ruby. Clif eyed the object before his finger depressed one of the large diamonds near the top. A pointed tip, as sharp as a butcher's blade, shot out of the bottom.

Clif smiled at the rod as he pressed the pointed tip against the stone floor and shoved it back inside the staff. He rose to his feet, lifting the candle with him.

He shuffled to the cave's entrance and took one last glance at his treasure. "Perhaps I'll return for you one day. Until then, I have bigger ventures to pursue."

He stepped from the cave and hurried up the passageway to the house. With any luck, he could sneak to the upper floor and surprise Henrietta while she haunted the widow's walk. He'd pay for it later if he pulled it off, but it would be well worth the look on her face.

A devilish grin crossed his features as he pushed the bookcase open. The smile faded from his lips as voices echoed in the dark house.

Clif's heart sped as he grabbed his pistol and readied it. Someone had followed them into Whispering Manor. And their intentions could not be pure.

CHAPTER 13

*H*enrietta stood on the widow's walk with her hair twisting in the wind that gusted from the sea. The white dress billowed in the breeze. She wrapped her fingers around the cool metal railing and stared out over the now-choppy waters.

Many a night she had stood on this walk and done the same thing. She had played at the reluctant widow, awaiting the return of her sailor husband. And it was from this very perch that she had faked her own death, pretending to throw herself to the ground below, too grief-stricken over her husband's death to go on with her life.

Her lips curled into a smile as she considered her life now. She preferred its freedom, and loved the adventure.

She puckered her lips as she pondered if her brother had completed his task yet. She eyed the sea cave in the distance, wondering if he remained inside or if he already returned through the passage his men had hewn from the rock.

A flicker of light caught her attention in the distance. She squinted her eyes as she stared into the pine trees surrounding Whispering Manor. Her chin dropped toward her chest as two men emerged from them and hurried toward the house.

They circled around it and disappeared on the front side. Henrietta chewed the inside of her lip. Who were they? And why were they approaching Whispering Manor in the dead of night?

She stepped to the metal door leading inside and yanked it open. Darkness yawned back at her. Voices floated from the lower floor. Henrietta strained to hear them, leaning into the house.

"…split up and search," a man's voice hissed.

"How sure are you?" another man's voice responded.

"Sure. They had to have hidden the treasure here."

Boots tramping across the hardwood sounded but stopped after only a few steps.

"Wait. What about the ghost?"

"Ghost? There are no such things as ghosts, you simpleton. Now get searching."

"If it's all the same to you, I'll keep my gun at the ready."

"Do whatever you'd like. Though if you do run into a ghost, I don't think a pistol will protect you."

Footsteps echoed through the house as the men traipsed around in search of the treasure rumored to have been hidden in the home.

Henrietta wrinkled her nose at the conversation. How dare these two nitwits enter her former residence, now her sister's residence, to rob it? She would teach them a lesson they'd never forget.

She stepped onto the stairs leading down and allowed the door to slam shut behind her. The footsteps quieted.

"What was that?" one man shouted as Henrietta descended the stairs to the upper floor.

"How should I know? I thought it was you banging around."

"It weren't me!" the man answered. Boots scraped against the floor as he hurried toward the entryway where Henrietta loomed at the top of the stairs.

"Oooh, do you think it was the ghost?"

"No, you moron, I do not. Ghosts aren't real, dummy."

"Then what made that noise?"

The two men met in the foyer. Henrietta held back rolling her eyes at the two disheveled simpletons standing below her.

"How should I know what made the noise?"

"A ghost, that's what!" the shorter man shouted, pressing his hands against his forehead on either side.

"How many times must I tell you... there are no such things as–"

"WHO GOES THERE?" Henrietta's voice boomed from the top of the staircase.

The shorter man yelped in fear, his eyes going wide as he shot a frightened glance at the other man. The taller man froze, standing stock still, focused on the shorter man.

"WHO ENTERS MY HOME?" Henrietta shouted again.

"Edgar!" the short man answered.

The taller man swatted at him and shook his head. "You fool. Do not answer!"

"But–"

The other man waved at him, signaling him to be quiet. "None of your business. Go back to Hell from whence you came."

Heat rose in Henrietta's cheeks and she balled her fists at her sides as anger coursed through her veins. "BE GONE FROM MY HOME BEFORE I DRAG YOU TO HELL WITH ME."

The short man winced, clutching at the other man's forearm. He patted it frantically. "Let's go. We angered the spirit of Mrs. Blanchard."

The taller man's gaze flitted around the room. "I'd like to see you try."

Henrietta thudded down a stair in her ethereal white dress, her chin held high. She stared down her nose at them. The shorter man gasped as he focused on her.

A shaky digit rose in the air, pointing at Henrietta. "Look! There she is! The ghost!"

The taller man squinted up at her, his jaw dropping open. "No, it cannot be!"

"Yet, it is. I am the ghost of Henrietta Blanchard. Returned to roam the house for all eternity and punish those who step foot inside for nefarious purposes."

The shorter man pressed his lips together and gulped. "Y-y-you hear that, Fred? It's the ghost of Mrs. Blanchard, and she's going to punish us!"

"If she's a ghost, she can't do anything to us."

Henrietta's gaze flicked to movement in the library. Clif crept to the doorway, his gun raised.

"I can harm you, and I will. Leave now or I will inflict my wrath upon you. When the bell rings thrice, I shall strike."

Clif receded into the darkness of the library. A moment later, a breeze rustled the lanterns hanging from the angels at the foot of the staircase and a bell chimed.

Henrietta eased herself down two more steps as the men shot a glance toward the library.

The shorter man gasped, his muscles stiffening. "Did you hear that? The bell chimed once already. She's called the winds of Hell upon us!"

"That's the breeze from outside. I smell the sea."

"How'd she bring it inside though? And how did she ring the bell?"

Henrietta stood still again and stared down at them with her arms outstretched. "Be gone or I shall rain fire upon you."

The bell chimed again, this time sounding like it came

from the sitting room. Henrietta held back a giggle as she pictured her brother flitting around the house with the servant's bell in hand.

The shorter man pulled his lips into a grimace. "Come on, Fred. That's the second chime. We're doomed if it rings again."

The tall man narrowed his eyes up at Henrietta, studying her. "That's not the ghost of Henrietta Blanchard. It don't even look nothing like her."

Henrietta struggled to keep her composure as the idiot below her rambled on about how she didn't look like herself. "Check the portrait in the sitting room. I assure you it is I."

"I-I-I saw the portrait, Fred. That's old Henrietta for sure. And how would you know anyway? You never saw her."

"Neither did you, outside of her portrait."

"That ain't true. I saw her once walking to post letters. Looks just like her."

"I still ain't convinced she can harm us." The tall man returned his attention to Henrietta. "If you can harm us, go ahead."

"Fine. I shall begin with you, Frederick Barnes." Henrietta pointed a finger at him, and the bell chimed one last time.

The shorter man squeezed his eyes closed as he clasped his hands together in front of him and bowed his head. Henrietta arched an eyebrow at the tall man who pushed his shoulders back and sneered at her.

"You can't harm me, you stupid bi–"

A loud bang cut off his words. Blood burst from his shoulder, discoloring his white shirt. He screeched in pain, grabbing at the wound as he doubled over.

"Fred?" the other man asked, snapping his eyes open and staring at him.

"I'm shot!"

"What?" Edgar asked, studying the blood oozing between Fred's fingers. "How?"

Fred pulled his hand away from the bullet wound and pointed a shaky, blood-stained finger at Henrietta. "She did it. The ghost did it!"

He gasped out a breath as he pressed his hand against his wound again. "I ain't never going to doubt again. Henrietta Blanchard's ghost is real! And I'll never deny it again. Come on, Edgar. Let's get out of here before she shoots me a second time!"

"Be gone, gentleman. And tell all who will listen of your frightful tale. Tell them Henrietta Blanchard will not allow thieves and pilferers in her home."

Edgar's chin bobbed up and down frantically. "We shall tell them, Mrs. Blanchard. We shall tell them!"

He placed a hand against Fred's back and led him out the front door. In their haste to escape, they left the front door swinging open. The two men lumbered down the stairs out front, racing away from the home.

Henrietta wandered down the remaining steps, a smirk on her full lips as they scurried away.

Clif stepped from inside the library, shoving his gun into his holster. "Well played, Ri."

She arched an eyebrow at him. "Your bell ringing was nothing short of brilliant."

"Really? And I considered the gunshot to be my crowning achievement."

Henrietta cocked her head and thrust out her lower lip. "No, the moving bell really set the tone." She swung the door shut before returning her gaze to her brother. "Did you get the rod?"

Clif retreated into the library and returned waving the golden staff in his hand.

Henrietta's lips curled into a smile. "Then I suppose our work here is finished."

"Shall we return to the ship? I am quite interested to know of our next destination."

Henrietta eased the door open and stared outside, scanning the surroundings. "Looks clear."

"We shall keep to the shadows, just in case," Clif said as he offered his arm.

They stepped from the house, securing the door behind them before they circled around the wraparound porch to a tree-lined side of the house. Clif leapt over the railing and reached up to help Henrietta over the wooden barrier. She shimmied over and hopped to the ground. They disappeared into the cover of the trees.

"Well, did you have fun haunting your former home?"

"I must admit, I did find it amusing to play the role of a ghost."

Clif held aside a pine branch as Henrietta stepped closer to the beach. "Will you be leaving the crew of *The Henton* to take up haunting on a regular basis?"

"As tempting as it is, no. I much prefer pirating to ghostly shenanigans."

Henrietta lifted her skirts as she climbed into the beached boat and settled onto the hard wooden seat.

"Really?" Clif asked, hopping in next to her and settling onto the bench. The skiff moved forward, pushed into the water by two other sailors before they leapt in and grabbed their oars.

"Of course. Especially with the bounty on the horizon."

Clif raised his eyebrows as the oars dipped in and out of the water, pushing them toward the ship hidden in the cove. A grin crossed his lips and he waved the golden rod in the air. "And what a bounty it shall be."

Henrietta stared at the gold, glinting under the moonlight. "May I see it?"

"Of course." Clif thrust the gold rod toward her.

Henrietta accepted the proffered item, balancing it between her palms as she studied it. Her eyebrows arched at the gemstones adorning it. She ran her fingertips over the wings, noting the fine detail in the craftsmanship.

"And you say we need this to access the City of Diamonds?"

"That is what I understand, yes."

"Hmm. I shall study it whilst we make our way to the next location."

Clif stood as they reached the ship, and the men worked to steady the boat. He thrust a hand out toward Henrietta to pull her up. "Good. If anyone can solve this puzzle, you can, Ri."

She handed him the golden rod before grasping the rope ladder and climbing aboard *The Henton*. She strode to the cabin, eager to reclaim her pirate clothes and dump the dress into the chest, hopefully never to be needed again.

She reached behind her and tugged at the fastening of her dress, freeing it as she slipped behind the screen. She shimmied out of the white fabric and slid her shirt over her head before tugging on her trousers.

A shout sounded from the deck. Henrietta ignored it, wrapping her belt around her after tucking her shirt in. As she pulled on her boots, more shouts resounded. With a sigh, she glanced at the door. "What now?"

"Ri!" her brother's voice called. "Come out here, please!"

"Oh, heavens," Henrietta huffed. She raised her voice and called through the door. "Just a moment!"

With a grumble, she shuffled to the door and tugged it open. Clif stood near the main mast, his arms crossed over his chest. In front of him, a worried Mr. Johnson clutched his hand.

"Here we are," Clif said, waving his hand in the air at her.

"Did I hear shouting? What is the problem?" Henrietta inquired as she strode toward them.

"Yes, you did," Clif answered, crossing his arms again and flicking a finger toward the consternated man in front of him. "Please explain to Johnson where we must go."

Henrietta stuck her hands on her hips and flicked her gaze to Johnson. "Moaning Isle."

A whimper escaped his lips.

Henrietta batted her eyelashes at the reaction. "Is there a problem?"

"Please, Captains, let us abandon this gambit."

Clif flexed his jaw and raised his eyes to the darkened sky.

Henrietta knit her eyebrows. "Abandon it? Whatever for?"

"Seeking the City of Diamonds is dangerous enough but Moaning Isle? No."

"What is the problem, Mr. Johnson?"

Johnson's face pinched with worry as he shook his head. "No one leaves Moaning Isle alive."

CHAPTER 14

Henrietta pondered the statement as Johnson's white-knuckled grip on his hat tightened and he continued his tale. "Terrible beasts prowl its jungles. Many a sailor has landed on the island and disappeared."

Clif lifted a shoulder. "And we shall not be among them."

Henrietta settled her hands on her hips, her thick eyebrows still pulled tightly together. "How do you know this about the beasts?"

"Stories get around, Captain," Johnson answered, his dark eyes going wide.

"Stories from whom? It cannot be survivors, you said there were none."

Johnson opened his mouth to answer before his brow furrowed. He clamped his lips shut as he studied the moonlit deck.

"As I suspected," Clif said. "Nothing more than wild tales told by drunken men."

"But–"

"Set the course, Mr. Johnson," Clif said with a nod.

Johnson flicked a pleading gaze to Henrietta again.

"Please, Captain. Surely you do not wish to step foot on a piece of land called Moaning Isle. Named for the shrieks heard when sailing past. And *that* is the truth! Many men have heard the terrible wails that drift from that island."

Henrietta's lips curled at the corners and a chuckle escaped from her.

"Gospel truth, Captain," Johnson said with his hand pressed over his heart.

"Mr. Johnson," Henrietta said, her mouth still stuck in a smile, "I lived in a house called Whispering Manor. I am certain I can stand it."

Johnson's shoulders slumped at her words. He opened his mouth again, but she waved her hand in the air to stop his response.

"Set the course, Mr. Johnson," Henrietta said.

He lowered his chin but offered a solemn nod. "Yes, Captains."

Their gaze followed him as he shuffled across the deck and lumbered up the steps as though walking to the gallows.

Clif shook his head before he strode away, pulling Henrietta with him.

"How in the world did you ever become a successful pirate with Bill "Cowardly" Johnson as your first mate?" she inquired as they returned to the privacy of the cabin.

Clif chuckled, circling around the desk and plopping into his chair. "Johnson likes to temper my wild nature with caution. I told you that."

"Caution?" Henrietta questioned. "I think you may have confused caution with cowardice."

"Johnson is a reliable sailor. And while he may not be as… brave as you, he is smart, loyal, and keeps good control of the crew."

Henrietta lowered her eyes to her feet as she considered

his words. "Is that what one looks for in a first mate? Intelligence, loyalty, and the ability to manage a crew?"

Clif narrowed his eyes at his sister and leaned forward, placing his clasped hands on the desk. "Among other things."

"What things?" she asked, glancing up at him.

"Why?"

Henrietta set her hands on her hips, eyeing her brother. "Just curious."

Clif arched his eyebrows at her before he pushed off the desk to stand. "A first mate must be your most trustworthy compatriot. He–"

"Or she," Henrietta interrupted, waving a finger in the air.

Clif snapped his head in her direction as he paced around the room. "Or she," he added, his eyes narrowing, "must oversee everything, particularly in your absence. You must also trust him… or her… to never betray you. Mutiny is not something you want on your ship."

Henrietta's eyes slid sideways as she considered it. "Mutiny," she murmured. "Does it occur often?"

Clif ceased his pacing, crossing his arms. "Ri, what are you getting at?"

"Merely asking. How do you manage to hold your crew together without mutiny?"

His eyebrows wiggled at the question. "If you do not know the answer to that after the time we've spent together on *The Henton*, you aren't as bright as I originally assumed."

Henrietta glared at him with an unimpressed stare. "Very funny, Clif."

"Another joke for my pub act," he said with a grin.

"I'm being serious. You push the men hard–"

"But not too hard," Clif said, raising a finger in the air.

"You are friendly with them–"

"But not too friendly."

"You give them harsh orders and demand much from them–"

"But not too much. The trick, Ri," he said as he sank into the chair again, "is to treat them with the same respect you wish to receive, be open to their suggestions, but take decisive action when necessary. You must be a leader. Harsh when you need to be, and pliable when the situation warrants."

Henrietta stared down at her younger brother. "And likable. Even as a child, people always liked you."

"People did not dislike you."

Henrietta stalked across the cabin and collapsed into the hammock. "Yes, they did."

"They did not. You were always scowling and fighting against people."

Henrietta swung forward, her feet smacking against the floor with her eyes wide. "Because–"

Clif waved a hand in the air to stop her argument. "I understand entirely. Life has been easier for me as a man. I would not argue that. I had free choice to do whatever I pleased and even when that choice proved… difficult legally, I did not receive flak from anyone."

Henrietta slumped back into the hammock, kicking her feet into it. It swung back and forth as the ship rocked on the waves. She clasped her hands in her lap and twiddled her thumbs, a scowl on her face.

"Stop scowling. You have made your own way in life, others be damned."

Henrietta kept her eyes lowered. "But I will never have the same acceptance as you."

"That is untrue. You already receive it. And it is quite a feat! You are a woman pirate captain. The men respect you, Johnson follows your orders, and you take quick and decisive action when needed. You are fierce, Ri. You have done what no other women have before and you do it quite well."

The corners of Henrietta's lips tugged up, though she fought back the glowing urge to grin.

"Yes, Ri, smile. You have achieved what few others could. Even me. I am one of dozens of pirates. Nothing special about me."

She flicked her gaze to him, and he grinned at her. "You are quite special. Not all pirates are as successful as you."

Clif leapt from his seat again and perched on the edge of the desk. "Quite right. Success is my mark."

She cracked a smile and nodded at him. "And only one other shall rival you."

"Oh?"

Henrietta cocked her head. "Me."

"Of course. I assume you will surpass me, actually. You always liked to be the winner."

"I have not changed in that regard."

"I should hope not. It is the sole reason I expect we shall be successful in our gambit to find the City of Diamonds."

Henrietta flicked her eyebrows up and offered a devilish grin at her brother. "I believe we shall."

"Speaking of, what led you to pinpoint Moaning Isle as our next destination?"

"Seeking to learn, are you?"

Clif rolled his hand as he bowed his head. "I set myself at the feet of the master."

She offered him an amused glance before she pointed at the desk. "Hand me the journal."

He gathered the open leather-bound book and passed it to her. She flipped a few pages back and forth until she found the reference she sought.

Poking a finger at the page, she said, "Here. See this note you made."

Clif squinted down at it, reading aloud, "The secrets are hidden by the wailing and gnashing of teeth." He furrowed his brow and glanced at Henrietta. "How does that point to Moaning Isle?"

"Simple," she flipped a few more pages. "Pair it with this reference. Map pieces are scattered and the women wail when men seek them."

"That likely means they are mourning the loss of their men as the rumors persist that they will be lost if they seek the treasure."

Henrietta shook her head and tapped the book. "No. The secrets are the map pieces. The map pieces are hidden by the wailing of women. The tales of Moaning Isle fit the description. And the tales of woe from anyone who seeks that island only added to my suspicion."

She flipped the page. "Then there is this curious reference. This is what really solidified it for me. Notice the information about a journey into a mountain cave. It fits with the description of the landmarks on Moaning Isle."

Henrietta called his attention to the notes. "A ring of trees surrounds the bottom. The mountain climb to a cave nestled on the north side. And this one." She tapped the page again. "A castle rises from the depths."

Clif's brow pinched further as he tried to piece the clues together.

Henrietta flicked her gaze to him. "You're getting slow in your old age, Clif. A castle rises from the depths. That island contains a volcano that resembles a castle. The bottom is surrounded by a ring of trees. I will bet you a fistful of diamonds there is a cave on the north side."

Clif rubbed his chin as he considered it. "You are correct. It does resemble a castle of sorts."

Henrietta raised her eyebrows and grinned at him. "Of

course, I am. This is why you tasked me with finding this impossible-to-find city."

He smiled at her and nodded as she swung in the hammock below him. "Correct. And it appears I have chosen well for the task. Which is another hallmark of an excellent captain." He waved his finger in the air before he crossed back to the chair and collapsed into it.

"I am so pleased I could add to your already enormous ego with my own success."

"Just wait until you see the size of my ego once we secure the diamonds. But for now, I am going to sleep." He kicked his feet onto the desk and pulled his hat over his eyes as he slouched down in the chair.

Henrietta returned to studying the notes, preparing for the journey into the cave to retrieve the second map piece. If her assumptions proved correct, their next stop would lead them to an Aztec temple. And from there they should be able to piece together the location of the lost City of Diamonds.

Henrietta laid her head back in the hammock and closed her eyes. She pictured herself striding through the jungle, shoving aside large green leaves before stepping into a clearing. A golden temple rose to the sky. Vines crawled the bricks to the top where a large diamond sat perched in a claw.

She stared up at it for a moment before she stalked forward toward the large structure. She climbed the stairs, finding an entrance to the structure halfway up. After ducking inside with Clif, she scanned the large space. Diamonds lay everywhere, some the size of goose eggs.

They'd done it. She bit her lower lip and grinned. They had found the legendary city of diamonds. They'd amassed a fortune and would become legends in their own time. She arched an eyebrow at the wealth laid at their feet.

She bent at the waist and reached for one of the larger

gems. Before she could grasp it, the ground under her shook. She wobbled on her feet, flailing her arms to stay upright.

A giant crack raced down the center of the floor, splitting the temple in two. The fissure widened as she struggled to stay upright. Beside her, Clif swayed, reaching to the nearby wall to balance himself.

"Leave the diamond, Ri!" he shouted. "We must run before the temple collapses."

She nodded, abandoning the gambit to retrieve the gemstone and spinning back toward the entrance. Before she could escape, the floor split again. Another gap bloomed between her and the doorway.

"Jump!" Clif shouted.

The floor continued to shift. She readied herself for the leap, taking a step back before flinging herself toward her brother. Her foot hit the edge and she slipped, plunging downward into the unknown blackness waiting below her.

Clif lunged for her, grasping her wrist and halting her fall. Henrietta dangled above the darkness, desperately reaching for Clif with her other hand.

"Hang on, Ri," he grunted as he tugged her upward.

She clung to him until her feet found the ground and she scrambled to safety, wheezing out a breath. A moment later, the floor holding them broke free and they both plunged into the darkness.

"Ri!" Clif shouted as they fell. "Ri!"

* * *

Henrietta's head rolled back and forth and her forehead pinched. "No," she murmured, "no!"

"Ri!" Clif called again, giving her a shake.

"No!" Henrietta gasped out, vaulting up to sit. She gulped

in breaths as she studied her surroundings. She swallowed hard, recognizing the ship's captains' quarters.

Her hammock swayed underneath her, and she wiped a bead of sweat from her brow. "What is it?" she asked Clif, flicking her gaze to him.

Before he could answer, the ship pitched hard. The hammock swung sideways, nearly smacking into the wall. Clif pitched forward, struggling to maintain his balance.

"What's happened?" Henrietta shouted over a deafening roar.

"There is a violent storm we've encountered. I need you to help me navigate it."

Henrietta nodded as she swung her legs over the side of the hammock and tried to stand. She fell back into the cloth as the ship rocked violently.

As it swayed back, she managed to climb from her bed and stumble across the floor, following her brother to the door. He flung it open to the thunderous sound of rain pounding against the deck. Sailors raced around in a desperate attempt to keep the ship from keeling over.

Shouted orders came from overhead. Henrietta stepped into the pouring rain, her clothes becoming drenched in seconds.

"Take over the wheel! Turn her upwind!" Clif shouted, pointing a dripping finger up toward it.

Henrietta hurried across the deck, clinging to the railing on either side as she climbed up to the quarterdeck. She waved at the helmsman to step away as she took over steering the ship.

"We've got to get ahead of this," Clif shouted to Johnson.

A massive wave crashed over the side of the ship, knocking several sailors off their feet and washing them toward the railing. Two of them righted themselves then disappeared below deck to escape the tumultuous weather.

Clif and Johnson fought their way toward the main sail's rigging, working to release it slightly so it would not tear under the pressure of the whipping winds.

"We need the storm sails!" Clif shouted.

"There's no time, Captain," Johnson responded.

Clif wiped at the water streaming down his face as he stared up at the main mast. "Then we need to lower our sails."

"Captain! We must keep on the move!"

"I realize that Johnson, but the winds are too high. They'll topple the main mast down or tear the sails."

Johnson stared up at the large pieces of fabric whipping in the violent wind as lightning tore across the sky and nodded. "Stow the sails!" he shouted to the few remaining crew members.

They worked to loosen the rigging when the wind caught one of the sheets.

Clif grasped hold of it, shouting for help, "Hold on! Do not let it go full!"

A small figure darted across the soaked deck and grasped the rope, tugging hard against it. Abby's feet slid across the deck and she struggled to hold on to the rigging. The wind whipped again, lifting her feet as the sails snapped.

Clif raced to the rope thrashing in the violent wind and smacking against the deck. He dove for it, grabbing hold of it and yanking it down.

Abby's feet settled back onto the deck boards. She gritted her teeth as she continued to keep a firm hold on the rope.

"Go back to your quarters, sailor," Clif shouted to her over the rumbling of the storm.

"No, sir! My help is needed, and I shall provide it."

Rain dripped off his hat and his chin. "You risk injury or even worse!"

"We risk more if this ship does not withstand the storm!" she shouted back.

He nodded in agreement, wiping the water from his nose. "Mr. Johnson, have Smith and Abernathy please help Miss Turner with trimming and removing the sails. I need to scout a path forward."

"Yes, Captain!" Johnson shouted over the crashing of the waves.

Clif scrambled across the deck, climbing the stairs to join Henrietta who worked to keep the ship moving at an angle as close to the waves as possible. He extended his spyglass, scanning the horizon.

His eyes grew wide as he spotted trouble. Land jutted out on their starboard side.

"Ri! Hard to starboard!"

"I can't!" she shouted over the din. "The waves will overcome us."

Clif hurried toward the wheel and thrust a finger toward the land he'd spotted. "There is land on the starboard side. The undertow will drag us in and smash us upon the rocks."

Henrietta glanced in the direction he indicated, tugging a wet strip of hair from her cheek. Her eyes went wide at the sight and she spun the wheel as quickly as she could, praying the ship turned fast enough.

The waves rocked them again, sliding them toward the land.

"Come on," Clif grumbled, his jaw tight.

"We're not moving fast enough," Henrietta shouted. "We'll be sucked right into the rocks!"

Clif's eyes flicked between the fast-approaching island and the horizon.

"We must let out the sheets a bit."

"We'll lose the main mast if we do that," Clif answered.

"Not if we time it right."

The wheel wobbled under Henrietta's hand. She braced her hip against it and flung a drenched arm toward the mast as the wind whipped. "We just need one good gust."

Clif eyed the sails as they went slack for a moment then nodded. "And more men. Hold that hard to starboard until we get the wind."

Henrietta nodded as Clif scrambled down the stairs. "We need two more men!" he shouted at Johnson. "We must let the sails full for an instant then trim them back immediately."

"Aye, Captain!" Johnson said. "I shall find two more brave souls."

Clif nodded at him before approaching Abby. With a rope wrapped around her waist and secured to the main mast, she remained firmly tethered to the ship. If it sank, however, she may not be so lucky.

"What is the plan, sir?" she shouted over the wind and thunder.

"We must let the sails out full for a short time to harness the wind and steer us away from the island. We'll be smashed upon it if we do not."

Abby nodded, not flinching at the order. "On your word, sir."

Clif grabbed hold of one of the riggings as Johnson returned, tying himself to the ship along with the two others he'd pressed into work.

"On my word, men," Clif said, shooting a glance at Abby, "and… women. We let the sheets out full and trim them back the moment the ship pulls away from the island."

With nods all around, Clif raised an arm in the air. He studied the whipping of the sails for a moment, flicking his gaze between them and the shoreline approaching faster than he'd like.

"Clif!" Henrietta shouted from the helm. "Now!"

Clif flung his arm downward and the sailors frantically scrambled to let the sails out full. The wind gusted and the sails snapped, billowing forward as they caught the burst. The ship sped forward, pulling away from the current that dragged them toward the island.

Henrietta quickly spun the wheel to angle into the hurricane-force winds as the ship threatened to keel. The main mast creaked, and Clif shouted orders to loosen the sails. The skeleton crew hurried to slacken the large sheets as the rain continued to batter them.

Another large wave crashed over the railing, splashing down on the deck as the ship rolled to the side. One man lost his footing and barreled toward the sea.

Clif dove toward him, sliding on the slippery deck boards and wrapping his fingers around the man's wrist before he disappeared into the turbulent waters. Their wet hands slipped as Clif attempted to haul him back.

Clif began to move backward inch by inch, tugged by an unseen force. He firmed his grip on the man as the ship righted itself. The sailor found his own footing and scurried to stand, quickly securing a rope around his waist.

Clif glanced behind him, expecting to find Johnson tugging on the line that tethered him to the ship. Instead, he found Abby. She offered him a salute before returning to her post.

After twenty more nerve-wracking minutes and careful sailing by Henrietta, the winds lessened and the rain died down. Soaked and tired, Clif climbed to the helm. Henrietta navigated the calmer seas.

"We were lucky," she said.

"No, we were smart," Clif countered. "And so is your new protege." He nodded to Abby who stuck next to Johnson like a shadow.

Henrietta flicked a glance at him, her lips turning up at the corners. "I told you she would be valuable."

"She's brave, I'll give her that."

"She is looking to make a name for herself. She cannot get away with the cowardice the men display at times. She would never make it."

Clif stroked his chin for a moment and flicked his eyebrows up. "I suppose you are correct. At any rate, we'd likely have lost Smith had it not been for her."

Henrietta snapped her gaze to her brother. "Nice to know my instincts were correct for once."

"Instincts?" Clif asked as Williams took over at the helm. "You merely felt sorry for her given her circumstances."

Henrietta plodded down the steps with Clif, both of them soaked through. "Not true! I could see the potential in her eyes. She had the gumption to seek help, to better herself, and to take an opportunity, however slim. I realized that would make her an excellent addition to my crew."

"Your crew, is it?" Clif asked with a chuckle, stepping through the door of the cabin behind his sister.

"Our crew," she said with a lift of one shoulder. "Ugh, I cannot wait to be dry."

Clif tugged off his jacket and wrung it out. Water splattered on the floor. He hung it over the desk chair to dry before peeling his shirt off. "Then we should likely return to the deck. Your island is not far off."

Henrietta disappeared behind the screen with a fresh set of clothing. "Then we shall see if I am a worthy member of your crew."

She emerged in dry clothes and retrieved a new hat. Its feather bobbed in the air as she affixed it on her head. "I really must stop ruining my hats."

"You must stop selecting them for fashion, Ri," Clif answered, sliding his own tricorn hat on over his wet hair. "We're pirates. Not high-society wives."

"I am uncertain why being a pirate must preclude me from being fashionable. It is the one true thing I enjoyed of my previous existence."

Clif eyed her before shaking his head. "If anyone can pull off that balance, it is you."

She lifted her chin, her feather wiggling in the air. "Thank you. I aim to be the fiercest and most fashionable pirate on the seas."

Clif tugged his belt around him and secured it before sliding his gun and sword into their holders. "I can imagine the quaking of those you overtake as you parade up and down their decks in your highest pirate fashion."

"When I am finished, they will say 'Black Jack, who?' We only know of Ravishing Ri. She strikes fear into the hearts of men and makes women envious with her fashions."

A shout came from outside the cabin. "LAND HO!"

"That would be your island, Ravishing Ri," Clif said with a bow.

She spun on her heel and stalked to the door, flinging it open and stepping onto the still-wet deck. The rain had stopped. A light mist rolled across the waters in every direction. From it, a dark blob rose in the distance. Thick fog clung to its form.

Henrietta leaned against the railing and stared at the large cloudy island. "At least the rain has stopped."

Clif pointed to a dim bulb hovering on the horizon. "With any luck, the rising sun will burn off the fog. Otherwise, exploring the island may be slow-going."

"Let us hope so. I detest delays."

They sailed closer to the island, slowing in their pace as they awaited more fog to clear. The thick nebula still obscuring the island's features settled on the volcano rising into the sky. Several peaks rose, resembling fluffy castle turrets.

Henrietta glanced at her brother, then back to the landmark. "There is your castle, brother."

"Indeed. Now all that remains is to find your cave."

"And the next piece of the map."

"If I remember my notes correctly," Clif said, rubbing his chin, "there are four pieces of the map."

"Correct. Combined they show the way to the City of Diamonds. And to access it, we need the staff."

"But we shall only have two and the staff. Where shall we find the others?"

"If we must find them, I have ideas."

"If we must?" Clif crossed his arms and narrowed his eyes at her.

"Perhaps we can identify the region with only two pieces. And even if we cannot, the reference to Moaning Isle says map pieces, not map piece. Perhaps all three are here."

The corners of Clif's mouth turned down and he nodded the statement. "You certainly are optimistic."

"We shall find them, Clif. I do not like to lose."

Johnson approached them as the ship floated in the waters far off the island's coast. "Captains, we dare not approach any closer with the fog. We may run aground."

"I agree, Mr. Johnson," Clif answered, letting his arms swing free as he studied the island. "Weigh anchor here and organize a search party."

Johnson pressed his lips together in a thin line. "Captain, I am not certain you will find many men willing to set foot on Moaning Isle."

Henrietta cocked a hip and placed her hand on it. "Is this a ship of cowards or pirates, Mr. Johnson?"

Clif raised his eyebrows and flicked his gaze to the first mate.

Johnson licked his lips and furrowed his brow. "I shall organize a search party." He offered a nod and stalked away from them.

"Moaning Isle has a reputation that causes even the bravest of men to quiver."

"I do not care if they quiver, but I will not tolerate the hiding under their bunks."

Clif's lips pulled back in a slight grin. "You really make an excellent pirate captain, Ri."

Men emerged from below decks, gathering at the railing to stare over at the misty island. A few remarked about its reputation. The wispy fog only added to the haunted ambiance.

Clif climbed a few rungs up the main mast and shouted over them. "Men! We have come to Moaning Isle in search of artifacts leading us to a great discovery. But we must form a search party. Who is with me?"

A few mumbles emerged from the group. The men jostled around as someone pushed from the back of the group and stumbled forward toward Clif.

The small form of Abby lifted a thin arm and saluted him. "I am, sir!"

Clif flicked his gaze to Henrietta before he nodded at the girl. "Noted. Who else?"

No one answered as murmurs continued. Henrietta stalked forward with her hands on her hips. "Really? No one? Not one man outside of this girl is willing to go ashore with us?"

"It's haunted, Captain!" a voice called. "Men do not come back!"

"I thought you were pirates. Did you quake in your boots whenever you overtook another ship? Did you tremble in your trousers when you clashed with other pirates?"

"No!" someone shouted. "But they ain't the ghosts that prowl on that island and suck the soul right from your body!"

"Soul-sucking ghosts?" Henrietta questioned. "Nonsense. Now, I require two search parties of six men each. We have one volunteer already. Who will be the other eleven? Anyone willing to go ashore will be guaranteed a larger share of the bounty."

Slowly, a few men pushed to the front and stood shoulder-to-shoulder with Abby. After a few more minutes, eleven men and Abby stood in a line in front of them.

Clif leapt from his perch and eyed them with a tight-lipped smile. "You shall be handsomely rewarded for your bravery. Now, ready the skiffs. We depart for the island immediately."

The crew disbanded with the search parties readying two boats. The others milled around on the deck, staring over at the ghostly form of the island.

Henrietta and Clif climbed aboard one of the dinghies before the crew lowered it into the water. Tension hung heavy in the air as they hit the water and untethered themselves from the large ship. They rowed through the misty fog toward the sandy shore of the island.

After dragging the rowboats ashore, they gathered at the tree line.

Clif rubbed his chin as he stared at the fog-laden trees before checking his compass. "North is on the other side of the island."

A groan resounded through the men.

"We should split into two groups. One should remain here and guard the beach. The other group should seek out the cave," Henrietta said.

"Captain, I shall do whichever you prefer," Abby said with a crisp salute.

Henrietta nodded at her. "You should be with the search party. Your strength is in your wits."

"She can have it," one of the men said. "I'll stay right here on the beach. I don't wish to go into that jungle."

"There is nothing to be frightened of, Warick," Clif said. "You're letting a silly legend stop you from what will be one of our greatest finds."

The man swallowed hard and tugged his hat lower on his head. "If it's all the same to you, Captain, I prefer to guard the beach."

"Fine. Who else shall join the search for the cave?"

No one spoke up for a moment before a gangly sailor

pushed forward. "Captain, I do not believe we should split the group. We shall need all the men to survive the jungle. Strange creatures prowl within, waiting to feast on men's flesh."

Clif let his head slide back between his shoulders. "The real danger comes from other pirates who may skulk in these waters. There is absolutely nothing–"

A low growl, followed by a shriek, cut off the remainder of Clif's statement. All eyes turned toward the thick trees leading to the volcano. Clif raised his eyebrows at the unearthly noise. He'd never heard anything like it before in his life. And he wondered if the caution urged by his men was not unwarranted. What lurked within the jungle? And would it cost them their lives?

CHAPTER 16

*A*nother hair-raising screech filled the air as the group stared at the tangle of trees in front of them. One of the men sucked in a sharp breath before he spun on a heel and raced away from the trees. His feet splashed in the ocean's waters before he leapt into the waves and swam toward the ship.

"Newbury!" Clif hollered after him. "Get back here!"

The man's hands flailed as he continued his strokes toward *The Henton.*

"Let him go. He shall forfeit his extra portion to the men and women who are brave enough to stay."

"That's not the reason I'm calling him back. These are shark-infested waters. They are–"

"Captain!" Warick shouted, his finger jabbing toward the water.

A fin cut through the waters, heading toward the retreating pirate.

"Newbury! Shark! Come back!" Clif shouted, racing down the beach.

"Newbury!" Warick yelled, following behind Clif.

Several other men from the crew hurried after them, all hollering for the retreating man to return to them.

Clif cupped his hands over his mouth and shouted, "Newbury! You won't make it. Come back."

The man stopped his swimming, his wet hair plastered to his forehead and neck. He spun in the water, searching for the fin. It circled around him as he trod water.

"Swim back! You may remain on the beach with Warick."

"I'll take my chances, Captain! I don't want to be anywhere near whatever's on that island!"

"No, Newbury," Clif called, "you won't make it. It's certain death!"

The man bobbed in the water, following the fin of the shark as it continued to slice the waves around him. The roaring growl resounded from the jungle again. The sound proved enough to scare Newbury further into the sea. He kicked toward the ship, his arms stroking high overhead.

The shark's fin changed direction in an instant, zipping through the water toward the thrashing man.

"Newbury! Look out!" Warick screamed. He slapped his hands against his balding head and shook it. "He'll never make it."

The fin closed in on the man's location, the shark swimming faster than Newbury could manage. Sailors aboard the ship readied to haul him up if he could make it before the blood-thirsty sea creature stopped him. The chance slimmed with each passing second.

A loud boom resounded, and the fin shimmied before blood bloomed in the water around it.

A startled Newbury gasped and spun around toward the shark as the fin disappeared below the water. His wide eyes flicked to the island before he resumed his frantic swimming back toward the ship.

"What in heaven's name?" Warick murmured.

Clif spun to search behind him for whatever Newbury caught sight of before returning to his retreat. Henrietta stood with her gun raised, one eye squeezed closed. She cocked her head as she let her eye slide open and lowered her weapon.

She puckered her lips at her brother as she returned the weapon to the empty holster on her belt. "What?" she asked him as he continued to stare.

He spun to search the ocean again. "There must be another shark out there."

"Why?" Henrietta asked as she joined him.

"That attacked the first one."

"I shot it, in case you missed that," she said, her arms crossed over her chest.

Clif raised his eyebrows and shot her a sideways glance. "You shot at it. I saw that. But shot it? I doubt it."

Henrietta's posture stiffened and her lips pulled down in a frown.

"Don't pout at me, Ri. That was an impossible shot. No one on the crew could make it. I couldn't make it."

Her features settled into a stony, unimpressed stare.

"Though if anyone can, you could!" Clif said with a cheeky grin.

"I did," she said with an arched eyebrow. She flung a hand out toward the man being hauled aboard *The Henton*. "As you can see, the shark did not attack him because I killed it. Evidenced by both his survival and the large pool of blood in the water."

Clif glanced out at the sea again before flicking his gaze back to his sister. "I still cannot believe you made that shot."

"Excellent shot, Captain," Abby said as she approached them. "And it seems to have frightened off whatever lurked in the jungle. I have not heard the screeching cry since you fired and killed the shark."

"Well," Henrietta said, planting her hands on her hips and eyeing Clif, "at least someone believes me."

Clif motioned toward the tree line and winked. "Come on, Ri, let's take those legendary shooting skills into the jungle and find your map piece."

Henrietta scanned the group of men standing on the beach. "If we can manage to find five more sailors brave enough to venture in with us."

"How about it, men?" Clif inquired.

After a few moments, they'd gathered five more volunteers. Leaving the remaining members at the beach, the group of eight set off into the jungle at the foot of the volcano.

Heat seared through the overhead foliage as the hot sun burned off the remaining fog and blanketed the island with bright beams.

Large leaves slapped against them as they trudged through the thick vegetation toward the base of the volcano. Calls of monkeys and birds echoed throughout the jungle.

Sweat beaded on Henrietta's brow, dampening her hat. She swiped at a bead that rolled down the side of her hair. "Ugh, I'll bet my feather will not survive this walk."

"You and that damned feather," Clif said, slicing at a thick leaf with his sword before trampling on it.

"I like it," she answered. "I find that it–"

A shrill scream cut off the remaining words of her statement. The search party froze, ducking instinctively as they scanned the trees and sky for a threat.

The other sounds of the jungle disappeared. Eerie silence replaced the signs of life that chirped moments ago.

A low growl ricocheted off the trees around them, seeming to come from every direction at once.

"What was that?" one of the men inquired in a whisper.

"Shh," the man nearest him cautioned, pressing a finger against his lips. He shook his head in silent warning.

Clif retreated a few steps, coming to a stop next to Henrietta. He scanned the area, his eyes sliding slowly up and down the trees.

"Do you see anything?" Henrietta hissed.

He gave a slight shake of his head. "You?"

Her eyes continued to search for the danger. "Nothing. But the silence convinces me something is there."

"Yes, and something frightening to the local wildlife."

They held their breath for several more moments, still unable to locate the source of the alarming sound.

"Perhaps we should slowly make our way toward the volcano," Clif breathed.

Henrietta offered a slow nod, lifting a foot and placing it delicately down on the forest floor. She blew out a controlled breath as she inched forward, taking a few more tentative steps.

She shot a look over her shoulder and offered another nod. "Follow me," she mouthed.

Abby tiptoed behind her, careful not to make noise with her footfalls.

Clif motioned for the others to follow, bringing up the rear behind them. Overhead, a branch snapped. The group froze, their gazes darting upward.

Another rumbling growl echoed from their left. They snapped their heads in that direction, still unable to spot anything.

Henrietta lifted another foot to move forward when the leaves rustled. Something dark shot through them, leaping from branch to branch. A shrill, panicked scream assaulted their ears.

Branches swayed and another shriek echoed. A monkey

darted from between the leaves, swinging from limb to limb, its beady, black eyes filled with fear.

It leapt onto Henrietta's shoulder, jumped to Abby's, and continued through the line of pirates until it landed on Clif's shoulder.

Clif shimmied his arm, trying to dislocate the monkey and send him scurrying back into the trees.

"Shoo, go!" he hissed at the animal.

Its tiny mouth opened in a frightened grimace before it swung its furry arms around Clif's neck and clung to him, one hand-like paw grabbing his chin.

Henrietta stifled a chuckle.

"Go on, then!" Clif said, pulling the paw off his chin. The white-faced monkey squawked at him again and grabbed his chin with the other paw.

Clif tugged it away. The monkey replaced its grip on Clif's face with the opposite paw. They continued the game for several rounds before Clif grabbed both paws, his eyebrows raising triumphantly at the animal.

The monkey swung from his hands before pulling a paw from Clif's grip and scrambling back up his opposite arm. He settled on the other shoulder, his long tail draping around Clif's neck.

The smile broadened on Henrietta's face. "Looks like you've made a friend, brother."

Clif wrinkled his nose at the animal perched on his shoulder. "Go away. Don't you have monkey friends to commune with?"

"I don't think he's going anywhere," Henrietta said.

Clif heaved a sigh and shook his head. "It appears we are stuck with him for the time being."

"Perhaps it is a good thing," Abby chimed in. "He may alert us to danger."

Henrietta's shoulders lifted as she chuckled at the small

monkey clinging to her brother. "I think it's quite a good thing."

Clif raised his eyebrows at her. "Really? Perhaps you would care to shuttle the little devil around the island."

Henrietta shook her head and waved her hands. "Oh no, he has clearly selected his protector."

Clif twisted his neck to face the monkey on his shoulder. He waved a finger toward Henrietta at the front of the group. "She shot a shark, you know? Perhaps you would be better served with her."

The monkey chirped and tilted its head as though considering Clif's words. After a moment, it clapped both paws on his cheeks and kissed him.

A hearty chuckle burst from the group.

Unimpressed, Clif squashed his lips together into a thin line and shook his head at the animal. "I am not impressed, my friend."

"She loves you, brother," Henrietta called from the front. "She will have no other but you. Her knight in shining armor."

Clif shot Henrietta an irritated look. "Very funny. And how do you know it is a she?"

"Women typically throw themselves at you, so it is merely an educated guess."

"At any rate, he or she is not leaving. We should proceed. Perhaps our journey will spook it away, and we may be rid of the thing."

"We shall see," Henrietta said as she twisted back to the jungle ahead of her.

"The sound of birds has returned, Captain," Abby said from behind her. "Perhaps the creature that has joined our party was the source of their silence."

Henrietta puckered her lips as she picked her way through the jungle again. "I would find that surprising."

"What else could it be?"

"I believe whatever it was is what sent the little monkey scrambling onto Clif's shoulder," Henrietta answered, hiking her knee high to step over a fallen tree.

"Something after the monkey?" Abby questioned, hopping over the log and pushing past a large leaf.

"Yes," Henrietta answered her fellow female sailor. "Though it seems to be gone now. All the sounds of the jungle have returned. Perhaps it is frightened of humans."

"That would explain why the monkey believes it is safe with us."

"Indeed," Henrietta answered. "Let us hope the trouble is behind us." She wiped a bead of sweat from under the brim of her hat as they neared the base of the volcano.

Before she could proceed the final few steps out of the canopy, Henrietta froze, her muscles stiffening mid-step. Her fists curled into balls and she swallowed hard.

"What is it?" Clif called from the rear. The screech of his new friend followed. "The damned monkey is quite agitated."

"I can see why," Henrietta said, her eyes fixed on a single spot. "I would suggest no one move until we sort the situation."

"What situation?" Clif called.

Behind Henrietta, Abby sucked in a gasp as she, too, found the source of Henrietta's alarm.

Henrietta gave another hard swallow, her fingers wrapping around the grip of her pistol. "I know what frightened the monkey."

CHAPTER 17

$\mathcal{H}$enrietta squashed her lips together to stop them from trembling. Her fingers closed around the butt of her pistol when she realized she'd not reloaded it after shooting the shark. A whispered curse escaped her lips, and she wrinkled her nose as she slowly released the weapon.

Her eyes focused on the threat in front of her. A large black cat, easily as tall as her when standing on its hind legs, stared at her with yellow eyes from its perch in the tree. Its long, thick tail swished as it licked its chops.

Abby's fingers closed around Henrietta's arm as she inched her hand toward the hilt of her sword. "Captain," she breathed, "there is another to our left."

Henrietta licked her lips as she flicked her gaze sideways. Another large cat stood stock still several yards from them, crouched low and hidden by leaves.

"I'm willing to bet there is another on our right," Henrietta answered. "Williams, moving only your eyes, scan the jungle on your right."

"What am I searching for, Captain?" the man asked. "I still

150

don't see anything."

"A large black cat," Henrietta said as calmly as she could muster as she grasped her sword and lifted it an inch from its sheath.

"Do not make any sudden movements, men," Clif said from the rear. "Close ranks, backs together."

The group tightened into a circle, each of them facing outward.

"This is rather odd, isn't it?" Henrietta questioned as her eyes flicked between the two cats she'd spotted. "Don't large cats typically hunt alone?"

"Apparently not here," Clif answered. "I found your third. By their size, I'd guess mother cat is in the tree and her two children surrounded us."

"Can we outrun them?" Abby questioned.

"Doubtful," Clif answered as the monkey scrambled to hang from his back, protected by the circle of sailors.

"What shall we do?" Williams asked, his voice quivering.

Clif twisted to eye the large mother cat still perched in the tree. She licked her chops with a large pink tongue. He caught sight of the monkey's arm extending from his shoulder.

"I'll throw the monkey–"

"Clif!" Henrietta groaned. "You will not."

Clif squashed his lips together and wrinkled his nose. "Probably not."

"Whatever we do, we should not get any closer to the offspring," Henrietta said. "Nothing will raise her hackles so much as suspecting we may harm her babies."

"We move as a group and try to reach the edge of the jungle," Clif suggested. "Perhaps without the advantage of the trees, they will leave us."

"Can't they outrun us?" Williams asked.

"Aye. Though they may not try on open ground." Clif

swung his gaze around, doing a check on the two cubs before he nodded. "On my mark, steady, slow even steps. Ready? Go."

Henrietta inched forward, blowing an unsteady breath out from her parted lips. The group followed her as she made a slow crawl toward the open area.

"Almost there," Clif whispered as they inched ever closer to the tree line.

A low growl emanated from one of the cubs, causing the monkey on Clif's back to shriek again. One of the cubs lunged toward the group. Clif yanked his pistol from its holster and fired.

"Clif!" Henrietta shouted, whipping her sword from its sheath and skirting the other members of the group to reach him.

The mother cat leapt from the branch, hurrying to her cub's side. It lay flat on the ground. The mother snarled at the group before nudging her baby.

"Did you kill it?" Henrietta asked breathlessly.

"No," Clif answered. "I shot into the air. It's merely frightened."

The mother panther nudged her cub again as the second cub stalked toward its family.

"Perhaps we should take our leave whilst she is attending to her children," Henrietta suggested.

"I agree," Clif said. "Back away slowly. Try to make no noise."

They inched backward toward the base of the volcano. The frightened cub rose to its feet warily, rubbing under its mother's chin. The mother licked at the cub's head before shooting a glance toward the retreating pirate party.

Clif raised his hands as he stared her down and continued his withdrawal from the jungle. "Easy, Mother, we mean you no harm."

The panther snarled before nudging her children away from the group. They loped deeper into the jungle, disappearing into the thick foliage.

The group cleared the tree line, breathing out a collective sigh of relief.

Henrietta slumped against the rocky base of the volcano. "Those creatures are likely the source of the disappearing men."

"Possibly," Clif said as he reloaded his pistol before stowing it in the holster.

Henrietta eyed him working, tugging her pistol from her belt and reloading it, too. She nodded at him as he glanced at her. "Good idea."

"We must return that way," Williams said. "I wonder if we can avoid it. I have no desire to run into those beasts again."

Henrietta straightened and stowed her weapon, adjusting her belt. "Let us worry about the return journey after we have completed our goal."

"She is correct," Clif said. "We must first locate the cave and seek out the map piece."

"The north face of this volcano should be the opposite side," Abby said. She glanced back and forth, seeking out a path. "Perhaps we should split the group and circle around the mountain in separate directions."

"I disagree," Clif answered. "Given the dangers on the island, we should remain together. It may take longer, but we shall have to risk it."

Abby flicked her gaze to Henrietta who nodded at the plan.

"I agree. While splitting the group would provide the fastest resolution, the danger on the island outweighs any potential danger in the sea." Henrietta tugged the compass from her pocket and eyed it, glancing up at the volcano. She pointed a finger to her left. "Perhaps this way will provide the shortest route."

They trudged along the narrow path in a single file line, squeezed between the jungle and the base of the volcano. In several instances, their shoulders brushed against the brown stone.

They reached the north face and craned their necks to stare up the rocky side.

Henrietta raised her hands to her side before letting them slap her thighs. "I see nothing."

"Nor do I. Not even a path," Clif answered, rubbing his chin.

Abby wandered a few steps away as they continued to discuss the predicament. "Perhaps if we climb higher," Henrietta suggested, setting a boot on the rock face and pushing herself upward.

Her foot slipped, and she crashed back down to the ground in a heap. She cursed the turn of events as Clif pulled her to standing and she brushed off her trousers.

He twisted to stare up the side again, his eyes narrowed. After a moment, he shook his head. "I see nothing. Perhaps the clue did not refer to this island."

"Every detail fits."

"That doesn't mean–"

"On top of that," Henrietta said as she paced the small space, "the island's reputation would provide the primary reason no one has found the other map pieces."

"Ri, sometimes–"

"No! I refuse to believe I am wrong. We are missing something!"

Clif huffed a breath, his nostrils flaring as his sister continued to pace in front of him. He'd let her have her moment before he encouraged them to return to *The Henton* and reassess.

"Captain!" Abby called from several yards away.

"Yes?" Henrietta and Clif both answered. Clif squashed his lips together and motioned for Henrietta to proceed.

She stalked ahead toward Abby.

"I believe I've found something, Captain," the woman reported as they approached.

She brushed at the rockface before inserting her foot into a small divot in the stone. "This appears to be a rung to climb with."

"I'd argue it is merely an imperfection in the stone," Clif said. "What makes you believe it is more?"

"Because, sir," she answered with a grin, pushing against the ball of her feet to rise in the air, "there are more."

She stuffed her hand into another handhold and stood clinging to the side of the stone.

"And another just there." She pointed to another dirt-filled dimple above her head.

A smile tugged at the corners of Henrietta's lips. "Clever, Miss Turner." Henrietta's eyes raised higher, trying to seek more climbing holds. Her eyebrows raised and her smile broadened. "And look there!"

She jabbed a finger upward. "A path."

Clif's eyebrow arched and he smirked at the two women. "Well, my apologies, ladies. It appears you both were correct."

Abby continued her scramble upward, pulling herself up with each handhold. Henrietta followed behind her as her feet left the depressions in the stone for the next one. The monkey leapt from Clif's shoulder and scrambled upward, landing on the path first.

"Onwards and upwards, brother," Henrietta called with a giddy grin over her shoulder.

Abby reached the path above, scrambling onto it and sending a shower of small pebbles down onto Henrietta and the sailors that ascended below her.

"Sorry, Captain!" she called from overhead.

"Help me up," Henrietta said as she pulled herself up and reached for the edge of the pathway.

Abby grasped hold of her hand, bracing her feet as she hauled Henrietta up. Henrietta scrambled up the side, running as Abby pulled her up. She gained her footing on the narrow path, skirting Abby and inching forward as she awaited the arrival of her crew and brother.

The precarious passage only allowed a single file line of them and Henrietta continued to inch forward to make room for each new man who made the climb. She'd nearly rounded the bend out of the sight from the handholds when Clif crawled onto the pathway. The monkey scrambled up, perching on his shoulder again.

He adjusted the hat on his head before he squeezed past the others on the path and joined Henrietta.

"This is quite precarious," he noted as he eyed the ground below them.

"Exciting," Henrietta said with a grin as she began to creep forward.

"You cannot possibly find this amusing, can you?" Clif inquired, treading carefully with a hand pressed against the volcano's wall.

"Amusing, no. Exciting, yes. Clif, we are on the verge of finding another map piece." A giddy grin crossed Henrietta's face and she took another step forward.

The rock crumbled away under her foot and she plunged downward. Clif dove for her, wrapping his fingers around her forearm to halt her fall.

Henrietta clambered back up onto the path, her chest heaving as she stared down at the ground far below her.

"Thanks," she said with a nod at her brother.

"You were saying how exciting this was?" he asked with a grin.

She narrowed her eyes at him as she tugged her vest down. "Funny. I still do find it exciting. Dangerous, too. But exciting."

"Shall we continue on with your exciting venture?"

"Yes," she said, leaping over the small hole in the walkway and flailing her arms to catch her balance on the other side.

They continued their trek up the mountainside, the climb becoming steeper and narrower as they wrapped around the volcano.

Henrietta shuffled forward until she came to a missing chunk of the path. She stopped, teetering on the edge and biting her lower lip. The two-foot gap would require a jump to make it across.

Pebbles trickled down to the rock below as she hovered on the edge, assessing the leap.

"That's a wide gap at this height," Clif said from behind her.

"Yes, I know," she answered, her voice unsteady.

She lifted her gaze, her brow furrowing. She narrowed her eyes and pointed a shaky finger ahead. "Look, a hole!"

Clif leaned around her, wobbling as he spied the dark spot. The monkey leapt down onto the broken path and squawked at the hole before searching the side of the volcano. "You may be correct."

"We need to jump this. It is vital that we explore that cave."

"Swap with me," Clif said, placing a hand on her shoulder. "I shall try the leap first."

"No," Henrietta said, returning her attention to the gap.

"It has nothing to do with your capabilities, Ri. I am taller. The leap is much more easily made by someone my height. If I make it, I can catch you when you throw yourself across."

"If? Clif, if you do not believe we can make the leap, you should not try."

"We can make the leap. But given the crumbling pathway, I do not wish to test the limits nor risk you falling."

"We should not risk you falling either," Henrietta argued.

Clif tugged one corner of his mouth back into a half-smile. "I shall be fine. Now, swap with me."

"You'd better be. Or else I shall scramble down the volcano, revive you, and kill you again."

"A frightening prospect. I shall be certain to make the leap with ease given that."

"Always a jester," Henrietta said as they turned sideways and switched positions.

Clif sucked in a deep breath and blew it out. He rocked backward before he threw himself across the hole in the path. He sailed through the sky, landing on the opposite side with both feet.

With a glance over his shoulder, he steadied his footing and spun to grin at his sister. "There, you see. Simple."

"Let us hope I make it with as much grace."

"I have no doubt you can."

Henrietta nodded and stared down at the gap again.

"Do not look down. Look across at me and leap."

Henrietta parted her lips and blew out an unsteady breath, raising her eyes to her brother. She licked her lips and took a step back before she launched herself across the hole.

Her foot hit the edge and slipped, but Clif grasped her and tugged her onto the pathway. "Thank you," she said with a nod.

They spun to face the others on the path. "We shall explore the cave on our own. Wait there for us," Clif ordered.

The monkey screeched as Clif took a step away from them. It pounded on the path, its mouth hanging open in a frightened scream. The small creature inched to the edge and peered down before shrieking at Clif again.

"He misses you, brother."

"Stay there, you rat. Climb onto Abby."

Abby scooped the small monkey into her arms. He waved his paws in the air and screeched again. "He seems upset."

Clif lifted his eyes to the sky and heaved a sigh. "Toss him over."

"Toss him, sir?"

Clif nodded and thrust his hands out. "Toss him."

Abby spun the monkey around to face forward and swung him back and forth a few times before she released him into the air. The tiny creature sailed across the gap and landed in Clif's open arms. He grasped Clif's shirt and scrambled up to his shoulder, clapping his paws together and laying his head against Clif's.

Henrietta suppressed another chuckle at the sight.

Clif spun on his heel and eyed her for a moment before he stalked further up the path. "Do not say a word."

"I said nothing," Henrietta murmured as she trailed behind her brother on the narrow path. Her fingertips grazed the rough stone of the volcano as she stared down at her feet, carefully placing her footfalls one in front of the other.

"Careful, Ri, the path gets even worse here."

She winced as she caught sight of the tiny passage, only allowing her to pass by placing one foot directly in front of the other. Pebbles skittered down and some dirt crumbled away as she inched forward.

Her foot slipped and her fingernails dug into the rock, scraping along it until they tore. She sucked in a breath as she pulled her foot up and steadied herself.

The monkey screeched as she fought to stay on the path.

Clif glanced over his shoulder. "You all right?"

Henrietta swallowed hard and tugged at her vest. "Perfectly fine."

"Almost there."

Henrietta blew out a long breath as the treacherous path widened near the dark entrance.

Clif stepped beyond the door and spun to face her, motioning for her to enter first. "After you, Ri."

She tipped her hat to him before she swept past him and ducked into the cave. It took a moment for her eyes to adjust to the darkness from the bright sunshine outside. Thick, orange-red liquid caked with a black film sloshed in the chamber, lighting the inside with a deep red glow. Heat rose from the magma.

Sweat beaded on her forehead as she stepped further into the chamber. Clif followed behind her, glancing around as he stepped inside.

"Amazing," Henrietta breathed as she studied the chamber.

"Has it fulfilled your thirst for adventure?"

She smirked at him. "Partially. Though I do wish to press on and find the diamonds."

"Then we should start looking for the map piece that will lead us there."

The monkey on Clif's shoulder screeched and waved his arms in the air. "Oh, quiet," Clif barked at him.

Henrietta cocked her head at the animal. "Is he warning us of something?"

Clif removed his hat and wiped at his sweaty brow with the back of his hand. "Likely the heat. We may as well be standing on the threshold of Hell."

Henrietta scoured the cavern in search of a clue toward the map piece. "Where could it be?"

Clif pointed across the chamber. "There is an opening over there."

"How do we get across?" Henrietta inquired as she stared at the dark hole in the wall.

Clif studied the cavern's features in search of a route toward the niche. His brow furrowed as he failed to find many options to help them cross.

"I am not certain," he answered, rubbing his chin.

"I do not see a way. The river over this red sludge is far too wide. And given the heat rising from it, we cannot wade into it."

"No, I should think not." Clif stepped to the edge of the rock jutting into the river. He eyed the platform across from them, then let his eyes slip down to judge the distance across. He shook his head and huffed. "It is too far."

"Can you toss me?" Henrietta asked, joining him and staring up at the ledge they wished to reach.

"I doubt you'd make it. And if you slip..." Clif shook his head, his voice trailing off. "It is not worth the risk."

Henrietta balled her hands into fists and stomped her boot on the stone. "We must risk it! We did not climb this volcano for nothing."

"Ri, it is not worth it. It is far too dangerous. We shall have to try to locate the city without it."

"But–"

The shriek of the monkey interrupted her words. He lifted his paws in the air before he leapt from Clif's shoulder. He grabbed a stalagmite hanging from the ceiling and swung from it before latching on to another. He worked his way across the cavern, swinging above the red-hot river and landing on the perch.

"Clif! The monkey has made it across!"

"Yes," he answered as he followed the small creature. The monkey disappeared from sight for a moment before it returned. It waved a rolled scroll in its paw, screeching at them.

A smile spread across Henrietta's face, and she clapped

her hands together. "He did it! Come back, little monkey. Come on!"

The monkey stuffed the scroll between its teeth like a bone and swung his way back across the chamber, landing on Clif's shoulder and passing the parchment to him.

"Thank you," Clif answered, accepting the proffered item and shooting a glance at Henrietta.

"Open it," she encouraged.

With a flick of his eyebrows, Clif unwrapped the leather holding it closed, and slowly unrolled the scroll. Henrietta tugged the first map piece from her pocket and held it up.

The smile on her face grew wider as she matched the edge with the new parchment. "It is a piece of the map!"

Clif smirked as he studied the growing map. "Yes, it is. And we are now one step closer to finding the City of Diamonds."

"Much closer. This map piece is twice the size of the first."

"Indeed it is. We should return to the ship and study it. Perhaps we can locate the city without securing another map piece."

Henrietta snatched the piece from him and rolled it together with Bill's map piece. As she stuffed the parchment into her pocket, the ground shook. The monkey screamed again, clinging to Clif's head and squashing his hat over his eyes.

"Stop it, you beast, I cannot see."

Henrietta flailed her arms as she attempted to stay upright. The red river burbled and flared, sloshing more violently than before.

Henrietta's eyes went wide as the ground shook again, sending her stumbling forward toward the fiery lava.

"Ri!" Clif shouted as she fell forward and rolled toward the river.

CHAPTER 18

*H*enrietta tumbled toward the edge of the rocky outcropping that jutted into the lava river. The ground shook violently underneath her as she desperately attempted to stop her forward progress.

"Ri!" Clif screamed as his sister flailed her arms, trying to grasp hold of something.

Her hat toppled off her head as she rolled further.

He dove forward, his arm outstretched to grab her before she tumbled into the molten hot river of lava. His fingers grasped the fabric of her blouse. He squeezed his hand closed around the white cloth. It tore as his fingers dug into it, but halted her forward progress enough for her to gain traction with her feet.

She scrambled closer to him, pushing away from the river as the tremors died down. Her hat continued bouncing down the rocky ground until it fell over the edge, plunging into the red-hot river with a hiss and burst of smoke.

"Damn," Henrietta said, still clutching Clif's arm. "Another hat lost."

Clif climbed to his feet, the monkey still balanced on his

"

arm despite his wild fugue to retrieve Henrietta, and offered his hand. He tugged her to her feet. "You really need to stop wearing these damned hats. They'll be the death of you."

"It's not the hat. It was the volcano. I think we'd better go and quickly."

Clif stared at the burbling river and nodded. "Yes. We need to get off this island."

"I agree," Henrietta said, casting one last glance over her shoulder. "At least we got what we came for."

Clif motioned for her to precede him to the entrance. "And I disagree with you. Those hats are unlucky."

Henrietta pressed her lips together and shot him a glance over her shoulder as she stepped into the bright sunshine. "They are not."

"They are too," Clif said as he stepped out of the cave.

"Captain!" Abby shouted, her finger pointing upward. "Hurry! We must descend."

Henrietta and Clif craned their necks to stare above them. The volcano, quiet when they'd arrived, now smoked from the top.

Henrietta waved a hand at them. "Go! Quickly. Begin your descent!"

The men behind Abby turned and hurried down the narrow path in a straight line.

"Jump, Captain!" Abby shouted from across the gap. Henrietta raced along the narrow path and leapt in the air. She landed on the edge of the opposite side, teetering as the edge broke away and her heel fell.

Abby grabbed hold of her arm and tugged her onto the path. Henrietta nodded and clapped a hand on her shoulder. "Go, Miss Turner. Quickly. I will be right behind you."

Abby nodded at her and spun on her heel, hurrying after the other sailors around the volcano. Henrietta scurried a few steps away before spinning to face Clif. Her face whitened, and her jaw dropped.

The gap that separated them had widened by a foot. "Clif!" Henrietta yelled. "Jump!"

Clif eyed the gap between them, his lips pulling into a frown. "Catch the monkey."

Henrietta hurried back to the edge as Clif tugged the animal from his shoulder and swung his arms. He released the animal, who shrieked as he flew through the air. Henrietta caught the small creature. He scrambled up her arm and perched on her shoulder.

She waved for Clif to make the leap. "Come on!"

"Stand back."

"No, I'll catch you. You won't make it."

"You cannot hold me. We shall both fall."

Henrietta's features pinched. "Clif, you won't make it!"

Another chunk fell from the edge, widening the gap even further. "Clif!" Henrietta shouted.

Clif's chest puffed with exertion as his prospects of survival slimmed further. He swallowed hard. "Get ready."

Henrietta nodded and widened her stance, her arms outstretched to grab him. He launched himself across the gap. His chest smashed into the side. His hands scratched at the rocky path to stop himself from falling.

Henrietta clamped a hand down on his forearm, stopping his descent. "Climb!" she grunted through clenched teeth.

Clif kicked his feet against the rock, slipping with each step. He slid further down. Henrietta slid closer to the edge. She plopped on her rear and dug her feet into the ground, leaning back to stabilize herself. The monkey dug into her shoulder, flinging his arms around her neck to steady himself.

"Let go," Clif groaned, sweat beading on his forehead.

"No."

"Let go, Ri. I'll drag us both down."

"No, damn it. Climb."

"I cannot. I cannot find a footing. Let go, Ri. Find the city."

Henrietta wrinkled her nose and set her jaw. "Then hold on."

She tensed every muscle in her body, leaning further back. Clif inched further up. She dug her feet in again and pushed her legs back to pull him up further. After another adjustment of her boots, she pushed her legs straight, a scream escaping her lips as she tugged his weight up.

With her third pull, she tugged his chest up onto the pathway. Clif wiggled his lower half to swing his knee onto the path. He scrambled up, glancing behind him at the fall he'd almost experienced.

The mountain trembled again and more of the edge broke away. Clif turned his attention to his sister, offering her his hand to pull her to her feet. "We must go."

Henrietta wiped the sweat from her brow and grasped his hand to stand. The monkey leapt from her shoulder to his and settled in with a screech. He waved his hands down the path and clapped.

Henrietta turned to hurry after the crew when Clif squeezed her shoulder. "Ri."

She twisted to face him.

"Thanks."

She patted his hand and nodded. "We protect each other. Always."

They set off down the path wrapping around the volcano, catching up with the remaining members of the group as they climbed down the rock face to the ground below.

"Go, Captain," Abby said as the final man scurried down the rock face, half-climbing, half-sliding his way to the ground.

"No, you go Miss Turner. Lead the group straight to the beach and ready the skiffs. We will be directly behind you."

"But, Captain–"

"Go," Henrietta ordered.

Abby pressed her lips together and nodded before swinging her leg over the side and placing her foot into the handhold.

Henrietta followed behind her a moment later. Another violent tremor shook the island. Henrietta's hand slipped from the perch. She fell backward a foot before something stopped her progress. Warm fingers wrapped around her wrist.

She glanced up to find Clif grinning at her. "One good turn deserves another."

"Now we're even," Henrietta said with a wink before she resumed her descent down to the ground.

Clif followed and they scrambled onto the ground within minutes.

"Captain, perhaps we should circle around to find an opening in the jungle. We do not wish to meet those panthers again," Williams said.

More smoke puffed from the top of the volcano, and the ground shook again. "No, we take the fastest route," Clif answered, pushing through the group to the front and leading them under the canopy. He glanced over his shoulder. "Ri, keep up."

"I will," Henrietta promised, grabbing hold of Abby's arm and ensuring she stayed with them.

They trudged through the trees with Clif hacking at leaves and branches that delayed their progress. The island continued to tremble under their feet as they hurried through the foliage toward the beach.

They reached the sand unaccosted by the large cats. The

other men waited near the skiffs, searching the horizon for the remaining members of their crew.

Clif waved them into the water as they raced across the beach. "Get the skiffs in the water!"

They pushed the two boats further out before climbing in and awaiting the others. Clif reached the water first, spinning to find Henrietta closing the gap between them. "Get in, quickly," he shouted at her as her boots splashed into the sea.

She dragged Abby along with her, shoving the girl into a boat before climbing over the side. The other men hurried toward the second skiff and piled in as Clif, the monkey still clinging to his shoulder, dove into the boat.

Henrietta tugged him aboard as the other crew members rowed away from the vibrating island. A massive plume of ash shot into the air as they put more sea between them and the beach. Red lava spilled onto the volcano's side, streaming down the rock in a thick, slow-moving sludge.

Three large black cats appeared from within the canopy of the jungle, pacing the beach as they searched for a way off the island.

Henrietta blew out a sigh of relief as they neared the ship. "Poor things," she murmured.

"Poor things?" Clif questioned as they bobbed in the water next to *The Henton.*

"Yes, their home is being destroyed." Henrietta shot him a glance, her eyes falling to his shoulder. "At least you saved the monkey. What will you name him?"

Clif shook his head at her as she ascended the rope ladder to the main deck. "Nothing!" he shouted after her.

"That's a terrible name, Clif. Surely, you can do better!" She climbed onto the ship and leaned over the railing, grinning at him.

Clif climbed aboard moments later, and the crew began

hauling the skiffs up. "I shall leave his naming to you, Ri. You are the writer. You should have loads of ideas."

"Captain," Johnson said, approaching them before Henrietta could answer, "what of the mission?"

"We retrieved another map piece," Clif said with a wiggle of his eyebrows.

"Your orders?" Johnson questioned.

Clif turned to Henrietta, his eyebrows raising.

She tugged the map pieces from her pocket as she spoke. "Set sail for Mexico. We seek an Aztec temple in a place called Cuetitlan."

Johnson's brow furrowed at her words. "I have never heard of such a place, Captain."

Henrietta waved him toward the cabin. Clif followed behind them as they pushed inside. She stalked to the desk and shifted the papers from the desk to expose a map.

She poked a finger at the map, indicating a specific area. "We shall need to travel quite a ways inland, but I believe we shall find our last piece of the puzzle there."

Johnson stared down at the area indicated. Clif furrowed his brow as the monkey leapt from his shoulder and perched on the chair. "Is this Aztec territory?"

"Traditionally, no. It is an unclaimed area between Aztec and Mayan lands. But I believe that is why no one has found the last piece and the City of Diamonds."

Clif rubbed his chin before he nodded. "Set the course, Mr. Johnson. We continue our journey there."

"Aye, aye, Captain," Johnson said with a salute and a nod before he hurried from the cabin, barking orders as he stepped through the door and onto the main deck.

"What makes you believe the next map piece is there?" Clif asked as the door banged shut behind Johnson.

"First, the references in your journal pointed to a temple that contained both a clue and pointed toward the city. My supposition is that the temple contains the final piece and is in reasonable proximity to the City of Diamonds."

Clif sank into the chair as the monkey climbed onto his shoulder again.

Henrietta narrowed her eyes at the small primate balanced on her brother's arm. She snapped her fingers. "Jack."

"What?" Clif asked, his brows knitting.

"His name. Jack. After your former self, Black Jack. We shall keep your memory alive." The monkey open its mouth in an amused screech and clapped his paws together.

"That's ridiculous. You cannot name the monkey after my former pirate persona."

"Jack seems to like it," Henrietta said, lifting one shoulder and puckering her lips.

Clif rolled his eyes as the monkey pulled his lips back into a grin and tilted his head. "Go on. I am still not convinced about your course."

The amusement on Henrietta's features faded, replaced by an unimpressed stare down her nose. She picked up his journal and plopped it on the desk in front of her, poking her finger at a reference.

"A round temple dedicated to the plumed serpent and hidden deep in the jungle."

Clif lifted his shoulder and shook his head, staring up at Henrietta for an explanation.

"The Aztecs are better known for four-sided temples, not round temples. Round temples are dedicated to Quetzalcoatl, the feathered serpent. This one is one of the fewer explored ruins."

Clif kicked his feet onto the desk. "How do you know all this?"

"Reading."

"Reading? About Aztec culture?"

"I have to research for my novels. I have read much on the subject as I find ancient cultures fascinating."

Clif puckered his lips and crossed his ankles, pulling a flask from his pocket and taking a sip. "And what is the second reason for your certainty?"

Henrietta stood and crossed to the desk, unrolling the map pieces and spreading them across the other chart. "This. I only had a brief look at it before the volcano went mad, but it convinced me I am correct."

She flattened the smaller map piece and slid the larger one obtained from the volcano cave into place above it. The lines met, forming a partial map with a rectangular hole in the lower right corner.

"This is Mexico. This is the temple we must visit, marked with a star," she pointed out on the new map piece before slapping her hand against the missing area. "And this area must be where the City of Diamonds is located. We need the last clue to find its exact location."

Clif studied the map as Jack badgered at him for a drink from the flask. He shooed the animal away with a shake of his head before rubbing his lips. After a moment, he flicked his gaze to Henrietta and raised his eyebrows. "I think we just may become famous."

Henrietta's full lips curled into a satisfied grin. "I wouldn't mind that."

"A female pirate who finds the City of Diamonds? You shall become a living legend, Ri."

She wiggled her eyebrows at him before she stalked across the cabin and plopped into the hammock, kicking her feet up. "You should get some rest. By my calculations, it will be a two-day journey on land to that temple."

Jack scampered across the floor and leapt into the hammock next to Henrietta, curling into a ball next to her hip.

Clif tented his fingers and arched an eyebrow. "Looks like you have a new friend."

Henrietta stroked the monkey's fur as his eyes closed. "I shall allow him to sleep here only because the desk is far too uncomfortable. Though I maintain that he is, in fact, your monkey."

Clif pressed his lips together into a thin line and shook his head before pulling his hat over his eyes and settling back in his chair with his feet propped on the desk.

Henrietta let her eyes slide closed as the movement of the ship rocked her hammock back and forth, lulling her to sleep.

* * *

Jack's screeching startled Henrietta awake. She jumped, nearly toppling out of the hammock as the ship swayed.

"What's happening?" she questioned, realizing only she and Jack remained in the room. She scrambled to her feet and hurried toward the door, wrapping her belt around her and fastening it before she stepped onto the main deck.

A massive boom sounded, and the water splashed onto the deck, pelting a few sailors who trimmed the sails.

"What is going on?" she questioned aloud, hurrying toward the sound.

Her eyes grew wide as she spotted the large sailing vessel off their starboard side.

"Welcome to the party," Clif said, sidling next to her and staring through his spyglass.

"What is happening?" she questioned, knowing the likely answer.

Clif slammed the spyglass closed and twisted to face her. "We are under attack."

CHAPTER 19

Another cannonball landed short, splashing into the water and sending a tall spray over them. Henrietta's eyes widened, and she shot another glance at the other ship charging toward them. "Can we outrun them?"

"I doubt it," Clif answered. "We must make a stand and fight."

Henrietta snatched the spyglass from his hand and expanded it, closing one eye as she stared at the ship in the distance. A frown formed on her lips and she smashed the spyglass closed. "Whitemane."

"Again."

"We escaped him last time. Perhaps we should try for the same strategy."

Clif shook his head, pushing off the railing and heading toward the helm. "No. He will be prepared for that. We used it once. We should not push our luck. We must make a stand."

"Can we win?"

Clif rolled his head and puckered his lips. "I certainly hope so."

Henrietta stuck her hands on her hips and stared at her brother. "That does not sound as confident as I'd like."

Clif arched an eyebrow and offered her a grin. "I do not plan on losing. Put her hard to starboard."

The helmsman spun the wheel until it stuck hard over and the ship began to turn.

"Clif! What are you doing?"

"I plan to sail straight at him."

Henrietta's jaw dropped open and she stared at him before she blinked her eyes and shook her head. "Are you mad?"

Clif wandered to the starboard railing and eyed the progress of their turn along with the position of the other ship. "Not at all."

"Why would you sail toward him?"

"Simple. First, sitting sideways we present a large target. I prefer to present a smaller one. Second, I plan to charge him."

Henrietta balled her hands into fists and stamped a foot on the ground. "Charge him?

"We are well-equipped to fight. Best case he turns tail and runs. Worst, we battle."

"What are our odds of winning?"

Clif lifted a shoulder as he started down the stairs. "Quite good in my estimation. His crew has proven themselves slow to react after our last encounter."

Henrietta followed him to the main deck. "But this time he shall be out for his revenge."

They reached the railing and Clif leaned over it, peering ahead as they sailed toward the warring ship. "Yes, quite right. Our advantage is lessened because of it. We must go in for the kill immediately. Disable his main mast. If possible, we should attempt to disable his rudder, though that may prove tricky."

"To disable the rudder we need someone on board."

Clif raised his eyebrows and nodded before shouting an order to Mr. Johnson. "Bring both sets of cannons to the starboard side. We will fire in rapid succession. Load the chain shot."

Henrietta chewed her lower lip for a moment before she flicked her gaze to her brother. "I shall disable the rudder."

Clif snapped his gaze toward her. "No."

Henrietta stuck her hands on her hips. "You are not my captain. You cannot order me to stay here. I shall board his ship, disable his rudder, and return."

"Ri, no," he said again, his features betraying his concern.

"I shall take two men with me," she said with a shrug before stalking across the deck in search of volunteers.

"Damn it, Henrietta, you will do no such thing," Clif said, storming after her.

"Stop playing mother to me, Clif. I am capable of this feat."

"It is far too dangerous. If you are caught–"

"I do not plan to be caught, dear brother." She stalked toward the stairs leading below decks.

"Of course not. No one *plans* to be caught. But if you are–
"

Henrietta ceased her strides and spun to face him. "Do you plan to shelter me always? Am I only to be half a pirate?"

"Of course not, but–"

Henrietta held up her hand, interrupting him. "Tell me, would you refrain from asking this of any other sailor on this ship?"

"Certainly not. Any of them are capable of this task."

"Then why not ask it of me?"

"Because…" He pressed his lips together and flung his hands in the air. "Fine. Go. Have it your way. Do not expect me to save you if you are caught."

Henrietta smirked at him. "I will not need you to save me." She disappeared down the stairs into the chamber below.

Clif chewed his lower lip, shaking his head in frustration until Johnson called for him.

"Captain! *The Pillager* approaches. Shall we veer off and take a defensive stance?"

"No," Clif said. "Sail straight on toward her. Do not turn until I tell you."

"But, Captain."

"I said no!" Clif snapped at him. "Straight on until I say otherwise."

"Yes, Captain," Johnson said with a salute before racing across the deck to carry out the instructions.

Clif squeezed his eyes closed for a moment before he disappeared down the stairs to the men's quarters below. Henrietta already stalked toward him, two sailors in tow.

"If you plan to make another attempt to convince me not to go–"

"No, no. I have a request."

Henrietta arched an eyebrow as he detailed his request. A sly grin spread across her features and she nodded to him. "Of course, brother. Consider it done."

"Ri," he said as she stepped past him toward the stairs, "be careful. And good luck."

Henrietta bobbed her head up and down with a wink. "I shall see you for the victory party."

"We'll celebrate with diamonds," he called after her. A pang of worry struck his heart as she disappeared onto the deck above him. He closed his eyes for a moment before he forced himself to return to his duties as captain.

He emerged from below deck to a flurry of chaos as sailors prepared for the battle. Johnson rushed toward him. "Sir, they are taking a defensive position, pulling to port."

"Let us not give them a wide target just yet then, shall we?"

Johnson shot a worried glance to the turning ship and nodded. "The cannons are loaded and ready."

Clif climbed to the helm and studied the ship through his spyglass. "We are not within range, and I do not wish to waste ammunition."

He flattened the spyglass and glanced at Johnson. "When we are within fifty yards, fire forward cannons. Not before then."

"Aye, Captain."

"Then initiate a turn, use the anchor, and fire all before turning back. And get a man in the crow's nest. Our best shot. Take out their helmsman."

"Aye, Captain, but they will replace him."

"It won't matter by then. Just do it," Clif retorted, shooing his own sailor away from the wheel and taking over.

He stared at the ship as it prepared to fire upon them. "Come on, Ri," he murmured.

* * *

Henrietta stared down at the rolling waves as the ship continued forward toward *The Pillager*. She glanced at the others next to her, now a complement of four men instead of two. They awaited her word. She climbed onto the railing and offered a nod before stepping off and plunging into the blue waters below.

The cold penetrated her as she sank under the waves. Whooshes tugged at her as her crew plummeted into the water next to her. She opened her eyes. Bubbles filled her vision, floating upward to reveal the other sailors.

She counted four men before poking a finger toward the oncoming ship. With a kick of her foot, she swam underwater toward it. They surfaced slowly halfway between the two ships before slipping beneath the surface again and continuing their journey.

The bulky form of the ship's underside cut through the water, approaching them. Henrietta and her crew closed the gap toward it and resurfaced.

She wiped the water from her face before tugging a knife from her waistband and clenching it between her teeth. She grabbed the nearest ratline and scrambled up the ship's side to the shroud. Whitemane stood on the helm, staring at *The Henton* through a spyglass.

She eyed him as she ascended the final few steps up the rope ladder with her crew following behind her. While she'd love to take his heart back for Clif, she had more important matters to attend to. Disabling the ship trumped disabling the man.

She leapt onto the deck and palmed the knife in one hand, her sword in the other. She fended off an attack from one of Whitemane's men, landing an uppercut with the handle of her knife and slashing a wide slice into his chest.

Two of her men pounded down against the deck boards next to her as sailors rushed toward them. She glanced across the ocean, a smirk forming on her lips as the forward cannons fired.

"Brace," she shouted to her men after the final three landed on the main deck.

One cannonball splashed in the water off the bow, but the other struck the ship, rocking it as it tore a hole into the wood.

"Williams, you're with me," she said as the ship stabilized from the impact.

Sailors scrambled to return fire. Cannons rumbled from below deck as they retaliated against Clif's advances.

Henrietta and Williams, with the assistance of the other

three men, fought their way to the stairs leading down. They parted ways, heading down into the bowels of the ship. Chaos ensued as sailors raced back and forth, retrieving cannonballs for counterattacks. Loud blasts sounded as cannons fired return volleys.

"Quickly," Henrietta said as they threaded their way through the men, "we do not have much time."

"Aye, Captain," Williams said as they reached the stern and located the rudder chain. With a repurposed lobster trap, Williams tangled the rudder chain, tugging against it to ensure it would not move. "Done."

A sly grin spread across Henrietta's face as she nodded. "Let's go."

They picked their way back through the turmoil below deck, climbing up into the open air. The others in their party had already abandoned the ship in anticipation of Clif's impending attack. Henrietta eyed Whitemane one final time.

"Captain, we must go. *The Henton* is preparing to fire," Williams reported, waving a hand at their ship.

Henrietta gave one last glance at the captain standing on the helm, her fingers wrapping around her sword. If she could off him, she could score a huge victory for them. She licked her lips, taking one step toward the helm.

"Captain, we should go," Williams insisted. "It will be enough to disable the ship."

Henrietta's lips formed a frown, but she nodded. Before they could mount the railing and dive into the ocean below, swords appeared under their chins. Henrietta stared down her nose at the tip glinting in the sun, her heart pounding.

* * *

Clif eyed the other ship with his spyglass. Three men leapt from the railing into the waves below. His sister remained on the ship. He jammed the spyglass closed with a frustrated frown.

"Your orders, Captain?" Johnson asked.

"Hold."

Johnson's features betrayed his disapproval, but he nodded, holding off on bellowing orders for the crew to fire upon the other ship.

"Perhaps the forward cannons–"

"No, I said hold," Clif growled.

Another few tense moments passed. Cannonballs sailed from the other ship, splashing in the water around them. One of them clipped the ship, grazing one of the foremast's crossbeams and splintering it.

"Captain?" Johnson asked again in a questioning tone.

Clif extended the spyglass and studied the other ship again, his jaw flexing.

"Sir, if we do not fire soon, we shall miss the opportunity and run straight into the ship."

Clif closed his eyes, weighing the odds. They had no more time to postpone firing. To save his ship and his men, he would be forced to fire upon the other ship while Henrietta remained aboard.

"Sir? Your orders?" Johnson asked again.

Clif opened his eyes, biting into his lower lip before cocking his head. He swallowed hard and said one word, "Fire."

Johnson spun to face the crew, barking orders. "Put her hard over and drop the port side anchor. Prepare to fire!"

The ship swayed as the helmsman spun the wheel until it would spin no more. The anchor plunged into the water, catching hold of something underneath and swinging the ship around. The men braced as the ship tilted dangerously to the side.

Clif studied the other ship as his own ship tilted back down, praying he witnessed two individuals leap into the water. He spotted no one.

His heart sank as Johnson screamed out the order to fire at will. The cannons blasted from under his feet, roaring with explosions. Cannonballs sailed from his ship one after the other toward the opposing craft.

The first few splashed into the water, missing their target. But the next several, fired during the second volley, smashed into the ship's side, tearing massive holes into it.

From the crow's nest, a single shot sailed over, striking the helmsman in the head. He keeled over before he could follow any orders shouted by his captain. Whitemane stared at the man for a moment before grabbing the wheel and attempting to turn the ship. He struggled to spin it, finding the task impossible.

Clif lowered the spyglass he'd used to keep track of the progress and search for Henrietta. She'd succeeded in her mission to disable the rudder chain. Where was she?

Chain shot sailed toward the ship as the third set of cannons fired. One smacked into the main mast, cracking it. It splintered, falling forward and crashing onto the main deck.

A final bevy of cannonballs sailed toward *The Pillager.* Their strike put the final nail in Whitemane's floating coffin. The first tore through the ship, splashing into the water on the opposite side as it left a hole through both the starboard and port walls. The second grazed the hull, knocking the frozen rudder askew. The third did the most damage, smashing through the hull into the ship's armory.

Shouts rose from the other vessel as Clif's crew pulled up their anchor and continued their turn away from *The Pillager.*

Moments later, a massive boom resounded and fire shot from the inside of the ship. An ear-splitting crack announced the splitting of the vessel. The stern tilted backward, sinking quickly as the bow plunged into the waters and bobbed up and down.

Bodies littered the water, clinging to the pieces of the ship or flailing their arms to stay afloat. Clif searched the waters for a woman but found none.

Johnson hurried toward him, a grin on his face. "Captain, *The Pillager* is defeated."

His smile faded as Clif's stony features stared back. "Captain? This is a great victory. We've done it."

"Tell me Henrietta is aboard."

Johnson swallowed hard. "I'm certain–"

"Certain?" Clif snapped. "Are you certain? Then show her to me."

"Well, Captain, I have not seen her."

"Have not seen her?" Clif growled, wrapping his fingers around Johnson's neck and forcing him back a few steps. "Then find her. And if she is not aboard, search the waters for her."

"Aye, Captain," Johnson said with wide eyes, his head bobbing quickly enough to knock his hat off.

He released his grip on the man, who scurried away in search of his other captain. Clif stalked to the railing, searching the sea for his sister. He wrapped his fingers around the wood, his knuckles turning white as he gripped it.

His stomach somersaulted, and his heart dropped. Had he doomed his sister when he'd fired upon *The Pillager?*

* * *

Henrietta clenched her jaw as she stared down the length of the sword thrust into her face. Pressed against her back, Williams, also facing a sword from another sailor.

"Captain," he whispered.

She gave a slight nod. "On three."

His muscles tensed as she began her count. She made it to "two" when a blast shook the ship. Cannonballs tore through the hull, rocking the vessel hard. The helmsman took a bullet to the skull, slumping away from the wheel and smacking onto the deck.

Henrietta stumbled forward as her attacker lost his footing and sprawled onto the deck. She drew her sword waving it in his face as she stepped onto his wrist. He dropped his weapon and she kicked it away before she spun to assist Williams with his battle against two opposing crew members.

She slashed at one man, drawing his attention away from her crewman. He brought his sword down against hers. They struggled for a second before she released the pressure against him, spiraling away and kicking him in the rear.

The force of her kick along with a second volley of fire from her home ship sent him rolling across the deck. A round of chain shot cracked into the main mast, splintering it.

"Williams!" she shouted. "Let's go!"

Williams plunged his knife into his assailant's chest as another volley fired from *The Henton*.

"Quickly," she said, fighting her way through the other sailors aboard who scrambled to save their badly damaged vessel.

One attempted to capture her, but she slashed at his arm, sending him reeling as blood spurted from a deep wound.

They reached the railing and climbed up. Henrietta glanced over her shoulder as the third round of fire slammed into the ship. Her eyes widened as the cannonballs hit their mark and shouts erupted from below deck.

A rumbling sounded and fire shot up from the ship's underbelly before an explosion blew the ship in two.

* * *

"Captain! Captain!" Johnson screamed, a deep expression of dismay on his rugged features.

Clif raced toward the man, his eyes wide. "What is it?"

Johnson licked his lips. "Sir..." His head fell to the side and his lips bobbed up and down but no words came out. Instead, he lifted a shaky finger and pointed at the water.

Clif followed it, staring at what it pointed at. A body,

burned beyond recognition, floated in the waters. Small in stature, with long dark hair, Clif eyed a body that could be his sister. Nearby, a hat bobbed with a wet feather poking into the air.

Clif's chest tightened and he struggled to breathe. "Br-Bring it aboard."

"Aye, Captain," Johnson said, passing orders along to the men to capture the burned body and bring it aboard.

"Sir," Johnson said again as Clif stared blankly ahead. "Should we be underway?"

Clif shook his head. "No, not until…"

Johnson raised his eyebrows, his chin sliding forward. "Sir?"

"Bring that body aboard, Johnson. We shall discuss plans after we have…"

"Captain, perhaps it is best for you to retreat to your quarters. I shall fetch you when we retrieved the body."

Clif swallowed hard, his eyes glistening as he nodded. "Fetch me, when you have… yes."

"Aye, Captain," Johnson murmured as Clif skirted past him and hastened to his cabin. He pushed through the door, tears spilling onto his cheeks. His shoulders shook with sobs as he stumbled to the desk.

Next to it, the hammock rocked with the ship's movements. In it, another hat with a feather jutting from it. Clif grasped it, clutching it to his chest as more tears threatened.

"Ri," he choked out. "I should never have let you go."

He wiped at his cheeks before reaching into his pocket and withdrawing his flask. With a shaky hand, he twisted off the top and took a swig. He screwed the cap back on, staring into the distance at nothing when a knock sounded.

"Captain," Johnson called, "we have the body."

Clif twisted toward the door, prepared to answer, but could not find the words. Instead, he set the hat on the desk and marched over to it, sucking in a deep breath before he flung it open.

The small charred figure lay in the middle of the deck. Clif pushed back the tears that threatened again and stepped into the bright sunshine. A group of men had already gathered around the body. They pulled the hats from their heads, placing them over their hearts in a sign of reverence for their former captain.

Clif pulled his tricorn from his head and stepped forward. The group shifted to allow him access to the body. He knelt at her side, his features pinching with upset.

"We have lost a great sailor, today," Johnson said. Murmurs of agreement went up from the group. Abby pushed her way through, dropping to both knees, her face a mask of anguish.

"Captain," she cried, tears flowing freely down her cheeks, "no!"

Clif bowed his head as Abby continued to sob. He licked his lips, knowing he needed to address the men but unsure he could formulate words.

His lower lip trembled when he opened his mouth to speak and he squashed it closed. Before he could recover enough to speak, another voice sounded from the back of the group.

"And just what is going on here? Do we not have business to attend to?"

Clif's jaw dropped open with a gasp as he slowly rose to his feet and spun around. The crush of sailors made it impossible for him to see who spoke, but he recognized the voice.

He motioned for them to part ways. They shuffled to form a break in their ranks. As the sea of sailors parted, Clif's heart skipped a beat.

Behind the crowd, hands on hips and an eyebrow arched

stood Henrietta. Still dripping wet, she managed to find a feathered hat to stick on her head.

Clif's features melted into a mix of surprise, relief, and joy. He barreled toward her, scooping her into a bear hug and lifting her off her feet.

"What is wrong with you?" she questioned.

"I thought you were gone," he explained as he set her down on the deck.

"What? Whatever gave you that impression?"

"I fired upon *The Pillager* before you abandoned the ship. And then…" His voice trailed off and he glanced over his shoulder at the burned body.

"Then?" she prodded.

"We spotted the body in the water. A feathered cap floated near it. I assumed…"

"That I died? Oh, Clif, I would never have been foolish enough to do that."

Clif set her on the deck and shook his head. "I fired. I had no choice."

"I know. I saw them. The chain shot took out their mast, though your final volley did more than disable their ship, brother. Well done."

"How did you–"

"Williams and I heard the shouting. We leapt into the water moments before the explosion. Being underwater when it happened likely saved our lives. We swam back as quickly as we could."

Clif breathed a sigh of relief before wagging his finger at his sister. "You will never do that again."

"What? Be useful?"

Clif pressed his lips together and shook his head. "That's not what I meant and you know it."

Henrietta clapped a hand on his shoulder. "Sorry to have frightened you, brother."

Clif drew in another deep breath before he spun to face his crew. "Well, men, we have achieved a great victory today. And we now know we have not lost our beloved captain."

"What now?" a man shouted.

Clif's lips pulled back in a devilish grin. "We press on to the City of Diamonds."

Johnson spun to face them. "You heard him, men! Prepare to make way!"

The sailors scattered, returning to their posts as they got the ship moving forward. Abby hurried toward Henrietta, offering her a salute before she threw her arms around her neck. "Oh, Captain! I am so pleased you are alive."

Henrietta eased her back. "As pleased as I am to be alive, this behavior is highly inappropriate, Miss Turner."

"My apologies, Captain," Abby said, a grin still on her lips. "I am overcome with joy. You are my savior and to think you may have…well, never mind."

"I am not dead, Miss Turner. But you will be if you do not return to your post."

Abby saluted again, adding a nod before she scurried off to assist with the sailing.

Clif and Henrietta returned to the captain's quarters. The little monkey scurried out of the hammock and scrambled across the floor on its hands and feet, climbed up to Henrietta's shoulder, and threw its arms around her neck.

Henrietta scrunched her features at the greeting.

"Looks like I was not the only one happy to see you."

"Apparently not. Between Jack and Abby, I just may be more beloved than you."

"If you lead us to the City of Diamonds, I have no doubt you will be the more popular captain on this ship." Clif collapsed into the chair behind the desk with a sigh.

"If?" Henrietta questioned, peeling the monkey from her

shoulder and cradling it as she plopped into the hammock. "When."

Clif grinned at her. "Did I ever tell you I love your spirit, Ri?"

"Many times. Also, my stories."

"I did miss those when you stopped writing."

Henrietta kicked her feet up into the hammock and set it to rock. "A dark time in my life which, thanks to you, is over."

"You blamed me for it happening to start with," Clif said, kicking his feet onto the desk.

"It was your fault! You left me to become a pirate and live an exciting life. I was stuck marrying whatever fat, middle-aged man proposed."

"Blanchard was well past the middle of his life," Clif said, rising to snatch an apple from the table in the room.

"You're digging your grave deeper."

"I am sorry, Ri," Clif said after a bite of his apple. "And I did not leave to become a pirate. I left to–"

Henrietta let her head fall back into the folds of fabric. "Escape the aftermath of Thomas's death, I know."

"I am sorry I left you to deal with it."

She turned her dark eyes to him. "We took the paths we were meant to take in order to shape us into what we would become."

"Living legends?" Clif asked with a cheeky grin.

Henrietta lifted her chin. "Of course. I cannot wait to reach the shores of Mexico."

"It should be smooth sailing now."

* * *

Clif clung to the railing as the storm rocked the ship. Waves crashed over the side, smashing onto the deck.

Sailors, tied to the main mast, worked to trim the sails as

they continued through the rough water, trying to escape the black skies.

"I thought you said smooth sailing!" Henrietta shouted over the rumbles of thunder and crashing of the sea. Rain battered her face and the wind gusts threatened to blow her hat from her head unless she kept a hand firmly clamped down on it.

"Mother Nature forgot to tell me her plans!" Clif yelled back.

"Just get us out of this," Henrietta hollered.

"Aye, aye, Captain!" Clif said with a salute before he climbed the steps to the helm and took over the wheel.

"Sir!" Johnson shouted to him. "Turn back!"

"No!" Clif called. "We shall come through it."

Henrietta spun, one hand still holding her hat tight to her head, and fought her way across the deck as the ship swayed on every swell. "Mr. Johnson, where may I be of assistance?"

"Trim back the main sails."

Henrietta nodded and hurried to the mast, grabbing hold of a line that whipped in the air. The wind gusted, pulling her up. She dangled in the air, her feet kicking in search of the deck.

Clif spun the wheel and the ship rolled back the opposite way. Henrietta's feet slipped across the wet wood. Another wave slammed into the ship, crashing over the side and smashing into Henrietta.

It knocked her off her feet. She landed hard on her backside and barreled toward the opposite railing.

Johnson grabbed hold of her as she slid past. Henrietta clamped both hands onto his arm, climbing to her feet as he hauled her upward.

The rough waters pushed the ship around, making it impossible to remain on course.

"Land ho!" a sailor shouted from the crow's nest, his

finger pointed to the left. Clif spun the wheel, trying to steer away from it, but the angry ocean pushed them closer and closer.

Henrietta's eyes went wide and she pulled her gaze away from the quickly-approaching land mass and stared up at her brother. "We're going to hit!"

The ship shuddered as a loud scraping drowned out even the thunder overhead. Henrietta braced herself against the mast as the vessel shook underneath her. She raced to the railing, squinting into the rain that still pelted her to assess the damage.

Clif joined her, balling his hands into fists and pounding them against the railing. "Damn it!"

Johnson hurried over, leaning over the rail along with them.

"Johnson, assess the damage," Henrietta said. "Find out how long before we can be underway again."

Johnson's head bobbed up and down as he shoved off the railing and hurried across the main deck.

"This will put a pin in our plans for the time being," Clif said.

"How far south are we? Perhaps we can disembark and journey from here while the damage is assessed and repaired."

Clif glanced up at the sky. "Let's consult the maps and make a plan. Perhaps by then, the rain will have subsided."

Henrietta nodded her agreement and they crossed to the captain's cabin while other sailors bustled about the ship. Clif headed for the desk, shoving papers aside to expose the maps underneath. Jack scrambled up to sit on his shoulder.

"We've run aground, little friend," Clif told him as he poked a finger at the map. "We were here at last check."

"And now?"

Clif cocked his head, tracing his finger along a pathway. "The storm blew us somewhere in here. Though I cannot be more specific than that."

He traced an invisible circle around a piece of land jutting out into the sea.

Henrietta dug her notes from the stack of papers. "This new location shortens the journey by half a day. Well done, Clif. Even with the storm knocking us off course, you have managed to win."

"Glad to oblige you by running aground, Ri."

"Let us hope the damage is minimal. But we should gather a contingent of men and set off as soon as possible."

"In the rain? Your feather will not survive it."

"Never mind my feather. And if I'm not mistaken, it sounds as though the rain has slowed. We may be in luck."

They stepped out onto the sodden deck, finding the dark clouds racing away and the rain subsiding. Johnson hurried toward them from the stairs leading below deck.

He flung his hand up in a salute. "Captain. The damage can be repaired, though it may take a day or more."

"Good," Clif said with a nod. "In the meantime, we shall go ashore and search for the City of Diamonds. According to our research, we are closer to the final map piece than if we had sailed into port. We should gather the men, leaving behind a contingent to repair the ship, and set off as soon as possible."

"Aye, Captain," Johnson said. "I shall ready the men to depart."

Within the hour, they were underway, heading into the jungle for the trek toward the Aztec temple.

As the dark clouds disappeared, the sun shone brightly overhead, raising the temperature quickly as they cut a path through the jungle. Henrietta wiped at the beads of sweat forming under her feathered cap when they stopped for a brief break.

"We should reach the temple by nightfall," Clif said as he sipped water from his canteen before passing it to Henrietta.

"We should have traveled at night. This heat is unbearable."

Clif glanced at her head. "Your feather is holding up well in the mugginess. Too bad the same cannot be said for you."

Henrietta thrust the canteen back at him, smacking it against his stomach. "I am holding up just fine. Onward!"

She removed her sword from its sheath and hacked away a few large leaves before proceeding forward. The tired men rose to their feet and continued their march through the afternoon. As the sun descended past the horizon, they closed in on the location of the temple.

Lit torches were passed among the group as darkness covered them and they continued forward. As the moon rose overhead, a scout raced back to the large group.

"Captain!" he called, his torch blowing in the wind as he ran.

"What is it, Smith?" Clif inquired.

"A group at the temple. Several tents."

"How many?" Henrietta inquired.

"Six," the man answered. "Has someone beaten us to it?"

"Doubtful," Clif answered. "Only we have the map pieces. I shall return with you now to determine how best to proceed."

"Mr. Johnson," Henrietta called. "Keep the men here whilst we scout the encampment."

"Aye, Captain," he answered.

"Ri–" Clif began.

"Do not even try to convince me to stay here. I shall be perfectly fine."

Clif nodded his acquiescence and they followed the scout forward, crouching behind trees to view the camp.

Lanterns glowed from within tents. Outside of one, a spectacled man balanced a sketchpad on his legs. He stared up at the temple, glowing under the moonlight before he swiped his pencil across his paper.

"Researchers," Henrietta whispered to Clif.

"Yes. Likely unarmed for the most part outside of the guides."

"An easy battle," she answered.

He nodded his head, pressing a finger to his lips, and retreated backward. As they strode back to their crew, he answered, "Yes. We should be able to take that camp without too much fuss."

"Perhaps they know of what we seek."

Clif grinned at her. "Yes, they may have made our job easy."

"We shall know soon enough. We should raid the camp in the cover of darkness."

"I agree," Clif answered as they rejoined their group. He passed along his orders. They would march on the camp with weapons drawn, seek out their leader to determine if the map piece had been located, and herd the others into one tent.

With orders given out, they extinguished their torches and crept forward toward the temple using only moonlight to light their way. Within minutes, they had the encampment surrounded. An unfortunate scout met the tip of Clif's sword as he backed him to a tree.

"Hello. I don't suppose you'd be willing to help us find a map piece."

The man raised his hands, his lips quivering as he bobbed his head up and down in agreement.

"Lovely. After my sister finishes binding your hands, you can lead the way to the temple," Clif answered with a grin.

Henrietta stepped forward with a gag and rope. She fastened the cloth in his mouth and secured the man's wrists behind his back before Clif stuck the tip of his sword into his back. "Straight to the temple, please, without a word."

They marched toward the massive, moonlit structure as their crew rounded up the others in the encampment. Johnson sought out the leader. He struck a man in the stomach, doubling him over before he bound his wrists and dragged him toward a nearby tree.

Henrietta continued along with Clif as they approached the temple and climbed to the top. She grabbed a lit torch as they ducked into the dark entrance and descended the steps into the heart of the temple.

"We are searching for a map piece, similar to these," Clif said, showing him the rolled-up parchment. "Perhaps in a box."

The man shrugged his shoulders and shook his head. Henrietta waved the torch around, searching the corners for the item.

"Has your group searched within the temple?"

He nodded his head and murmured something. Henrietta tugged the fabric from his mouth. "James," he gasped out.

"James is the leader of your outfit?" Clif inquired.

He nodded as Henrietta secured the gag.

"I suppose we should check with James, eh, Ri?"

"It would certainly make things faster," she murmured as

she waved the torch over the decorated walls, studying the images. "Fascinating."

"You can ogle the walls later. We have work to do."

She shot a sideways glance at her brother, a smirk on her lips. Voices called down to them. Clif answered and soon footsteps reached them.

Mr. Johnson and Williams, both carrying torches, entered the large rectangular space. "The camp is secured, Captain."

"Good," Clif answered. "Have you found a man by the name of James?"

"Indeed, sir. He is hanging from a tree."

"By his neck?" Henrietta asked, spinning to face him.

"No, Captain," Johnson answered.

"We shall need to speak with him at once. Cut him down and bring him to us."

"Aye, Captain. And what of the others? We grouped them within a tent."

Henrietta handed her torch off to Clif. "I shall deal with them. Take me there."

"Aye, Captain," Williams said, motioning for her to precede him up the steps.

Henrietta climbed into the night air, allowing Williams to pass her and lead her to the tent at the foot of the temple.

Williams pulled the tent flap back and ducked inside. Henrietta leaned into the tent as the lantern flared to life. A sailor shoved it toward the prisoners, huddled on their knees with their hands bound behind their backs. The light illuminated the frightened face of a blonde woman, her light hair escaping the hairstyle she'd tucked it into earlier.

Tears streaked her face, and she struggled to hold in a sob, shying away from the light.

Henrietta's muscles stiffened and her jaw dropped open. She let the flap drop closed as her mind parsed what she'd just witnessed.

"No," she breathed. She stood for a few more seconds before her feet moved her back toward the temple. Still reeling from the scene in the tent, she sucked in a deep breath and mounted the stairs.

Leaving the moonlight behind, she ducked into the temple again. Voices floated from the depths, and she made her way down to them.

Flickering light filled the space as she re-entered the large room. A man knelt in the middle of the floor. Clif struck him across his face, knocking him to the floor below.

His glasses flew from his face, clattering across the stones and landing at Henrietta's feet. She stared down her nose at them for a moment before raising her eyes to her brother and Mr. Johnson.

"He's not very cooperative," Clif lamented with a sigh, "but we shall soon remedy that."

Johnson hauled the man back to his knees. "When the captain asks you a question, you answer!"

Clif stared down at the man with raised eyebrows. "It would be wise to heed his advice."

He pushed his shoulders back, his jaw flexing as he prepared for another blow.

"Nothing to say?" Clif questioned.

The man pressed his lips together.

Clif shrugged a shoulder. "More's the pity." He raised his arm, preparing to strike the man again.

"Clif," Henrietta shouted.

Clif froze with his hand still raised in the air, flicking his gaze to his sister.

"A word."

Clif's arm fell, slapping against his side before he flung them both out. "I'm in the middle of something."

"This is more important."

"More important than ascertaining the location of the final map piece and the City of Diamonds?"

"Infinitely," Henrietta answered.

Clif waved for her to continue. "I am all ears."

Henrietta shook her head and flicked her gaze to Johnson. "Mr. Johnson, take this man to his tent. Keep him under guard."

Johnson took a step toward the prisoner when Clif held his hand up. "Just a moment, Johnson. What's all this about? I am not finished with him."

"You are for now." She bobbed her head at Johnson who pulled the man to his feet and shuffled him toward the stairs. His already swollen, blackening eye gleamed in the flickering flames of the torches, along with the trail of blood from the corner of his lip.

As Johnson passed her with the man, she said, "There is a woman among the prisoners. Bring her here immediately."

The prisoner's eyes grew wide as she spoke the words. He twisted to face her. "No!" he cried.

Henrietta waved for Johnson to take the man away. He wrangled him up the stairs as the man continued to shout at them about the woman.

Clif stared at a few of the murals decorating the walls as Henrietta joined him. "Might you now tell me the meaning of this?"

Henrietta flicked her dark eyes up to her brother's, letting her hands fall onto her hips, and shook her head. "You're not going to believe this."

CHAPTER 22

"*P*lease do not tell me you've found another wayward girl in need of rescue," Clif said, crossing his arms over his chest.

"Not exactly, though it does involve the woman I mentioned earlier."

"We cannot save them all, Ri. Besides, we have other things to do. We are on the verge of finding the last map piece and the City of Diamonds. Well, we were until you stopped me from extracting the information from that man."

Henrietta shook her head at him. "You will be glad I did."

Clif raised his eyebrows at her. "Really? Intriguing. Explain how I shall be pleased with this interruption."

Henrietta cocked her head, staring at him with an unimpressed expression. "Simple. You will not want to have beaten him within an inch of his life when you discover who he is."

Clif's eyes slid from side to side before he narrowed them at Henrietta. "And who is he exactly?"

Henrietta raised her eyebrows as she stared into her brother's cocoa-brown eyes. "Carolina's husband."

Clif's expression melted from coy to shocked in seconds. He swallowed hard. "What? How do you know?"

"The woman in the tent," Henrietta answered, "is Carolina."

Clif's eyes widened. "It cannot be."

Henrietta shrugged as she stalked across the room. "See for yourself. That is why I requested her brought here. You said she was out of town."

Clif's gaze fell to the stone floor as he considered. "Yes, but…"

"But what? Is not her husband a university professor leading an expedition?"

Clif chewed his lower lip for a moment, joining his sister in the shadows at the far end of the room. "Unbelievable. Are you certain?"

Henrietta cocked a hip and stared at him. "Are you really asking that question of me?"

Clif pressed his lips together in a thin line as footsteps sounded on the stone steps.

"Here they come. You'll see for yourself in just a moment. Remain in the shadows if you'd like, though I am not wrong."

Seconds later, Johnson and another man entered with a woman, her head bowed and her hands bound behind her.

"Here she is," Johnson said, shoving her forward a few steps.

"Light," Clif called.

The second sailor passed his torch to Johnson who shoved it nearer the woman. She turned her face away from it, but the sailor grabbed her, giving her a shake as Johnson squashed her cheeks between his hands and tugged her face closer to the light.

Clif's eyes went wide as the flames lit her face and he gasped.

"I told you," Henrietta said, sticking her hands on her hips. "Now what?"

"We cannot take the map piece and leave without revealing ourselves to her."

Henrietta puckered her lips and heaved a sigh.

"Do you object?"

With a shrug of her shoulders, Henrietta shook her head. "I do not. Though it will likely shock her."

"Indeed. Hopefully pleasantly," Clif whispered before raising his voice. "Carolina."

The woman's brow furrowed, her lower lip trembling as Clif stalked forward. The shaking extended from her jaw to her whole body. Only the strong arms of the sailor holding her stopped her from collapsing.

"Please, sir," she choked out as Clif closed the gap between them, her eyes downcast and tears streaking her cheeks.

Clif grazed her chin with his finger. She shrank away with a gasp, an expression of disgust stuck on her features. Johnson shoved her head forward again. Clif tapped her chin again, tilting her head upward.

Her eyes remained fixed on the floor even as he moved her head up. With gasping breaths, she licked her lips and slid her eyes upward, her expression switching from horrified to shocked.

A grin spread across Clif's face. "Carolina."

A sob escaped the woman and tears fell to her cheeks. Her lower lip trembled again and her forehead crinkled. "Clif?"

The smile on his face broadened and he waved behind him. "And that's not all."

Henrietta stalked forward toward her baby sister. Carolina's eyes bulged as the torch's flames illuminated her features. "Henrietta?" she gasped out.

Clif wiggled his eyebrows at his sister, still grinning.

"No," Carolina said, her head shaking vigorously. "No, you're dead. Both of you. Dead. This cannot be."

Clif shrugged a shoulder at her. "Mere trickery. Rather an excellent plan on Ri's part. As you can see, we remain very much alive."

Carolina sucked in breaths as her gaze fell to the stones below her feet. She glanced back at Clif, then Henrietta before shaking her head again.

"Cut her loose," Clif said to Mr. Johnson.

Johnson cocked his head. "Captain–"

Clif clapped Johnson on the shoulder. "Easy, man. This is my baby sister, Carolina. She means us no harm."

With a frown affixed on his features, Johnson tugged a knife from his belt and sliced through the rope around Carolina's wrists. She pulled them forward, rubbing at the red marks. She stumbled forward a step as Clif tapped the sailor's arm in a silent order to let her go.

She flicked her gaze between the two of them again before she stretched an arm out and touched Clif's cheek. She jerked it back as her fingers touched his flesh, the expression of shock still etched on her features.

"Clif?" she whispered.

Clif held his hands out to the sides and offered her a bow. "In the flesh."

"But–" She bit her thumbnail, flicking her gaze away from him before she raised her eyes to Henrietta. "You died. You both died."

"I told you," Clif answered, circling to stand in front of his younger sister, "a clever deception orchestrated by Ri. She faked her suicide and then I faked my shipwreck."

"Why?"

"You did not honestly believe I would throw myself from the widow's walk over a man, did you?" Henrietta huffed.

"You were so distraught," Carolina answered.

Clif arched an eyebrow at Henrietta. "I told you your acting skills would be sufficient."

Carolina's eyes widened, and her hands balled into fists. She lunged toward Henrietta and pummeled her with her clenched hand. Henrietta's eyes went wide and she stumbled back, shoving her younger sister off her as Clif caught Carolina and dragged her back a few steps.

"Have you gone mad?" Henrietta questioned.

"I thought you were dead! Both of you!" Carolina spat, tears forming in her eyes again. "I grieved you! I wept over you! My heart ached when I learned you took your life."

She sniffled and flicked a tear away before raising her still-glistening eyes to Clif. "And you! The news of your death just months after Henrietta's crushed me."

Henrietta lifted her eyes to the ceiling, her head shaking. "Of course, it did."

Carolina drew her chin back, an incredulous expression on her features. "What do you mean by that?"

"Of course, Clif's death crushed you. You idolized him."

"I idolized you both!" Carolina shouted, poking a finger at Henrietta. "You, my big sister, so strong and proud. So independent. So brilliant with your novel writing. When the Captain died and your mind went…well, when I *thought* your mind went, I felt so terrible about it. I wished for you to recover. I prayed for it nightly. When I learned of your death, I felt awful. Your death shocked me, Henrietta. I had wished we could become closer, but I did not know how to reach you. You were always closer to Clif. You despised me."

Henrietta crossed her arms over her chest and puckered her lips. "No, I did not."

"You did! You detested when Mother thrust me upon you. I was a burden for you."

"Carolina, that is not true. You were always too busy being a goody-goody to appreciate anything I did."

"I was not. I could never live up to you. So I stuck my nose in a book because I couldn't do anything else." Carolina covered her face with her hands as she wept.

Clif shot Henrietta a pointed glance. She lifted a shoulder in a silent question to him. He raised his eyebrows, waving a hand at their sobbing sister.

Henrietta pressed her lips together and rolled her eyes, taking a step toward Carolina. She put her arms out, letting them flail in the air for a moment before she wrapped them around her sister's shaking shoulders, shooting Clif a glance to wordlessly inquire if the action appeased him.

"There, there," Henrietta said to her sister.

Carolina's shoulders heaved as she continued her crying, uncovering her face to fling her arms around her sister tightly. Henrietta stumbled back a step as Carolina clung to her, burying her face against Henrietta's shoulder.

Clif offered a half smile at his older sister's surprise as she wrapped her arms around his other sibling and stroked her hair. "It's all right, Carolina. We are not dead. Either of us. You can see us any time you'd like."

Carolina sniffled, pulling back from Henrietta and nodding. She wiped at her eyes before she threw herself into Clif's arms. Clif stroked her shoulder as she cried for a few more moments before recovering.

With a shaky breath, she finally released her hold on her brother and wiped at her cheeks. Henrietta offered a handkerchief and her sister accepted, drying her eyes with it. "You still never explained why. Why would you do this? I felt so alone."

"We did it to protect you," Clif said.

Carolina's features pinched as she sniffled again. "What?"

"Another pirate threatened your life," Henrietta said. "Clif and this man's father were enemies and Clif…well, let's just say the man no longer sails the seas. We worried he would seek his revenge by harming you."

"So, you disappeared."

"To protect you," Clif said, his head bobbing up and down.

"Will this man not find out you are alive now?"

"He may. But rumors will abound first. And it bought us enough time to strengthen our forces if needed."

"You mean to fight. You will go to war with him."

Clif nodded and Carolina's lips pulled down into a frown.

"We will not lose, Carolina," Clif assured her.

Henrietta flicked her gaze to her sister, whose eyes remained trained on the floor. "Clif never loses a battle."

"Yet he had to fake his death to win before."

"To protect you. Now, you are married. And obviously much harder to find. He will likely not waste his time tracking you down but spend it chasing after my ghost," Clif answered.

Carolina chewed her lower lip as she considered it for a moment before changing the subject. "How did you manage to find me?"

"We didn't," Clif said with a glance at Henrietta.

Carolina's brow furrowed at the response and she glanced up at him, a questioning expression on her features.

Henrietta answered for her brother. "We stumbled upon you by accident. We are in search of the City of Diamonds and our research pointed to this temple to contain the final piece of the map."

"Thank heavens Ri recognized you," Clif added.

Carolina winced as she tamed a wayward lock of blonde hair behind her ear. "I shudder to think what may have become of me had the pirate captain *not* have been my brother."

"And sister," Henrietta said.

Carolina screwed up her face.

"Ri is an excellent pirate," Clif said with a grin.

"You mean to say you do not simply sail with Clif but that you…" Carolina's voice trailed off as she waved an upturned finger at Henrietta.

Clif wrapped an arm around his older sister, a grin beaming from his chiseled features. He wiggled his eyebrows at Carolina. "Fights like a pirate, sails like a pirate, is a pirate."

A proud smile spread across Henrietta's face, and she lifted her chin in the air as she turned her gaze to Carolina who fluttered her eyelashes.

"And you enjoy this?" she questioned.

"I feel as though I finally have the life I wanted."

"Sailing about on Clif's…your ship?"

Henrietta cocked her head and arched an eyebrow. "And searching for adventure."

"I am not certain I could stomach that," Carolina admitted as she stalked a few steps away.

"Says the woman whose husband dragged her into the jungle," Henrietta responded.

"That's rather different," Carolina countered. "And look what happened! I was nearly sick when your men took over the camp. I almost died of fright."

"Good thing you didn't, sister," Clif said. "Now, about that. We need to speak with James about this map piece."

Carolina licked her lips, furrowing her brow. "What sort of map piece?"

Mr. Johnson's arrival postponed further conversation.

"Ah, Mr. Johnson," Clif said as he appeared at the bottom of the steps. "Please bring Dr. Edmonton down at once. We must finish our conversation."

"Right away, Captain," Johnson answered, scurrying up the stairs.

"I am not certain what sorts of things James has cataloged already," Carolina answered. "I have spent most of my time sketching the murals on the walls."

"I am certain James can clear it up quickly. Particularly now that we have a connection," Clif said with a grin.

"I am not certain–" Carolina began when footsteps scraped against the stone floor. Johnson shoved James forward into the room. He stumbled a few steps, catching his balance despite his hands still being bound in front of him.

He scanned the space, his eyes going wide as he caught sight of Carolina. His face twisted into a mask of anguish as he raced toward her. "Carolina, are you all right?"

She nodded, her features pinching as she took his face in her hands.

"Are you hurt?"

She shook her head, unable to find words as she stared at the black, swollen eye on her husband's face.

Before she could speak, James pushed in front of her. "Let her go."

"There's no need for that," Clif said. "We–"

"Let her go, I said!" James shouted, his face reddening.

Clif sighed and tried again. "If you'll listen–"

"She has nothing to do with whatever you're after. Now, let her go. I–I'll cooperate with whatever demands you have, but you must let my wife go and promise she will be unharmed."

"James, please wait," Carolina said, tugging on his shoulder.

"No, Carolina, I must do all I can to protect you from these vicious brutes."

"But, James–" she tried again.

"You cannot trust them. They are pirates. Barbarians."

He flicked his gaze back to Clif. "I will tell you whatever you want to know the moment she is free. You have my word."

"No one is going anywhere," Henrietta said.

"How can you do this?" James burst out. "You, a woman. How can you subject another woman to what she will go through at the hands of these ruffians?"

"She will go through nothing," Henrietta said, offering an unimpressed stare at the man.

"I don't believe you," James spat.

Henrietta rolled her eyes at him and strode forward. James swallowed hard as she approached him. "If you would shut your mouth and listen, you would learn the reason her safety is assured."

"Oh? Spit it out then, wench!"

"James!" Carolina shouted as Clif stormed forward.

"Now, see here, sir!" Clif shouted as he grasped James by the collar. "That is my sister you are degrading and I will not have it!"

James's nostrils flared as he stared into Clif's eyes. "With your concern for her apparent, you ought to understand mine for my wife."

"Of course, I do," Clif answered. "Because she is also my sister."

James's eyes went wide and he stumbled back a step as Clif let go of his collar. He flicked his gaze to Carolina, confusion apparent on his face.

Carolina's lips formed a trembling smile as she slid a hand onto her brother's shoulder. "Clif is my brother. And Henrietta is my sister."

"And while we would never harm our little sister, if you call me a wench again, I will slice you in two," Henrietta said to the man.

"But..." James's voice trailed off as his gaze wandered

from face to face. "You…they…they're dead. You said they were dead."

"I thought they were," Carolina admitted, a tear falling to her cheek again. She flicked it away and sniffled. "They are obviously not."

James snapped his gaze to Clif and Henrietta. "Why would you do this? Carolina was devastated!"

"We have explained the circumstances to Carolina already. If she chooses to share them with you, that is up to her," Henrietta answered. "What is of consequence at the moment is a very particular item."

James's face morphed from confused to obstinate in an instant. He stormed forward, pushing between Clif and Carolina. "I still do not understand why I should help you!"

"Look, James," Clif said, clapping the man on the shoulder, "normally in these situations, I would demand that you help and give you little other choices. You've already experienced a bit of that. Though since you are my brother-in-law, I'm certain we can come to an understanding that suits everyone here."

"I will never help you, pirate!"

"I'd think again," Henrietta said. "You may be interested in what we seek. From an academic perspective."

"And what is it you seek?"

"The City of Diamonds," Henrietta answered.

The man's expression changed again, first to surprise before it melted to amusement. "The City of Diamonds doesn't exist."

"Doesn't it? Then why have we found a map pointing to it?" Clif asked.

"And with one last piece, we shall have the complete chart to it," Henrietta added.

Clif stalked toward him. "And there is a share in it for you if you were to help us locate the last piece and the city itself."

James squared his shoulders and raised his chin, his lip lifting into a sneer. "I would never share anything with a pirate."

"James…" Carolina breathed, grabbing his arm.

"No, Carolina!" James barked. "We must not give in to scoundrels like this."

Henrietta lifted her eyebrows, crossing her arms as she shot a glance at Clif. His jaw tensed.

James spun to face his wife. "I am sorry, but we must stand firm. I know they are your siblings and I have no doubt this unexpected reunion has warmed your heart. But that does not mean we can support this lifestyle of criminal behavior."

"Clif is not a criminal!" she shouted.

James shook his head. "Oh, Carolina, I said nothing in the wake of his supposed death, but he is. The rumors are true. And it is obvious even after his supposed demise he continues the lifestyle he led before."

He spun back to face Clif. "Which is why I cannot give in to your demands."

Clif's lips formed a scowl and he narrowed his eyes at the man. He balled his hands into fists. "Then we shall have to do something about that."

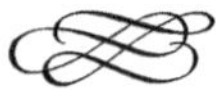

"No, Clif!" Carolina begged, racing in front of her husband to shield him.

"Ri, take Carolina to her tent," Clif said. "Dr. Edmonton and I need to have a private discussion."

"No!" Carolina shouted again. "I will not go."

"Carolina, it is for the best. You trust Clif, don't you?" Henrietta said, wrapping an arm around her sister's shoulders.

Carolina wriggled free from her sister's grasp, her face pinched with upset.

"You don't trust him, do you?" James said. "You know what he is."

Carolina's features twisted further.

Clif held his hands out to his sister. "Carolina–"

"No!" James shouted, interrupting his plea. "Do not attempt to play the caring brother!"

He stepped toward his wife, a pleading expression etched in his eyes. "Carolina, please, do not listen to them. They are pirates! Thieves!"

Fresh tears streamed down Carolina's pale skin again.

Her lower lip bobbed up and down as her gaze flitted from face to face.

James straightened and stared at Clif. "We cannot help you."

Clif opened his mouth to respond when Carolina blurted out, "I will give you the map piece."

"Carolina!" James spat.

Henrietta's shoulders slid down, and she arched an eyebrow. "You have it?"

"Yes, I believe so," Carolina said. "A piece of parchment in a curious wooden box."

"Take me to it," Henrietta said.

"Carolina, do not do this," James pleaded.

"I'm sorry, James, but I must. It is of no consequence to you if they take it and depart."

"This is ridiculous," James said. "The City of Diamonds is only a legend. It is not real."

"Then why do you care if we take the map piece and search for it?" Clif asked him as he sauntered closer to the man, cutting off his view of Carolina.

"I–I–It is not right. In the event the legend turns to truth that site should be cataloged and its contents given to a museum for all to enjoy."

"I offered you a share," Clif said. "Give us the map piece, and we shall all benefit."

"I do not wish for a share. I wish for these sites to be preserved and studied."

"You can preserve and study your share to your heart's content, brother-in-law. All in exchange for one tiny piece of the map that my sister is willing to give me for nothing."

James tensed his jaw, his nostrils flaring as he stared at Clif.

Clif narrowed his eyes when the man didn't respond. "Last chance, James."

"Over my dead body," James spat back. He reached for the knife in Clif's belt, withdrawing it and backing up a step, pointing it forward with his bound hands. "Or yours."

Henrietta drew her sword as did Johnson, both of them quick to point it at James.

"You are a dead man if you even so much as nick him," Henrietta said.

"Drop the knife, James. You do not wish your new wife to see you dead, do you?" Clif questioned, holding up his hands.

"No!" Carolina screamed. "Stop this!" She buried her head in her hands as she wept.

"You cannot be trusted," James answered, his hands shaking as he continued to hold the knife out.

"You may not believe it, but I would never harm my sister. That extends to you, as harming you would harm her. Now, drop the knife before the situation becomes unfixable," Clif said.

James's jaw trembled as he stared down the two blades pointed at his chin.

"You cannot win. Put the knife down and take the olive branch my brother offers before it is retracted." Henrietta said.

James's gaze flitted around the room for a moment from face to face before he lowered the knife. It clattered to the ground as he doubled over. Carolina raced to him, wrapping her arms around his shoulders. He straightened and pressed his forehead against hers.

"We can trust them, James. I promise," she breathed.

"I want to go with you," James answered after a moment.

Clif collected his knife from the floor and secured it in his belt as Henrietta and Johnson sheathed their swords.

"No!" Carolina said. "It may be dangerous!"

"It is a monumental discovery if it exists. Seeing it would be life-changing."

"For your bank account, too," Clif said with a grin.

"Just a moment," James said, stepping around Carolina again, "I wish to be perfectly clear. Anything found will go for the greater good."

"As I said," Clif answered, "I care not what you do with your share. Give it to your university. Give it to the poor. I don't much care. What I do care about is retrieving our share."

"What is the split to be?" James inquired.

"You may have twenty percent."

"Twenty percent?" James questioned.

"I am being generous. Had you not been my brother-in-law, you would have received none."

James bit his lower lip before he nodded. "Fine. We shall leave at daybreak after consulting the map."

"We shall leave immediately," Clif answered. "Give us the map piece and we shall set our course."

"Now? In the dark?"

Clif closed the gap between them, leaning closer to James. "What's the matter, doctor? Are you frightened?"

"The jungle is a dangerous place. We have a perimeter at the camp for a reason."

"And we have swords and guns for a reason, too," Clif answered. "We leave as soon as we have identified the final destination."

James shifted his weight from side to side as he considered it.

Clif waved a hand in the air. "You do not need to go, doctor. I shall happily send your cut to you."

James licked his lips and shook his head. "No, I prefer to go. I may be able to help."

"I shall go, too," Carolina answered.

"Absolutely not. You will stay here in the camp with the others."

"James!" Carolina protested when Clif interrupted her.

"We will all go. That will lessen the chance of one of your men betraying us."

"I prefer that Carolina not make this journey."

"Carolina will be fine," Henrietta answered.

James glared at her as Clif bolstered her statement. "Ri's right. I am certain if she made the journey here, she will make it to the City of Diamonds. After all, we wouldn't want her left here alone and defenseless, now, would we?" Clif grinned at him, his teeth gleaming in the flickering flames. "Now, the map piece."

"Untie my hands," James said.

"I think not. Not until we are ready to depart from this camp."

"You tell me to trust you, but you will not even free me."

Clif stalked around him, his hands clasped behind his back. "After you pulled a knife on me, no."

James shot him a sideways glance filled with annoyance.

Clif clapped a hand on the man's shoulder. "The map piece."

"It is in my tent amongst the things we have removed–"

"I know where it is," Carolina interrupted. "I shall retrieve it."

"I will accompany you," Henrietta said, sliding her arm around her sister's shoulders and guiding her to the stairs. "Perhaps that will give you men a chance to come to terms. We cannot have you bickering with each other at every step."

Carolina sniffled as she glanced over her shoulder at her husband, battered and bruised before she mounted the stairs with her sister.

"Which is your tent?" Henrietta asked as they emerged into the night air.

Carolina pointed to a dark tent near the center of the encampment. "There, on the left."

They descended the stairs, hurrying to the large canvas structure. Carolina pushed inside and crossed to a table, lighting a lantern before she lifted it in the air and scanned the messy space.

"James is not neat," she murmured.

Henrietta closed the tent flap behind her, securing it before she spun to face her sister. "Carolina, I think we need to have a frank discussion before we go any further."

Carolina stopped and stared at her, the flickering lantern's light casting ever-changing shadows across her face. Her features pinched and tears welled in her eyes again. "James will not survive this, will he?"

"No, no," Henrietta said, shifting her gaze to her feet, "it's not that. Clif is a man of his word. James will come through this unharmed. Unless he does something incredibly stupid like he did with the knife."

Carolina sniffled again, wiping at her eyes and nodding. "Oh. I shall make sure he does not."

Henrietta snapped her gaze to her sister's face, studying it. "Can you?"

Carolina's features pinched at the question and she drew her chin back. "I–"

"Can you really ensure that, Carolina? It does not appear so."

"I trust my husband."

"But can we?"

Carolina swallowed hard and flicked her gaze back to the cluttered worktable.

"Carolina, I am being serious. James seems to behave rashly with little thought to you–"

"That's not true!" Carolina spat. "His first thought was to me. He bargained with the map piece to save my life."

"And after he found out we would not harm you, he behaved foolishly. Clif, while a man of his word, is not a man to cross. And I will not allow your husband to harm him either. Neither will any member of our crew."

"I told you I would speak with him to ensure his cooperation."

Henrietta narrowed her eyes at her sister. "Fine. That is not what I wished to speak about anyway."

"What else would you like to berate me over now, sister?" Carolina said, leaning over the desk to shuffle a few items.

"That attitude is exactly what I wish to discuss."

"I am sorry, but I have no other attitude. Particularly after this latest incident in which you disappeared from my life without even a thought to my feelings. And you took Clif with you."

"Yes, I understand Clif's loss would affect you, but we did it to ensure both your and his safety."

"And yours," she said, still refusing to make eye contact.

"There is a lot of bitterness between us, Carolina. I know not why, but I wish for it to end."

Carolina whipped around to face her, setting the lantern on the desk. "You know not why? Honestly? Even after everything I explained in the temple? Well, then I do not know what to tell you, Henrietta. Apparently, our hostility toward each other will continue."

She spun back to the table.

"I have no ill feelings toward you. I do not understand why you developed so much toward me."

"No ill feelings? You hated me! You resented me as a child. You resented how Mother treated me. You refused to spend time with me. You detested me. Do you think I did not know this? Do you think it did not affect me when you snipped at me at any chance?"

Henrietta heaved a sigh, casting her eyes downwards again. She slung her thumb through her belt and bit her lower lip. "I did not resent you, Carolina."

"You did!"

"I didn't!" Henrietta said, raising her voice, her eyes snapping to her sister. "I resented my life. Not you."

"You took it out on me," Carolina said, a frown forming on her face. "I thought you hated me."

"Of course not. I hated how you seemed to enjoy your existence. You seemed happy. Clif seemed happy. While I was miserable."

"How could you be miserable? You were so smart, so sophisticated. You indulged in all the latest fashions. You knew exactly how to behave. You had multiple marriage proposals…"

"None of which I wanted. Do you think I wanted to be married to that barrister?"

Carolina drew her chin back before she nodded. "Yes."

"No! He was twenty years my senior! Fat, old, and far too dull for my taste."

"Then why did you accept him?"

"I had few other choices."

"That is not true. You were so attractive. Men's eyes followed you wherever you went."

Henrietta lowered her gaze to the floor again. "Men's eyes following me do not always imply the wish for marriage. And besides, I did not want it. I wanted to be free. To make my own way."

"I do not understand any of this. Why did you have such little choice? Surely, you could have made a match that would have suited you better. Was it Clif's departure that affected you? Father and Mother said it troubled you terribly."

"Yes, it did."

"But–"

"Leave it, Carolina."

Carolina lowered her shoulders, narrowing her eyes at

her sister. "You said you wanted to have it out. So let's have it. Why did you treat me the way you did?"

"I already told you, I was unhappy with my life."

"Your life was your making."

"I suppose that is true," Henrietta said, tears glistening in her eyes. "But I was too young to know better."

"Know better from what?"

"Do you remember Thomas Cranston?"

"The man Edwina married? The one shot by some wretch in the street and left to die?"

Henrietta bobbed her head up and down. "Yes, that's the one."

"What has he to do with this?"

Henrietta stalked to one of the cots in the tent and sank onto it with her back to her sister, her eyes staring at nothing. "Once upon a time, I thought he would marry me. It turns out he was one of those men whose eyes followed me, but not for marriage."

"Then for what?"

Henrietta flicked her gaze over her shoulder and cocked her head. "You are a married woman, Carolina, I'm certain you can figure it out."

Carolina's pale face flushed and her jaw dropped open. "No, surely not. Thomas Cranston was a gentleman from a fine family."

"Yes. On the night of his engagement party, he made it quite clear he would like his cake and eat it too. There was a quarrel between him and Clif. It came to blows. But that did not stop him. Even after, he tried to ensure I could make no decent matches. And when I would not give into him, he attempted to force me."

"Oh, Henrietta," Carolina said, rushing toward her sister and wrapping her arm around her.

"Clif killed him in that alley that night," Henrietta said as a tear rolled down her cheek. "I am the reason he left us."

She buried her face in her hands as she cried. "And you married the Captain because you felt you had no other choice."

Henrietta righted herself, wiping at her cheeks. "Yes. And when he died, Clif returned. We patched our fractured relationship and he offered me the freedom to live as I choose. And when that freedom, and you, were threatened, we reacted."

Henrietta took her sister's hands in hers and squeezed them. "I did not hate you, Carolina. I merely hated how content you were in your life whilst I could find no happiness in mine."

"Contentment is subjective," Carolina said, spinning away from her sister.

"Are you not content now?"

Carolina forced a smile onto her lips and faced Henrietta again. "I am."

Henrietta narrowed her eyes at her sister's seemingly forced response. She opened her mouth to respond, pausing as her forehead crinkled. Her nostrils flared and she gave the air another sniff. "What is that?"

Carolina inhaled deeply, choking and coughing afterward.

"Smoke," Henrietta murmured. She shot a glance over her shoulder, her eyes growing wide. Her lower lip trembled as her heart sped up. "Fire!"

CHAPTER 24

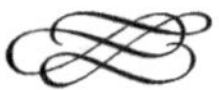

"What?" Carolina questioned, leaping from the cot. She slapped her palms against her cheeks, her jaw hanging agape. Across the room, flames shot from the lantern which now lay on its side. "Oh, no!"

"Get out, Carolina. I will retrieve the map piece."

"No, I can find it faster."

Thick smoke filled the tent as the flames spread to other items on the table, burning papers and dancing around relics.

"No, Carolina," Henrietta shouted as her sister darted around the cot and raced toward the flames.

"Get out, Henrietta! I shall join you as soon as I secure the map piece." She covered her nose with the crook of her arm, coughing and choking. Her eyes narrowed from the heavy smoke and tears filled them.

Henrietta hurried across the tent to her sister as Carolina reached into the flames for something on the table. "Here!" she called, grabbing at a wooden box. She dropped it, shaking her fingers and yelping in pain.

The small wooden rectangular cube bounced across the

floor, landing under a chair. Carolina dove for it. The smoke made it difficult to see and she smacked her head off the chair's corner. Blood gushed from a wound on her forehead as her limp form collapsed to the ground.

Henrietta choked and coughed as she crossed to her sister. "Carolina!" she called, shaking her. Her sister did not move.

Henrietta's features pinched as she reached past her sister for the small box, still warm from the fire that charred its side. She shoved it into her belt before grabbing her sister's wrists and straightening.

With her lungs burning, she hauled her sister's listless form toward the exit. Flames caught the canvas on fire, spreading quickly toward them and blocking their path toward the opening.

"Damn it," Henrietta choked out as she wiped at the tears stinging her eyes. She changed course, heading as far from the flames as she could toward the wall opposite the table.

Her eyes struggled to stay open as the smoke burned them and the shallow breaths she took made her feel dizzy. Shouts sounded outside the tent. Clif's voice screamed her name before arguing ensued.

She could not gather enough breath to call out to him. Instead, she knelt at the tent wall, tugged the knife from her belt, and slashed a hole into the canvas. The infusion of fresh oxygen fueled the flames. They burned hotter, inching closer toward them as Henrietta grabbed her sister again and shoved her through the slit.

With her slack form hanging half out of the tent, Henrietta crawled through the opening into the night. She gulped in the fresh air as she continued coughing, her nose and eyes still stinging from the smoke.

With her chest heaving, she grabbed Carolina and

dragged her all the way out of the tent. She collapsed to her knees at Carolina's side, patting her cheeks. "Carolina. Carolina, wake up! Come on, sweetheart, wake up."

Henrietta swiped at the tears on her cheeks with her sleeve as her heart hammered in her chest. "Carolina! You've got to wake up."

She grabbed her sister's shoulders giving her a shake. "No," she cried when her sister did not respond.

"Henrietta!" Clif's panicked voice called again.

"Here!" she answered, patting Carolina's limp hand. "Help!"

Clif rushed around the corner of the burning tent, his eyes going wide. "Ri!"

He raced toward her, sliding to his knees next to her and pulling her into a tight embrace. "What happened?"

"The tent caught fire from an overturned lantern. Carolina hit her head trying to retrieve the map piece from the flames." Her voice caught in her throat as she talked. "I cannot revive her."

"Carolina," Clif said, tapping her cheeks with his palm. "Carolina, wake up."

"I have tried that," Henrietta said, her voice still shaking. She tugged a handkerchief from her pocket and dabbed at the blood on her forehead. "She hit her head. And there was so much smoke."

"Carolina," Clif said again, leaning over his sister. He jiggled her body, giving her a hard shake.

Sharp shouts came from around the corner and James, followed by Johnson, plowed toward them. James's eyes widened and his lower lip trembled as he caught sight of them.

"Carolina?" he cried, panic lacing his voice. Johnson hurried forward, dropping to a knee on one side of her.

"We cannot awaken her," Henrietta said, pressing a palm to her forehead.

"What have you done?" he growled at them. "My poor Carolina!"

"The lantern tipped and we did not realize until it was too late," Henrietta said.

James's face twisted with fury and he lunged toward Henrietta, knocking her onto her back. Her vision of the starry sky was obliterated by James's ire-filled face hovering over her before he swung his bound hands to smack her in the chin.

He pulled them back for a second strike. Before he could swing, he toppled backward. Clif landed a blow against his jaw, sending him stumbling sideways.

Clif pointed a finger at the man. "I warned you about attacking my sister." He landed another blow against the man's cheek.

"Your sister killed my wife. Out of spite, like the low-life pirate she is."

"I did not!" Henrietta shouted as she pushed herself to her feet.

Clif drew his sword, pointing it at the man's chin. "Apologize and I may let you live."

James spat on the ground before raising his chin. "No."

"I said apologize to her!"

James narrowed his eyes at Clif, silently daring him to follow through on his threat.

A choking cough sounded from behind them. Henrietta and Clif twisted to face their sister. Johnson patted her back as he held her rolled onto her side.

Carolina continued to hack for a moment longer before Johnson eased her onto her back. She gulped in breaths as tears fell sideways to her hairline.

"Carolina?" Henrietta asked, tears welling in her eyes again as she dropped to a knee next to her sister.

James raced to his wife, shoving Henrietta aside as he knelt near her. "Carolina!"

Carolina flitted her gaze between each of them before she pushed herself up to her elbows.

"Easy, Miss," Johnson said, keeping a hand on her shoulder. "Do you feel lightheaded?"

"That's Mrs. Edmonton to you, pirate," James said, glaring at the man as he tried to take Carolina's hand in his.

Carolina coughed a few more times before she glanced at Johnson. "I think I am all right. Will you help me up?"

"Of course," he answered with a smile that showed the dimples on his cheeks. He rose to his feet and pulled Carolina up to stand. His hands lingered on hers as she continued to stare into his eyes, a smile playing on her lips.

Henrietta shot Clif a glance, puckering her lips and arching an eyebrow over the scene.

"Mr. Johnson," Clif began, stepping forward to grab Carolina's elbow and guide her to a seat.

"Take your hands off my wife this instant!" James shouted at the man.

Johnson pulled his hands away from Carolina's, sending her stumbling forward a step. Clif steadied her as her eyes lingered on his first mate. "Thank you, Johnson. Perhaps there is another matter you need to attend to?"

"No, Captain," the man answered.

Clif cleared his throat. "I am certain there is."

"Perhaps the camp's other occupants," Henrietta added.

Johnson's gaze flicked back and forth between Clif and Henrietta before he lifted his chin, understanding dawning on him. "Yes, of course, Captains. If the lady takes a turn, I shall be–"

Clif bobbed his head up and down, shooing the man away. "We know where to find you, Johnson."

Clif wrapped his arm around his sister's shoulders as he guided her toward the temple. Henrietta stepped to her other side, wrapping her arm around her sister's waist.

James trailed behind them. "Untie me at once."

"No," Clif said as he eased Carolina onto the stone steps leading up the temple's side. "Are you all right, sister?"

"Yes, I think so. I have a slight headache but nothing else."

Henrietta took a seat next to her, wrapping her arms around her baby sister and pulling her close. "Are you certain?"

"Yes, I am." She pulled back and looked at her sister's sooty face. "What happened?"

"They tried to kill you," James spat.

"That's not true!" Henrietta barked at him.

"Yes, it is! You attempted to murder your sister and take the map piece for yourself."

Clif drew his sword again and leveled it at the man's chin. "What did I tell you about maligning my sister?"

"Stop this!" Carolina shouted, leaping to her feet. She wobbled for a moment, before plopping back onto the stone and massaging her temples.

"Carolina?" Henrietta asked, her tone questioning as she grabbed her sister's shoulders.

"I am all right. But the bickering must stop. My sister would never harm me."

Clif sucked in a deep breath, sheathing his sword as James leaned forward, pleading with his wife, "But, Carolina–"

"No," she said. "Henrietta likely saved my life. The last thing I recall is a fire breaking out. I tried to retrieve the map piece but I hit my head. Everything went dark."

"I tried to drag you out, but the flames blocked the exit. I had to cut the tent open."

Carolina faced her sister, squeezing her hands and smiling. "Thank you." She flicked her gaze to Clif. "I am sorry, Clif. The map piece is likely gone."

Henrietta tugged a hand free and pulled the box from her belt. "I managed to retrieve it."

Carolina's smile broadened and she glanced up at Henrietta. "So, you saved the map piece and my life."

"Perhaps we can hold back on the applause," James complained.

Clif shot the man an annoyed glance as he relieved Henrietta of the box. "Good work, Ri. On both counts."

"And are you all right?" Carolina asked Henrietta.

"Yes, I am quite fine. Merely worried about your head bump." Henrietta smoothed Carolina's blonde locks away from the bloody wound and studied it. "Mr. Johnson should have a look at this."

"Perhaps not," Clif murmured.

"What?" Henrietta asked.

"Nothing. Quite right. Johnson is an excellent almost-doctor. He should assess it before we set off."

"Set off? Surely you will not make her trek through the jungle with her head split open?" James asked.

"I want to go," Carolina answered, her hand still holding tight to Henrietta's.

"Our guide is a medic. I would prefer him to attend to Carolina's wound and assess her before we go any further."

Clif narrowed his eyes at the man before nodding. "Fine."

"Untie me."

"For the last time, no. You can oversee her care with your wrists bound," Clif answered as Henrietta helped Carolina to stand.

They walked her to another tent, sending for the camp's guide and medic and leaving Abby and Williams to oversee her care and James's captivity.

They stepped back under the canopy of stars, striding to another tent to study the map.

"I would have preferred Johnson look at her wound," Henrietta said as they crossed the camp.

"I would not have."

"Why? I thought you trusted him."

"When it comes to matters of the sea, I do," Clif said as he held open the flap of the tent.

Henrietta ducked inside and glanced at Clif as he stepped in. "But not in medical matters?"

"Of course, I trust him in medical matters. I don't trust him with Carolina. Did you see the way he looked at her?"

Henrietta smirked as she unraveled the map pieces and rolled them out on the table in the tent's center.

"Why are you smiling?"

"It was no different than the way she looked at him."

"That is what bothers me."

"Why?" Henrietta asked as she grabbed the box from her brother's hands and popped it open.

"Ri, she is a married woman. And quite frankly, I am shocked that you are not concerned. Given your...colorful history with men, how can you not be?"

"My colorful history with men as you so eloquently put it did not involve men who stared admiringly at me as Johnson does to Carolina."

"She is a married woman. I cannot believe Carolina would behave in such a manner."

"Unhappily from what I understand. And why not? Johnson is a handsome man."

Clif's thick eyebrows knit. "When did her marriage turn unhappy? And what do you mean Johnson is a handsome man?"

Henrietta shrugged as she untied the string around the newest map piece, unrolled it, and placed it in the empty slot.

"Just a feeling. And the other is obvious. Dark curls, dark eyes, chiseled features with dimples…"

"Allow me to stop you there. I need not hear more of Johnson's virtues as a man. I cannot believe what I am hearing. And a feeling? You are willing to allow Johnson's chiseled features and dark eyes to ogle your baby sister over a feeling?"

She leaned forward, spreading her arms across the desk as she studied the map. "I am not allowing anything. They are two adults, and if the moment arrives when counseling is needed, I shall provide it."

Clif stood speechless, his attention on his sister instead of the map.

"There," Henrietta said, jabbing a finger at the final location on the map and grinning.

"How can you say that?"

"Simple. It specifically references it as the City of Diamonds. Well, it's in Spanish, but still quite easily recognizable. Really, Clif, I thought you better at maps than this."

She glanced up at her brother's stony features. He narrowed his eyes at her, crossing his arms over his chest. "You find this funny, do you?"

"I don't find it anything," she said, flinging her arms out. "I do not understand the concern."

"The concern is a man like Johnson ogling our baby sister."

"A man like Johnson? When did we become so high and mighty? Mere days ago, Johnson was a loyal first mate. Now he's a 'man like Johnson.'"

"Do you really wish that for Carolina? A pirate?"

"I do not wish for her the ass she is married to, so I suppose a pirate is an improvement. Look, Clif, nothing has come of it."

"For now," Clif interjected.

"Let it be. Carolina is an adult. Now, will you please focus on the matter at hand? We are *this* close to finding our prize."

Clif crinkled his nose as Henrietta gave him a playful shove. He stared down at the map spread on the table. "That is several hours journey on foot. If we leave now, we may make it just after daybreak."

Henrietta's lips curled into a smile. "Perfect." She gathered the map pieces from the table, carefully rolling them up and securing them in her pocket. "Let's gather the men and prepare to set off."

"Perhaps we should leave Carolina here," Clif said as they stepped from within the tent.

"She said she wanted to go."

"But–"

Henrietta rolled her eyes as they strolled to the tent housing her sister. "If this has to do with Johnson again–"

"No," Clif interrupted. "She hit her head. Perhaps she is too woozy."

"You propose leaving her here alone then?"

"Of course not," Clif said.

Henrietta smirked at him. "Perhaps we can leave Johnson behind to protect her."

Clif narrowed his eyes at his sister as they approached the tent. "You are bound and determined to taunt me over this."

Henrietta let out a chuckle. "Because I find it laughable. Clifton Nichols, Black Jack himself, twisted into knots over his sister's love life."

"I'd hardly say twisted into knots. Though I do find your revelation about Johnson's appeal disturbing, to say the least."

Henrietta tugged back the tent flap and shook her head at her brother, a playful smile on her lips. "Oh, Clif, you poor dear. I'm afraid you'll need to toughen up."

She patted his chest before ducking inside. Clif rammed

into the back of her as he followed, sending her stumbling a step forward.

"What are you doing?" he questioned as she stared at something across the tent, her jaw agape.

She shot him a shocked glance. "They're gone!"

CHAPTER 25

*M*uffled cries came from Williams who sat with his wrists bound behind his back and his ankles tied together, a gag stuffed in his mouth.

Henrietta raced to him, tugging the gag from William's teeth before she unfastened his bindings. "What happened?"

"He said he urgently needed to relieve himself. He over-powered me and tied me up, forcing me back in here. They overpowered Abby and forced her to go with them."

Henrietta shot to stand, her eyes wide as she glanced at Clif. "We must find them."

Clif readied his gun and sword as he nodded. They hurried into the night air, scanning the surrounding jungle for the foursome.

"There!" Henrietta called, jabbing a finger toward a lone torch moving through the thick undergrowth. She drew her sword and they hurried after the others. Williams emerged from the tent behind them, following as they trekked through the wilderness.

"Williams," Clif murmured under his breath, "circle around quickly and cut them off."

With a nod, Williams veered off, using only the moonlight to navigate as he slipped away from them. Clif and Henrietta continued to close the distance between them and the fleeing party.

Henrietta squinted ahead into the torch's dim light. James, with his hands now free, dragged a bound and gagged Abby along roughly as the guide tugged Carolina by her elbow.

"Going somewhere?" Clif called out in a loud voice as they neared the others.

James froze, tugging Abby closer to him and wrapping an arm around her throat. He held a knife up, his face scrunching. "Take another step and your concubine will wish you hadn't."

Abby's eyes widened as the knife grazed her neck.

Clif raised his sword. "She is not my concubine, and I would not threaten such things if you are not willing to follow through on them."

"Oh, I am more than willing," James said with a sneer.

"James, stop!" Carolina shouted as the medic held her arms.

"No, Carolina, we cannot allow these...people to do what they are doing to us."

Henrietta raised her sword toward the medic who held her sister. "You were so concerned about Carolina's injury and her traveling, yet you are dragging her through the jungle trying to escape her own family."

"You are no family to her!" James shouted as he tugged back on Abby, bending her spine into a painful backward curve.

"Let her go," Henrietta ordered.

"Let us go," James countered.

Clif shook his head, his sword still leveled at James. "I will not have you dragging my sister into the jungle to escape from nothing. You put her in more danger this way than by simply following through with the plan."

"I refuse to be involved with criminals. I am an upstanding citizen. I will not have my reputation marred by you."

"That's too bad, but I advise you to give in and accept the offer still open to you before I no longer feel as generous."

"I fail to see how you can force me into anything. I am holding all the cards."

"That is where you are wrong," Clif said as Williams emerged from behind James, pressing his sword into his back. "You see, you are surrounded. Trapped. So, I'd give in if I were you before your options begin to disappear."

James pressed the knife tighter to Abby's neck. "If I am to lose, so shall you."

"Do not harm her," Henrietta shouted, her eyes never leaving the man she covered with her sword.

Before Clif could respond, Abby unraveled the rope binding her wrists, pulled her arm, and snapped it back into the man's gut. He groaned, the air leaving his lungs as he doubled over. She grabbed the arm that had been around her neck and swung it forward and down. The man flipped over, landing on his back, the wind blowing out of his lungs a second time.

His face scrunched with anguish as three swords descended on him. The guide released his grip on Carolina, fleeing into the woods as she stumbled forward a step.

"Please do not harm him," she pleaded, sliding a hand onto Clif's shoulder. "Please, Clif."

Clif slid the sword into its sheath and tucked the gun into its holster. "You are lucky my sister speaks for you. Bind his hands, Williams. And this time ensure that he cannot escape."

"With pleasure, Captain," Williams answered, snugging rope roughly around James's wrists.

Henrietta placed a hand on Abby's shoulder. "Are you all right? Did he harm you?"

"No, not really. He was only a little rough when securing my bonds."

Henrietta shot James a glaring glance.

Abby lifted her chin and firmed her jaw. "Nothing I could not handle, Captain."

Henrietta raised her eyebrows at the girl. "Apparently. Quite an interesting tactic. I should like to learn it."

"I will be happy to teach it to you," Abby said with a beaming smile. "I learned it from my time at the brothel."

Carolina's eyes widened at the statement as they began their walk back to the encampment. "We have our course set," Clif said, "we shall leave as soon as we gather the crew."

"Carolina is in no condition to make this trek," James shouted as Williams marched him back to the camp at the tip of his sword.

"Yet you were willing to parade her into the night in a desperate attempt to flee from her own family," Clif said. "Mr. Williams, please gag Dr. Edmonton."

"I am all right. Mr. Jenkins tended to my wound," Carolina said. She flicked her gaze up to Clif. "And Mr. Johnson will be with us to see to me if anything else is needed."

Clif avoided her stare, a frown settling onto his features as Henrietta shot him an amused glance.

"I will oversee you myself," Clif said, wrapping an arm around his younger sister's shoulders as a muffled complaint came from behind him. He ignored it as they stepped back into the camp's boundaries.

Abby scurried off to retrieve the others and within a quarter of an hour they set off on the excursion, setting a moderate pace and keeping their prisoners between them.

Henrietta led the way with Abby and Williams, who still

kept an eye on Dr. Edmonton. After their first rest break, they removed his gag, leaving it hanging around his neck and warning him he'd earn it back if he continued to disrupt their journey.

They marched along in silence for several minutes, listening only to the sounds of the jungle in the wee hours of the morning.

"Why do you do it?" James asked after a few moments.

"Do what?" Henrietta responded, hacking at a leaf with her sword.

"This," he spat out.

She shot him a confused glance and shook her head, lifting her shoulders.

"This lifestyle. Why? You are a beautiful woman. Surely you could find a suitable match for a comfortable life."

Henrietta slashed at a large leaf. "I do not wish to make a suitable match."

"What an odd statement," James said. "I am not certain I have come across a woman who prefers to sail about the seas on a pirate ship rather than live a comfortable life."

"Now you have."

"Do not assume every woman can achieve a comfortable life with a man," Abby piped in. "I have received nothing but misery from them."

"Well said, Miss Turner."

James glanced between the two women, his eyebrows shooting up. "I suppose you do not care about my opinion. It appears you have both made your choices."

"Actually," Henrietta said, "there is something I would very much like your opinion on."

James glanced at her, his features pinching in question.

"What do you think of my hat?"

* * *

Clif side-eyed his younger sister as they followed the rest of the group through the jungle. "How are you feeling?"

"Perfectly fine," she said, glancing up at him before swiping at a bead of sweat on her brow.

"Are you certain? Do you need to rest?"

"No."

"No, you are not certain, or no, you do not need to rest?"

"I do not need to rest. And I do not need this much concern, Clif. While appreciated, I am not as delicate as you may imagine."

They took another few steps in silence as Carolina rose to her tiptoes and peered over the shoulders of the men in front of them. "How does she know where she is going?"

"Ri is quite adept at reading maps and following a compass."

"I am still quite shocked that she chose this life. I imagined her remarrying to someone even more prominent and living a high society life."

"Ri is more independent than you give her credit for. Her dreams of high society living were not her true goal in her marriage. Freedom was."

"Freedom," Carolina repeated, her brows knitting. "Yes, she always was fiercely independent, wasn't she?"

Clif smiled down at his sister as they marched ahead. "She still is." He chuckled.

"It appears so," Carolina said as she watched her sister thwack down another branch, the feather in her cap bobbing from side to side.

"And what about you?" Clif asked.

"I fear I am not as independent," Carolina answered.

He slid his eyes sideways to gauge her reaction. "But are you happy?"

She cast her eyes downward, studying her feet as they marched down the cut pathway. "Yes."

"That sounds less than convincing."

She flicked her gaze up to Clif, a fleeting smile crossing her lips. "News of the deaths of both of my siblings within a month of one another made for a difficult start to our marriage."

"Oh?" Clif inquired.

"It is past us."

"Carolina, is there something you are not saying?"

She shook her head, forcing another smile onto her lips.

"If there is, now or ever, you can tell me. Or Ri. She is an excellent listener and a wonderful problem solver. Ri's never met a problem she could not work out."

Carolina licked her lips as she studied her sister at the lead of the group. "Is she happy?"

Clif flicked his gaze to his sister, a smile crossing his lips as he studied the feather poking from her hat. "She seems to be happier than at any other point in her life. Particularly if she has a feathered cap."

Carolina chuckled as she side-stepped a thick branch on the path. "A feathered cap?"

"Yes, she is intent on being a fashionable pirate."

"That would be Henrietta, yes," Carolina said with another chuckle. She studied her sister for another moment. "She is so very brave."

"As are you," Clif said, pushing a wayward lock of hair from his sister's cheek.

"Not like her. I did not realize how brave she was."

"Until you saw her as a pirate?"

Carolina shook her head. "No, I...she told me about what happened. Why you went away. I did not realize what she'd been through. What you both had been through. And yet she reinvented herself over and over. How did she do it?"

"I told you, Ri has never met a problem she could not face and beat."

Carolina's eyes shifted to Abby. "Who is the other woman? Did you already have a woman pirate on your crew?"

Clif shook his head as he helped Carolina over a fallen log. "No. That is Abigail Turner. She was a former prostitute at a brothel in Tortuga. She ran away and begged Ri to help her escape for good."

Carolina's eyebrows raised as she studied the girl, who chattered away to Henrietta. "And Henrietta helped her?"

"She is more tender-hearted than you give her credit for," Clif answered. "Henrietta insisted we help her. She shot a man to ensure the girl's freedom and nearly cost us both our lives. But she insisted the girl needed help, and she would provide it."

"Hmm," Carolina murmured.

The group continued forward, torches blazing in the night as they trekked further into the jungle. After several hours of hiking, they stopped for a rest as the first signs of daybreak painted the horizon yellow-orange.

Clif and Carolina trudged up to Henrietta at the front of the group. "How much farther?" he asked his sister.

She took a long sip of water from her canteen. "We are on the final leg. I would say another thirty to forty minutes."

"How will we know when we have arrived? Is it a large temple?" Carolina questioned.

James snorted a laugh but gave no commentary after receiving a glare from Henrietta.

"I do not believe so. The map makes it appear as though it is in a cave or somehow underground from the drawing."

"An underground city," Clif pondered. "Yes, perhaps linked to the diamond mines that produced the gemstones."

"Indeed," Henrietta answered as she slung the canteen's strap over her head and pushed it backward on her hip. "Shall we go?"

Clif nodded, signaling for their captives to be brought to their feet. Groans erupted from them as his crew tugged them to stand and pushed them forward.

Clif motioned for Henrietta to precede him and they continued along their journey as the jungle began to awaken. Bird calls filled the air as more glints of sunshine brightened the skies. The torches were extinguished twenty minutes later as light filtered through the thick canopy.

A monkey screeched in the distance and Henrietta shot Clif a playful glance. "Perhaps you will find another friend for Jack."

"Do not even mention him to me. I am pleased he remained on the ship."

"I am certain he would have preferred to come with you. You locked in him the cabin, poor fellow."

"You have a monkey?" Carolina questioned.

"Yes," Henrietta said with a coy smile, "Clif picked him up on Moaning Isle. He scampered onto his shoulder and would not let go."

"He is just as fond of Ri," Clif claimed.

"He is not. He loves you, Clif. You are his hero."

Clif shook his head at his sister, offering her an unimpressed roll of his eyes. Carolina flicked her gaze between the two of them as they bantered, a smile creeping onto her face. As she took a step forward, her foot caught on something and she tumbled forward.

Clif reached out to grab her arm, breaking her fall as James shouted from behind. "Carolina!" He attempted to rush forward, but Williams barred him. "Let me go to her!"

"Are you all right?" Clif asked.

"Yes," she said, kicking at a thick vine with her foot. "I trod on something here."

Henrietta squinted at the vine, cocking her head.

"She is unwell. You are pushing her too far," James

shouted, earning himself an elbow to the gut and the gag replaced between his teeth.

"There is something there," Henrietta said, hacking at the vine and yanking it away.

"You are correct, Captain," Abby said as she sliced through another portion of the thick foliage. "This vine has grown around something."

"Uncover this," Clif shouted to a few crew members, who hurried forward to remove the rest of the vines. The shape of a giant serpent formed as the leaves and stems were pulled away. Several crew members scurried up a nearby tree to cut away the leaves covering the snake's head.

Henrietta gasped as she spotted the final few feet of the statue, soaring above her head. A massive diamond was clutched between the serpent's fangs.

CHAPTER 26

"Look!" Henrietta said, jabbing a finger at the serpent. "A diamond."

A grin crossed Clif's lips as a cheer went up through the men. "We are close," he said. "Spread out and search the area!"

The crew members fanned out, tearing away leaves and slicing through vines to check for any other hidden statues or cave entrances.

Henrietta crossed her arms, staring up at the snake.

Clif eyed her. "What are you thinking, Ri?"

"That the snake has more to tell us than we know."

"I see no carvings or writing."

"No, but…" Her voice trailed off as she narrowed her eyes at the statue. "It has ruby eyes."

"Yes, so?" Clif prodded.

"So, the staff we retrieved from your former treasure stash also has a ruby."

Realization dawned on Clif as he leaned his head back. "You believe the serpent is the key to entering the City of Diamonds."

"Indeed."

Clif stared at the base of the statue before his eyes climbed it. "I see nowhere to place the staff."

"I do," Henrietta said.

He furrowed his brow. "Where?"

She pointed at the top. "Its head. The staff must go in its mouth or the top of its head. I would guess the top so that he wears the ruby as a crown."

"I shall find out, Captain," Abby said with a salute before she scurried up a nearby tree, crawling out onto a branch that shot toward the snake's head. She froze as a cracking noise filled the air and the branch swayed.

"Careful, Miss Turner," Henrietta called up to her.

She nodded, her lips pulled into a grimace as she continued to shimmy toward the snake statue.

"It's going to give way!" Williams shouted, pointing at the base of the branch.

A large split formed at the top as the branch bowed toward the ground.

"Jump!" Clif shouted to Abby.

Another crack sounded and the branch splintered further. Abby sat up and reached for the statue with her foot. Her toes glanced off the edge, slipping as the branch wobbled under her.

She tried again, stretching her leg as the branch shifted lower. Her foot caught the snake's hood and she launched herself forward, falling onto the snake's head. She clutched at the scales as she scrambled up, clinging to the statue to stay on top.

"Ha! She did it!" Henrietta said with a grin. She raised her voice, cupping her hands around her lips as she shouted up to Abby. "What do you see?"

"There is a round hole in the top of its head, Captain. Could the rod go into it?"

Henrietta raised a finger, motioning for her to wait. "We shall find out."

"Williams," Clif said, "bring the staff."

A murmuring went through the crew as the ruby-topped, golden rod made its way to the front. Clif took hold of it and lifted his gaze to the woman crouched atop the snake statue. "Can you catch?"

"Toss it, sir," she answered with a nod, stretching her hands out.

Clif flung the staff upward. It soared to the snake's lower jaw before falling back to the ground.

"Try again, sir," Abby encouraged.

"Use a little effort, Clif," Henrietta said with a coy smile.

Clif rolled his eyes as he scooped the staff from the leaves below. Abby swung her legs on either side of the snake and leaned forward. Clif tossed the rod again. This time, Abby managed to wrap her fingers around it, bobbling it for a moment before she tugged it upward.

"Press the diamond to open it," Henrietta called.

With a glance at Henrietta, she nodded and depressed the large gem. The blade like bottom shot out of the rod. She lined it up with the opening at the top. With a shove, the golden staff slid down until only the ruby shone at the top.

The snake's ruby eyes glowed to life. Henrietta's jaw dropped open at the sight.

"What's happening?"

"I think you'd better come down," Henrietta shouted as the ground began to shake.

"Perhaps not," Clif answered, flinging his arms out and shoving his sister back a few steps as the earth rumbled underneath them.

Dirt fell away and the scent of fresh earth penetrated their nostrils. At the foot of the snake statue, a panel slid away, showering the stone steps hidden below it with leaves and dirt.

Henrietta and Clif exchanged a glance, grinning at each other.

Henrietta raised her eyebrows. "I believe we just found the entrance to the City of Diamonds."

Abby, who rode out the quake on top of the snake, called down to them. "Shall I remove the staff, Captain?"

"No, leave it for now. I hope we do not need it again," Henrietta said.

With a nod, Abby scrambled down the snake's curved back and leapt onto the ground. "Shall I scout the passage, Captain?"

"No, Miss Turner, Clif, and I will proceed first with a search party which you are welcome to join."

"I should like to go," Carolina said, lifting a hand in the air.

A grumble sounded from her still-gagged husband behind them.

"Pipe down," Williams said, smacking him in the gut and doubling him over.

"Captain, I shall go with you," Johnson said, pushing his way to the front, his eyes lingering on Carolina.

Clif wrinkled his nose at the scene. "Perhaps you should stay here with the crew and organize–"

"Perfect," Henrietta interrupted. "You, me, Carolina, Abby, Johnson, and can we have two more volunteers?"

In short order, four additional men agreed to go, making their party nine rather than seven. With torches in their hands, they hovered over the stone steps leading into the earth.

Henrietta flicked a glance at her brother before she took her first step down. The scent of must filled her nostrils as she descended further down, leaving the sunny morning behind.

Clif shuffled down the steps next to her with his sword drawn, his gaze darting around the space in search of dangers.

"Do you believe we will encounter trouble?" she questioned as they reached the bottom.

"Better to be prepared in the event that we do," he answered, studying the moss-covered pillars holding a stone ceiling at bay.

Henrietta slid her sword from its sheath. Abby followed suit.

Clif scanned ahead of them. "We stay together, keep a tight formation as we move forward. Carolina, stay in the middle."

The others circled around Carolina, pushing her to the center of their group. With Clif and Henrietta in the lead, they marched forward toward a large set of stone doors on a raised platform.

"Do you think the diamonds are behind this door?" Henrietta asked as they approached it.

Clif swung an arm out to stop her from climbing the stairs. "Perhaps."

They studied the carved illustrations on each door depicting skeletons withering away and falling into a deep pit.

"That's rather morbid. I do not see a way to open the doors. What does this writing say?" Henrietta asked, waving a finger toward the Aztec symbols ringing the edges of the door.

"I do not read Aztec," Clif answered.

"I do," Carolina said from behind him. "Move aside."

"Careful, Carolina," Clif warned as she pushed in front of him and climbed the steps, peering at the doors.

Henrietta joined her, eyeing her sister as she tilted her head to study the symbols. "Can you make sense of it?"

"James is a bit better than I, but I believe this says, 'Beyond these gates lies the holy city. To enter a person must place their faith in the sun and the moon for the spirit of the great god Quetzalcoatl guards this entrance.'"

Henrietta crinkled her forehead as she studied the stone carvings. "What does that mean?"

"Given the number of skeletons depicted, I am not certain I wish to find out," Johnson chimed in from behind Clif.

Carolina reached out and caressed the carvings, her fingertips lingering on a skull of a falling skeleton. Her brow furrowed and she pressed against the smooth, round cranium. She snapped her hand back as the skull retracted into the door and a clicking noise echoed throughout the long underground chamber.

They searched the area for whatever mechanism had engaged.

At the back of the group, a sailor thrust his arm out toward the rear of the chamber. "The floor! It's disappearing!"

"Oh, no," Carolina murmured as she stared at the rippling floor.

"There must be a way to stop it," Henrietta said, swinging around to face the door again.

"Press them all?" Carolina inquired as she motioned toward the other skeletons.

"No," Henrietta said, staring at the symbolic writing rimming the door.

"Are you certain?" Clif inquired, shooting a worried glance over his shoulder.

"Try them all," Johnson said, offering an encouraging nod at Carolina.

"No!" Henrietta repeated.

"I must try," Carolina argued. She pressed another skull.

Clif winced as he glanced behind them and turned back. "Wrong. The floor is now disappearing faster than it did before."

"I told you," Henrietta said, slapping away her sister's hand.

"Think faster, Ri. We are about to lose a few crew members if we cannot open these doors."

Henrietta bit into her lower lip staring at the door. She pointed to the words. "What did it say again?"

"Beyond these gates–"

"No, the next bit. Skip that."

Carolina nodded, tracing the words around to the next part. "A person must place their faith in the sun and the moon for the spirit of Quetzalcoatl guards the entrance."

"Faith in the sun and moon," Henrietta murmured.

"Faster, Ri," Clif urged.

Henrietta scanned the door, a smile forming on her lips as she thrust a finger toward an object. "A sun!" She continued searching, the smile broadening. "And a moon!"

"Press them," Carolina gushed.

Henrietta nodded, pressing the sun and then the moon.

"It's not working," Clif announced in a sing-song voice. "Try something else."

"But why?" Henrietta said, pressing a palm to her forehead.

"Because the floor is still rippling, Ri, that's why."

"No, why is it not working?"

"Think faster," Clif encouraged as another man tried to pile onto the steps, knocking two off and toward the quickly disappearing stone floor tiles.

"Sun and moon," Henrietta mumbled. "Are there more?"

"Ri!" Clif said, bouncing up and down.

"We're not going to make it, sir!" Johnson shouted.

They all twisted to stare behind them as the floor continued to fall away, leaving only a few tiles between them and the first man who would fall to his death.

The final unoccupied square started to flip and fall when the mechanism ground to a halt. The massive stone stood straight in the air, revealing the gaping chasm below it.

The remaining floor tiles did not budge. Clif spun, his eyes wide, to stare at his sister, whose hand remained pressed against the door.

Henrietta swallowed hard and snapped her gaze to him. With a nod, she blew out a sigh of relief. "Solved."

"How?" Clif inquired.

"The feathered serpent," Carolina said as Henrietta pulled her hand away.

"Quetzalcoatl was the final guardian. I pressed the stone likeness of the feathered serpent and it stopped the mechanism and unlocked the doors." Henrietta motioned toward the crack between the doors where one had popped into the next chamber.

"Shall we enter?" Carolina inquired, glancing from her sister to her brother.

Clif stared at the crack between the doors. "Stand back. Let Henrietta and I enter first. There may be another trap."

Clif pushed around her, approaching the door. Carolina stepped back, sliding into the waiting hands of Johnson who steadied her.

Henrietta suppressed an amused grin as Clif narrowed his eyes at the scene. "Come on, Clif. Let's find a fortune."

Clif blew out a breath as Henrietta placed a hand on the open door and began to push. Darkness met their gaze as the crack widened.

Henrietta glanced at Clif before she waved her torch inside.

Clif placed his hand on her arm. "Careful, Ri. It could be a trap."

"There's only one way to find out."

She peered inside again, the torch barely beating back the shadows of the massive chamber. Henrietta rolled her shoulders back, lifted her chin, and, after a long, deep breath, lifted one foot and crossed the threshold.

CHAPTER 27

The flames flickered off the stone walls as Henrietta stepped through the door onto the stone platform. Something glinted in the light and she narrowed her eyes at it as Clif slid through the opening next to her.

His nostrils flared as he detected a familiar scent in the musty air. "Fuel," he murmured.

Henrietta waved her torch next to her. "There is a channel here." She dipped her fingers into it, rubbing her thumb against the oily liquid clinging to her skin.

"Light it," Clif said.

Henrietta shifted her torch down to the stone channel. It burst into flames as the fire touched it. The light raced around the room, springing to life and illuminating the space.

Henrietta craned her neck to stare up at the massive statue of Quetzalcoatl across the space. Clutched in its open jaws sat a massive diamond. Her eyes widened, and she clutched Clif's arm as a gasp slid from her lips.

"Clif!"

"I see it."

Her eyebrows arched as her gaze slid around the space. Diamonds littered the floor in front of them, some of them the size of goose eggs. They lined the walls around tunnels leading further deeper into the underground chambers.

Henrietta reached toward the silty brown dirt and grabbed a large gemstone. She held it up to the light, noting how it sparkled and reflected the flames. "Beautiful."

She flicked her gaze to Clif and grinned. "We did it."

Clif grabbed the diamond and held it up. "We did it."

They spent another moment basking in their find before Clif handed the diamond back to Henrietta. "This is yours, Ri. You found it. You deserve the first one."

Henrietta accepted it, staring at it again with a grin before sliding it into her pocket.

"Are you pleased?" he asked.

"Indeed," she answered. "Now, let's make certain the entire crew is pleased."

"I shall call the men to bring the bags. This will be quite the haul."

She grinned as she nodded at him, turning to survey the diamonds sparkling in the firelight lining the chamber. Clif ducked through the door, passing along the message to the others.

Carolina slipped through the doorway first, followed by Johnson then the rest of the search party who hooted and hollered at the sight before them.

"Begin collecting as many as you can," Clif said.

"We may need more bags, Captain," Johnson said as he surveyed the volume of diamonds in the room.

"Indeed, Mr. Johnson. And we shall have them as soon as we find another way out."

"No need, Captain. The floor tiles returned to their original space, filling in the gaps after you entered."

"Wonderful," Clif said, clapping Johnson on the back as

the men spread out in the large chamber, filling sacks with the diamonds that littered the floor.

Carolina wandered to the middle of the room, picking up a large diamond and holding it up to the light. "This is amazing."

With a grin, Henrietta twisted to face her as she gathered an armload of diamonds. "Isn't it?"

Carolina studied her for a moment. "This truly does make you happy, doesn't it?"

Henrietta arched an eyebrow at the statement, her smile never fading. "It does."

Carolina's eyes scanned the room, studying the architecture, stone decorations, and writing on the walls. "This is truly astounding. I wish James could see it."

"Perhaps he can," Henrietta said. "If he is willing to behave himself, I'm certain Clif will agree to bring him down."

"He does not mean to behave as he does."

Henrietta straightened, the gems jangling in her arms. "What do you mean?"

Carolina opened her mouth to answer when a noise distracted her. Her brow crinkled, and she stared at one of the black holes leading deeper underground. "What is that?"

Henrietta swiveled to eye the low tunnel. "I'm not certain."

Men continued to chatter behind them, making it difficult to discern any noise as they continued to load their bags among hoots and hollers.

The women crept closer to the hole, peering into the darkness. "Do you think there are more diamonds in these holes?" Henrietta asked.

"I am not certain. Given the diamonds already available, I am not certain there is any reason to find out," Carolina answered, squinting into the darkness.

A hissing sound emerged from the hole. Henrietta's eyes widened. "There is the noise again!"

"Yes, I heard it, too."

"Ladies, is there a reason we are not gathering diamonds and instead are staring into a dark hole?" Clif inquired from behind them.

"There is some noise coming from this hole," Henrietta answered.

"Noise?" Clif inquired. "Who cares? May I remind you of the diamonds that were the primary draw to this location?"

He rolled a large, sparkling gem between his fingers.

Henrietta set a hand on her hip. "No, you mustn't remind me. Where do these lead, though? Perhaps to more diamonds."

"More diamonds? Ri, you will sink the ship!"

Two crewmen hauled several overflowing bags of diamonds through the door as others continued to fill their bags.

Mr. Johnson joined them, glancing between Clif and Henrietta. "What's this about sinking the ship?"

"Ri would like to crawl through the tunnel in search of more diamonds."

"There is some odd noise coming from the tunnel," Carolina said, waving a finger toward it.

"Ah," Johnson said, his eyes falling to her as he rubbed his finger along his chin, "perhaps something to investigate."

Clif screwed up his face. "Let's focus on the diamonds."

Henrietta rolled her eyes as she shook her head. "Forget the diamonds, Clif. We are *all* interested in the tunnel."

"Forget the diamonds? What kind of pirates are you?"

"The kind that likes to investigate," Henrietta retorted, grabbing a torch from Clif's hand and waving it toward the black hole.

"Do you see anything?" Carolina questioned.

Mr. Johnson pushed between them, snatching the torch from Henrietta's hand and peering into the darkness. "Allow me. I shall get to the bottom of this."

Carolina hovered close to him, peering around his shoulder. Henrietta backed up a step, biting the side of her finger as she flicked her gaze to Clif.

He shot her an unimpressed glance, shaking his head. Henrietta held back a laugh as Johnson leaned further into the tunnel.

He gasped, pulling back suddenly before diving back into the tunnel.

"What is it?" Carolina questioned.

"Eyes," Johnson breathed. "Odd, yellow eyes."

"Eyes?" Clif questioned as Johnson straightened again.

He nodded, swallowing hard. "There is something unsettling about those eyes."

Clif blinked his eyes as the man shuddered. He pushed past him, waving his torch toward the tunnel when a shout arose from across the space.

Clif whipped around, scanning the space in search of the commotion. One of the men dropped his bag of diamonds, racing from the room. Abby stared after him, her brows knit.

He straightened, narrowing his eyes at the man. "What is going–"

"SNAKES!" the remaining man shouted as he backed away from one of the tunnels.

Snakes poured from every opening around the room. The doors to the exit slammed shut as the space filled with brown-black snakes. They slithered through the room, hissing and snapping at the occupants.

"Quetzalcoatl guards the treasure," Henrietta repeated.

"Literally," Carolina breathed as Clif shoved his sisters behind him, waving his torch in front of him to keep the snakes back.

"Do you believe them poisonous?" Henrietta asked Clif.

"I do not wish to find out the hard way."

"They are," Carolina said. "Extremely."

"How do you know?" Clif asked, continuing to push them back.

"When we arrived in the camp, one of our guides was bitten by a similar-looking snake. He died within days of the bite despite the instant removal of most of the poison and constant care."

"Similar or the same?" Henrietta breathed.

Johnson shielded Carolina as she clung to her sister. "Similar. They appeared identical only much, much smaller."

The snakes slithered closer and closer, turning the dirt-brown floor almost black. Suddenly, the sea of snakes parted.

"What are they doing?" Johnson asked.

Clif followed the newly formed dirt path they had created, his eyes rising to find another form that made them go wide. "Uhhh…"

Henrietta followed the line of his gaze, her jaw dropping as she spotted what caught his attention.

The group huddled together and drew their swords. Johnson took a post next to Clif, shielding Carolina further from what approached.

A massive black snake, standing as tall as a man when rearing up slithered through the path created by the smaller reptiles. Its forked tongue flicked in and out of its mouth as it approached them.

"I believe the wisest thing to do may be to attempt to find a way out, Captain," Johnson said, his sword swinging from the large creature approaching the other snakes surrounding them.

"I agree. Ri," Clif said, turning his head toward her with his eyes never leaving the colossal snake sliding toward them, "might you be so kind as to figure a way out of this room?"

Henrietta gave a slight nod, her eyes still stuck on the mammoth snake. "I would be more than happy to."

She threaded her way through the group, returning to the doors behind them. After pushing and pulling, she studied them again. "Carolina, do the words on this door say something different than they did on the outside?"

Carolina squeezed through the tight group, joining her sister at the rear of the chamber. The crease between her brows pinched tighter as she studied the writing. "Umm, no, this is different."

"What does it say?"

"Uh…"

"Quickly, Carolina, what does it say?" Henrietta snapped.

"I'm trying. I am not an expert at this."

Henrietta glanced over her shoulder as the snake closed the gap. She set a hand on her sister's shoulder and squeezed. "I know. But the general gist as quickly as you can, please."

Carolina bobbed her head up and down as her fingers traced the words ringing the door's edge. She swallowed hard, her forehead pinching together.

"It starts out saying something about the space being guarded by the feathered serpent."

"Does it say how to defeat the feathered serpent or get it to go back to its lair, by chance, sister?" Clif called over his shoulder.

"It says…" Carolina murmured, crouching to trace the words to the bottom corner before swinging back up the other side.

Clif aimed his gun at the serpent as it reared back, his sword also at the ready.

"Which pieces do I press, Carolina?" Henrietta asked.

Carolina straightened, her eyes wide as she stared at the door.

"Carolina!" Clif shouted.

She swallowed hard and faced Henrietta, her pale face even whiter than usual and contorted with fear. "It says…" She paused as she flicked her gaze back to the door, then let her eyes slide back to Henrietta. After another hard swallow, she continued. "It says the space is guarded by the feathered serpent. All who enter shall die."

CHAPTER 28

"What?" Henrietta gasped.

"I'm not pleased with that answer," Clif called as the snake struck near him. He slid sideways to avoid it.

Henrietta waved a hand at the door. "Neither am I. Does it say anything else? Nothing about opening the door?"

"It does not mention opening the door. There is more but I am not able to make it out."

"Try," Henrietta insisted, positioning her sister in front of the second door.

After a moment, she swiped a hand across her forehead and shook her head. "I'm not certain."

"Carolina," Henrietta said, restraint filling her voice, "you do not need to be perfect. The general meaning will do."

"But that's just it," Carolina cried, "I do not know it. I... One misstep could cost our lives."

"You know more than we do," Johnson called to her. "Without you, our lives are forfeit."

Carolina glanced at the man before she set her gaze on the door again, a determined expression tightening her jaw muscles. "It says something about trials. One of the body, one of the mind, one of the spirit."

"Does it say how to defeat them?" Henrietta questioned.

Carolina studied the large serpent. "This must be the trial of the body. It says only the bravest soul with the meekest steps will survive."

Clif screwed up his face. "What?"

The remaining crewman, Smith, offered his opinion as the large snake dived toward them again. "I say we slay them, Captain."

"We will never kill all of them fast enough," Henrietta argued. "And if we attack one, it may anger the others."

"Anger them? They seem fairly angry already," he responded.

Clif shook his head. "No, she has a point. They await some sort of signal. They have not moved to attack us. Why?"

Henrietta weaved through the men to return to Clif's side. "Everyone be silent."

She waved a hand in front of the large snake reared back and swaying in the air, narrowing her eyes at it. She slid her sword from its sheath and thrust it within inches of the towering serpent.

"Ri, are you crazy?" Clif inquired.

"No," she said in a low voice, sliding the sword into its holder and stepping forward, "merely testing a theory."

"What theory?"

"This snake is blind. A test of the body. Only those with meek steps. If we set foot on the ground it protects, it will attack. It cannot see us though, it can only hear us."

Henrietta inched down the stone steps, carefully setting a foot onto the dirt. She glanced up at the large snake looming over her before she shot a glance at Clif. He squashed his lips together and shook his head at her.

She pressed a finger to her lips in a signal to be silent.

With her teeth digging into her lower lip, she held her breath as she took another step toward the large reptile.

She carefully set her heel down in the dirt before leaning forward to take another step. After several painstaking minutes, she reached the snake. Sweat beaded on her brow, and she swallowed hard. Keeping her breathing shallow, she tiptoed sideways before continuing down the narrow path between the mammoth serpent and the smaller ones that writhed next to it.

With careful footwork, she reached the far side of the chamber and climbed a set of stone steps that disappeared around a corner. As she rounded the bend, a large doorway yawned open at the top. Her lips curled into a smile and she hurried back down and waved at the others, miming that she'd found a door.

She pressed her finger to her lips again, reminding them to remain silent as they crossed the space. Clif sent Carolina next, but Johnson stepped in front of her, grabbing her hand and tugging her behind him as he crept forward.

As they reached the tail of the large creature, Clif sent Abby across. They crept across the space one by one until only Clif remained. While the others bypassed her, continuing on to the next chamber, Henrietta waited on the stairs as Clif took his first step to the ground.

He stared up at the large snake who remained ready to strike as he inched forward, careful with his footfalls. As he passed the snake, a shout came from the other chamber. The snake whipped around in search of a victim, snapping toward Henrietta.

"No!" Clif shouted.

The snake twisted, striking near him. Clif leapt forward, somersaulting across the ground toward the stairs. The other snakes slithered toward him as the large one spun around in search of its victim.

Henrietta dashed down the stairs, hitting the ground and sprinting toward her brother. She grabbed his shoulders and tugged him back as he kicked with his feet to propel them back faster. She scrambled backward up the stairs as the smaller snakes snapped at the soles of his boots.

Clif climbed to his feet and continued climbing up, pulling Henrietta along with him. They reached the top and hurried into the next chamber, gasping for breath.

"Who shouted?" Henrietta demanded. "You very nearly cost Clif his life."

"Apologies, Captain," Smith said, "but the door across the space is closed."

"Carolina," Clif said as he approached his sister who studied the door, "are there instructions?"

"Only the quick-witted will survive," she answered, flicking her gaze to him.

Clif glanced over his shoulder at his older sister. "Ri, this one is for you."

She slid her eyes to her brother as she stared at a series of different-sized jugs in the center of the floor, her arms crossed over her chest. She peered inside the stone containers, finding them empty before she shot a glance to the ceiling.

Spouts hovered over two of the jugs but not the third. She narrowed her eyes at them before she circled around the setup. Three levers protruded from the stone pedestal under the first two jugs.

Henrietta tromped on one. Liquid poured from the ceiling, filling the jug. A mechanism squealed before springing to life, pushing the walls in toward them.

Clif slid his eyes from side to side, studying the two walls that threatened to smash them. "Tell me you know what to do, Ri."

Henrietta stepped on the second pedestal, sending the

water from the large jug to the third jug. She stepped on the pedestal under the smallest container. Water splashed down from the ceiling, filling it. "Carolina, tell me what these markings say."

Carolina hurried toward the stone pedestal housing the three jugs. "These are numbers. Five, three, and four."

"Measurements," Henrietta murmured.

"Ri? The walls aren't getting further away. What must we do?"

"I believe we must pour a measure of four into this jug. No more, no less."

"How can we do that? That lever sends a measure of five to the jug. This one would send three. We cannot measure four," Clif said.

Henrietta stepped on the sole pedal under the jug marked four. The water drained away, leaving it empty. She bit her thumbnail as the walls continued their slow march toward them.

"Ri," Clif prompted after a moment.

"What is this lever for?" she murmured, standing in front of the first jug. She filled it with water, then stepped on the third pedal she had not tried. It sent the water to the middle jug, filling it and leaving a bit in the first container.

She narrowed her eyes at it.

"Ri," Clif tried again. "Please tell me you know what to do."

"Three in this jug, two in this one," Henrietta said to herself. She narrowed her eyes at the jugs. She stepped on the lever sending the measure of two to the final jug before she emptied the three-gallon jug.

"I need two more," she said to herself. She filled the five-measure container again, emptied it into the three-measure, then sent the remaining two measures to the last jug.

The walls shuddered to a stop and the door across the

space popped open. She spun to face Clif, a triumphant grin on her features.

"I am impressed," he said with a smile at her.

"On to the next," she said. They continued forward to the final chamber, dragging the sacks of diamonds they'd managed to fill in the first chamber with them.

They climbed the stairs, pushing through the heavy stone doors into the next chamber. Henrietta stopped short as they entered, teetering on her toes at the edge of the platform.

Clif grabbed her arm, tugging her back. They stared down at the large chasm filled with deadly spikes. Henrietta's lips turned down into a grimace as she stared at the skeletons impaled upon them.

"Test of the spirit," Clif murmured.

"Seems to be a rather difficult test," Henrietta answered, her eyes glued to the skeletons.

"The spirit," Clif answered. "Will? Willpower."

"Willpower to do what? Withstand a spike through your belly?" Henrietta asked, her voice incredulous.

Clif scanned the space, eyeing several rungs on the wall. He followed them up to the ceiling. More rungs spanned the large space, leading to a doorway on the opposite side.

"We must swing from rung to rung," Clif said.

Carolina stared up at the metal rungs. "I am not certain I can."

Clif gauged the distance between the two platforms.

"I am quite strong," Abby said. "I can try for it."

"It is likely too far for any of the women," Clif answered. "The rung placement is quite wide. I am not certain they can even reach between them."

"But–" Abby said again.

"How do you propose we cross?" Henrietta interrupted.

"We will need to carry you."

Henrietta stared across to the other platform. "Clif, it's

too far. You cannot carry us whilst swinging between the rungs."

"There isn't a choice."

"We will be forced to leave the smaller sacks of diamonds here," Henrietta answered.

"No. Tie the sacks around your waists. Then I shall take Carolina, Abby will go with Johnson, and Ri with Smith. Carolina, you must hop onto my back, and–"

"Wait," Henrietta said, holding a hand in the air. "This is not sound."

"Sound or not, we have little other choice if we hope to leave this chamber alive."

Henrietta shook her head. "I meant the pairings."

"I do not see what difference it makes. Any man should be able to carry a woman across."

"That is untrue and if we hope to maximize the chances of all of us escaping with our lives, we should structure this in the most sensible way."

"What do you propose?" Clif asked.

"You are the tallest male with the broadest shoulders in our party."

"Indeed. I should have an easy time carrying Carolina."

"Yes, because she is quite small. Only Abby is lighter than her, though taller. And I am both as tall as Abby but stouter. Therefore, I should cross with you."

"Then you'll switch and Carolina will go with Smith."

"Smith is lighter than Johnson and taller. He should take Abby."

Clif opened his mouth to object when Johnson spoke up. "A solid plan, Captain. I shall manage quite easily with Carolina."

"We shall go first and test the rungs," Henrietta said with a nod as she secured two pouches of diamonds to either side of her waist. "Clif, turn around."

"You did that on purpose, didn't you?" he asked over his shoulder as she wrapped her arms around his neck and leapt onto his back.

"I did not. It is common sense. Now, up we go."

"Oof," Clif said as he straightened and lifted himself onto the first rung, his feet scraping the wall to steady himself. "You are stouter than when I carried you to Whispering Manor all those years ago."

Henrietta slapped his arm. "I am not amused."

"Neither am I," Clif said as he twisted and leaned toward the first rung suspended over the chasm.

He swung to the first bar. They dangled over the pit as he reached for the next. He continued forward rung by rung until they reached the middle of the chamber.

"The next rung is quite a bit farther than the others have been."

"Willpower," Henrietta said.

Clif let go with one hand and reached, sweat beading on his brow before he snapped his hand back and clung to the original rung with both. "I will try again. Let me rest for a moment."

"You cannot reach with my weight holding you back."

"I will–"

"I can steady us," Henrietta said. "Let me grab the rung here and slide my weight forward whilst you reach."

Clif nodded, shimmying his hands to one side to make room for Henrietta to grab the metal rod.

She grasped it, heaving herself up toward the ceiling. "Go," she strained.

He let go and extended his arm forward, straining to reach the rod in front of them. His fingertips grazed it. "Almost."

"Lean," Henrietta said, tilting to allow her legs to move forward as he reached.

Clif's fingers clamped down on the bar and wrapped around it. "Got it. Let go, Ri."

She let her fingers slip from the metal rung as he swung forward, clutching at his neck to avoid toppling backward. Her hat wobbled before slipping off her head and plunging into the chasm below.

"Damn it," she cursed as it became impaled on one of the spikes.

"I shall buy you another," Clif grunted as he swung closer and closer to the exit.

"I suppose better my hat than the diamonds."

"The others took out several sacks. We shall survive it."

They reached the final rung and Clif swung his legs forward, his toes reaching for the platform.

"Leave me on this rung and leap across," Henrietta said.

"I'm not leaving you."

"I should hope not. I expect you to catch me when I swing over."

Henrietta grasped hold of the metal bar with both hands before slowly allowing her legs to dangle. The bar shimmied as Clif swung his lower half back and forth before he let go, propelling himself through the air and landing neatly on the platform.

He spun to face Henrietta, red-faced from the effort to remain clinging to the rod with the small sacks of diamonds weighing her down.

"Swing to me," he instructed.

Henrietta blew out a breath as sweat rolled down her cheek and kicked her feet to propel her back and forth.

Clif leaned forward, grabbing hold of her belt. "Let go, I've got you."

She released her grip on the rung, swaying backward for a brief second before Clif counterbalanced her and tugged her upright onto the platform.

Across the room, Abby helped Carolina climb onto Johnson's back before he began the trek across.

After a bit of similar finagling in the middle, they managed to make it to the last rung. Clif and Henrietta hauled them both over together before Abby and Smith began their trek. With little trouble, both of them made it to the opposite side.

"Well," Henrietta said as she hefted one of the sacks of diamonds into her arms, "time to make our triumphant exit."

"The men will be pleased with this haul," Clif said as he jangled the bag of diamonds he carried.

They stepped through the doorway and mounted the steps leading up to a door. Bright sunshine filtered in through the crack between the stone slabs closing it off.

"I hope there are no puzzles to open this one," Abby chimed in from behind them.

Henrietta shot her a smile over her shoulder before they climbed the last step and leaned against the doors. They burst open into the jungle.

Clif and Henrietta stepped out first, followed by the others. Abby bumped into Henrietta as she stopped short. Her muscles tightened and she swallowed hard, staring down the length of a sharp spear leveled at her chin.

CHAPTER 29

*H*enrietta and Clif leaned backward, their hands rising in the air as the men pressed the spears closer to their faces.

"Hello," Clif tried, earning another poke of the spear at him.

"They do not seem friendly," Henrietta whispered.

"Not at all," Clif answered.

"They are natives from a neighboring village," Carolina answered, pushing forward between her siblings. She bowed her head toward them and uttered a word neither of them understood.

"What are you saying?" Clif inquired.

"I greeted them," she said. "I do not know much more of their language. Our guide speaks with them mostly."

The man crinkled his forehead before saying something back to her.

Carolina winced, holding her palms up in front of her. "I am sorry, I do not speak your language. I was with the group at the Aztec temple."

The man barked something else at her.

"Temple. She used her hands to form a pyramid. Camp. Men." She did her best to speak through her hands and actions.

The man twisted and spoke to another man next to him in their native tongue. The second man shouted to the others with them. A smaller man ran up from the rear of the group, eyeing them.

"Miss Caro," he said with a toothy grin.

"Zuma," she said with a breath of relief. "Hello."

"Miss Caro, are you bad?"

"Certainly not!" Henrietta said, placing her hands on her hips. The man poked the spear in her direction again and she raised her hands up.

"No," Carolina said with a shake of her head. "He does not mean bad. He is questioning if I am in a bad way. No, Zuma. This is my brother and sister."

"Brother," the man said, his dark brows crinkling. His dark eyes lit up, and he pointed at Carolina before wagging his finger at Clif. "Ah, brother! Family."

"Yes," Carolina answered with a nod. "Family." She patted his shoulder, then Henrietta's. "Family."

"Family. Mr. James said bad."

Carolina scrunched her nose and shook her head. "Mr. James is mistaken. Confused. They are not bad."

Zuma narrowed his eyes, sliding them between Carolina, Clif, and Henrietta.

Clif grinned at him, lowering his voice as he turned his head slightly to Carolina. "Tell him we can offer their village diamonds as a peace offering."

"Oh, yes," Carolina said, grabbing a pouch from Clif's hands and shaking a few diamonds from it. "My brother offers these to you to prove himself."

Carolina thrust her hand out. A large diamond sat in her

palm, surrounded by smaller gems. She smiled and nodded, encouraging him to take them.

"Oh!" Zuma said, his eyes going wide. "Diamantés."

"Yes," Carolina said with another nod, "diamonds."

Zuma flicked his gaze to Clif. "You give?"

"Yes," Clif said, "we give these to you to prove our friendship. We mean you no harm. We mean Carolina and her group no harm."

He waved his hands in front of him for a moment before he slowly slid one around Carolina's shoulders and pulled her close to him. "Family."

Zuma nodded and bowed, curling his fingers around the gems. "Family, yes. You and me now family. We care for each other."

"Yes, that's right. And I am quite a good friend to have. If you should run into any trouble, I should be glad to assist you in defending your village."

Zuma cocked his head, placing a finger on his chin. "You help?"

"Yes," Clif answered, "I have helped a number of small villages in the past against men eager to destroy them and steal their riches."

Zuma nodded again and spoke a few words to the men on either side of him. They answered in their native tongue before Zuma pointed at Clif, murmuring more unintelligible words. They all nodded and the men lowered their spears.

Zuma grinned at Clif. "You help."

Clif glanced at Carolina before returning his gaze to the small, dark-skinned man. "What help do you need?"

"A vicious monster hunts near our village. He kills many. You hunt him. Bring back his head. Then we become safe."

"A monster?" Clif repeated.

Zuma's head bobbed up and down quickly. "A large ocelotl."

Clif's forehead wrinkled and he tilted his head, trying to discern the meaning of the word.

Zuma placed two fingers on top of his head and pulled his lips back, barring his teeth. He hissed as he hunched his back and stalked around.

"Oh," Carolina said, her eyes going wide, "ocelotl. That is the word for…" She crinkled her brow as she tried to recall.

"Yes?" Henrietta inquired.

"Cat. Um, it is a cat." She snapped her fingers. "Jaguar. He wishes you to hunt and kill a large jaguar that has been disturbing the village."

"Kill a jaguar?" Henrietta balked. "Wait, why did he not ask James and your party to do this."

"We did," Zuma answered.

"And?" Henrietta demanded.

Zuma grinned at her.

"Why are you staring at me like that? What happened when you asked James's party to kill the jaguar?"

"You make a fine wife. Very brave."

Henrietta shook her head at the small man. "Think again. I have no desire to enter into the bonds of marriage with anyone. Now, why did James's men not handle the jaguar."

"Mr. James too weak," Zuma answered. "He frightened. He cannot hunt."

"Well, at least he has one thing right," Clif said. "Look, Zuma, Henrietta and I will handle this issue for your village. You must promise you will let my men pass with their cargo unscathed and allow James's men to return to their encampment."

Zuma nodded at him. "Yes, yes, yes. Of course, of course."

Clif spun to face his men. "All right, gentleman…and Abby, you heard the man. Straight to the ship with the cargo. Henrietta and I will join you as soon as we have handled the problem." He turned back to Zuma. "We need to find the rest of our men. They are at the entrance to the mines. Can you take us there?"

Zuma agreed and led them through the jungle, emerging where the rest of his sailors knelt on the ground. James, now untied, stood over them with a watchful eye.

He hurried forward as they approached. "Carolina, are you quite all right?"

"I am fine, James. You should not have told these men the pirates are bad."

"But–" he began when Zuma approached the leader of the group. He passed the latest developments along to the party of natives holding the group hostage. They lowered their spears, stepping back from their aggressive stance.

"What are you doing? They are the enemy!" James shouted.

"Sorry, friend," Clif said, clapping him on the shoulder, "not anymore."

"Your men are free to go," Zuma said.

Clif nodded a thank you to him before addressing his group, giving them instructions to return to the ship and ready for departure. They parted ways with James's group returning to their camp with Carolina, the sailors setting off for *The Henton*, and Clif and Henrietta returning to the village with the natives after a promise to visit Carolina before leaving.

After a brief hike through the jungle, they arrived at the small village. Zuma introduced them to the village elder who offered a blessing upon them as they embarked on the dangerous mission.

Zuma pointed out the location where the jaguar had been spotted on several occasions before Clif and Henrietta set off into the jungle.

"How do you propose we track and kill a jaguar?" Henrietta inquired as they trekked through the foliage.

"Carefully," Clif answered.

"Very funny, Clif. I'm serious. We have limited knowledge of this large cat's tendencies."

"Not really. Jaguars tend to be solitary predators. We may stumble upon a nest where they tend to take their prizes. We can lie in wait for it and kill it at an opportune moment."

"Opportune moment?" Henrietta inquired, her nose wrinkled.

"You said you wanted adventure. Are you pleased?"

"I am less pleased about hunting a vicious beast than I was about seeking the diamonds."

Clif held a branch aside, ushering Henrietta through before following her. "I do have some experience in this, you know."

"Oh? Have you hunted wild cats before?"

"Once, in Africa. A small village, quite bothered by the English on numerous occasions was also troubled by a lone lion."

"Don't lions live in packs?"

"Normally, yes. Though the pride had mostly been killed. The lion attacked any human it came across."

"And what happened?"

Clif sliced through a vine as they continued their hike. "I hunted it and killed it."

"You killed a lion?" Henrietta questioned.

Clif shot her a glance. "Don't look so surprised. I am quite adept, you know."

"I've no doubt, though slaying a lion is not a feat I ever imagined for a pirate."

"Sometimes I tell the others I killed it with my bare hands just to make the tale more interesting," he said with a grin.

"Perhaps you should be the writer."

"No, I shall leave that to you. Just remember to have your fictional Black Jack strangle the lion with his bare hands."

"I certainly will," Henrietta said as they entered a small clearing. Her nostrils flared and she covered her nose. "Ugh, what is the stench?"

Clif tugged back a few leaves piled on the ground. Flies buzzed around rotting meat and bones.

"Ugh," Henrietta said, squeezing her eyes shut.

"Looks like we found our nest."

Henrietta glanced around, wrapping her arms around her midriff and shivering.

Clif scanned the area in search of a hiding place. "We will wait here until it returns."

He found a space well-hidden on a large branch in a nearby tree. They scrambled up and settled in for the wait.

Hours passed before they spotted any movement. As the sun descended in the sky, a swishing sound met their ears. The thick leaves of the jungle parted and a large cat stalked into the lair, dropping a maimed animal near the pile of rotten meat and bones.

Clif bit his lower lip, inching forward on the branch with his pistol in his hand. He aimed at the large cat as it nosed through its stash, sending a flurry of flies buzzing through the air.

Clif sucked in a breath, holding it as he cocked the gun. The noise drew the attention of the large cat. It flicked its golden eyes in Clif's direction, its nose sniffing the air. A growl emanated from the beast as it stalked closer.

"Damn it," Clif said, following the cat's movements with his weapon before he fired.

The shot hit the animal in the shoulder, eliciting a cry of pain, but not deterring the animal from defending itself. It barred its teeth, leaping up toward Clif in an attempt to drag him from the branch.

"Stay back, Ri," Clif warned as he unsheathed his sword.

The cat's frantic scrambling shook the branch. Clif

managed to maintain his balance, but Henrietta toppled from the unsteady perch, landing hard on the ground below.

The cat raced toward her as she curled into a ball, shielding her head.

"No!" Clif called, leaping down to the ground below and brandishing his sword.

His shout drew the attention of the wild cat. It spun to face him before flicking its gaze to Henrietta then back to Clif with a hiss, showing its large front fangs.

Clif widened his stance, his sword at the ready as the wounded cat leapt into the air. He danced to the side, but the cat's claws caught him, spinning him around and sending him stumbling backward.

He slashed his sword at the animal, missing it. It turned with lightning-fast reflexes and leapt again, knocking into him before he could thrust his sword.

He tossed the weapon to the side as he focused on shoving the angry cat's head away from him as its jaws snapped open and closed it in an attempt to tear his flesh from his bones.

His features pinched as his muscles struggled to fend off the jaguar's strength. With a shove of his foot against the ground, he rolled the large cat off him, scrambling away as the cat wiggled on the ground before rising to its feet.

Clif rolled toward his sword, grabbing it and reeling back toward the beast. The jaguar leapt at him with a battle cry, knocking the sword from his hand as it slammed into his arm. Clif cried out as the weight of the cat smashed down on him. He struggled to stop the cat from tearing him to pieces.

His heart thudded in his chest as the angry cat's teeth sought to clamp onto any piece of him. He wouldn't survive this, his mind told him. He only hoped to give Henrietta enough time to escape. In his struggle, he wasn't certain if she'd already fled, but he hoped so. If he could distract the cat long enough, she could disappear and hopefully find her way back to the village or the camp.

The cat snarled and hissed as it snapped at Clif's face, each strike coming closer and closer to sinking into his flesh as his muscles began to tire.

He winced as he braced for the inevitable pain, his eyes squeezing shut when the cat let out a squeal. Clif popped his eyes open as blood trickled down on him. The animal cried out as it stumbled to the side, staggering with each step.

Clif kicked his legs out, scrambling backward in search of his sword as the animal limped away before giving them another hiss. He shot his eyes sideways, his jaw falling open as he spotted Henrietta, sword tinged in blood, standing beside him.

She gave him a nod before she offered her arm to pull him to his feet. He made short work of the wounded animal, ending its pain and retrieving the token requested by the village as proof of their safety.

As they trudged back through the jungle toward the small village, Clif asked, "Why did you not run, Ri? That animal could have killed you."

"Or you," she said, flicking her gaze to his moonlit features. "Did you really believe I would leave you?"

"It may have been better if you had. Had I lost the battle, you would have been its next victim."

"I was there to ensure you did not. We are a team. Unstoppable when we work together."

Clif offered her a smirk and a head shake as they approached the village, going directly to the village elder's tent. After declining to stay for a celebration to honor them, they returned to the encampment near the Aztec temple.

The moon still shone down as they approached, finding Carolina pacing the pathway between the tents.

"Carolina," Clif whispered as they approached.

Carolina raced toward them, flinging her arms around them both as tears escaped her eyes. "I did not believe you would return."

"Of course, we would," Clif answered. "We did not have the chance to say goodbye before we sailed."

Carolina let her gaze fall to her feet as she lowered her arms.

"Carolina, are you quite all right?" Henrietta inquired.

"I will miss you both greatly."

"We will visit again," Clif promised with a squeeze of his sister's arm.

"But when?" Carolina asked, a sob breaking her voice.

"We shall visit as soon as you return home," Henrietta answered.

Carolina sniffled, wiping at her cheeks and offering a weak nod.

Henrietta flicked a gaze toward Clif before addressing her sister again. "Carolina, are you certain you are all right here?"

"I will miss you both. Terribly."

"Come with us," Henrietta said, pushing a lock of hair behind her sister's ear.

Carolina hesitated for a moment before shaking her head. "I couldn't."

"Why?"

She snapped her gaze up to Henrietta, her features scrunching with emotion. "I am a married woman. I have made my choices."

"Do not let a poor choice dictate the rest of your life, Carolina," Henrietta answered.

Carolina wrapped her arms around her midriff, stalking away from them. "It was not a poor choice."

"Then why are you so sad?" Henrietta asked.

"I told you," Carolina said, spinning to face her, "I will miss you both terribly."

"And that is all?"

Carolina lowered her eyes, her features pinching again. "Please let us leave it at that." Tears fell to her cheeks again.

Clif pulled her into his arms, pressing her head against his chest.

"We will leave it at that as long as you promise that James has not harmed you."

Carolina pulled back from Clif, wiping at her cheeks again as she gave a slight shake to her head.

"Carolina," Clif said, cupping her face in his hands, "if he has laid a hand on you, you must tell us."

A rustling drew their attention to one of the tents. James stepped from within, narrowing his eyes at the scene.

"I must go," Carolina said, sidestepping the question. She pulled them both into a tight embrace. "Promise me you will be safe."

"We promise," Henrietta answered, giving her sister a squeeze.

Carolina's features melted into a mask of tears as she nodded and turned to stride away.

"I do not like this," Clif said as they watched her duck into the tent with James.

"Neither do I, but she is a grown woman. And a married one. She must make her own choices. We cannot force her to do as we wish."

"The last time I left my sister with a man she should not have been with it nearly ended in disaster."

"Let us hope that does not happen this time."

Clif stared at the tent flap, his fingers wrapping around the butt of his pistol.

Henrietta laid a hand on his arm. "Clif, we should go. We will monitor her closely."

Clif's jaw flexed as he stared for another moment at the

tent before stepping away and offering a silent prayer for his younger sister.

* * *

Henrietta tipped the chair backward as she sipped at her ale, her feet kicked up on the table.

Abby entered the tavern, scanning it before hurrying across toward her. She flung her hand up in a salute. "Captain! Everything is prepared."

A smirk formed on Henrietta's lips, and she set the mug down on the table after one last sip before she rose to stand. They stalked out into the night air and down to the dock. *The Henton* bobbed in the water. Henrietta and Abby continued past it, walking to the end of the floating dock and staring up at a larger vessel.

"What do you think? Too big?" Henrietta asked, her arms crossed.

"I think you shall need a bigger feather in your cap, Captain," Abby said with a grin, her hands set on her hips.

"Another feathered cap?" Clif inquired as he strode up from behind them. "I dare say you can afford it with the haul we had."

"That and much more, brother," Henrietta said, shooting a gaze at her brother before returning it to the vessel in front of her.

"That's quite a ship," Clif said.

"Indeed."

"*The Grandmistress*. It is quite grand," Clif noted.

A smile crossed Henrietta's lips at the statement.

Clif glanced down at her. "Why do you look so pleased with yourself, Ri?"

"Because I am."

"Oh?"

"What would you say about expanding our interests?"

"Expanding them? Do you mean another adventure?"

"In a way," Henrietta answered. "*The Henton* feels a bit crowded, wouldn't you say?"

"I hadn't thought of it, really. I am quite happy there."

"But wouldn't you be happier with more than that?"

Clif shot a glance at the large ship floating in front of them. "Are you saying you wish to get rid of *The Henton* in favor of something larger?"

"No," she said with a shake of her head, "I am saying we should not sail one ship. We should sail a fleet of ships."

"A fleet of ships?"

"Two ships, in particular. One for you and one for me."

"Your own ship?" Clif asked. "What's wrong with mine?"

"Well, ours, but there you have it. It is yours. And so it should be."

"So, you want your own ship?"

"Not want," Henrietta corrected, her eyes flicking to the large vessel, "have."

Clif's jaw dropped open. "Have? Have you purchased this ship?"

Henrietta raised her chin and puffed out her chest. "I have. I am the captain of *The Grandmistress*."

"Ri!" Clif said, shock still apparent on his face. He closed his mouth, turning it into a pout. "I thought you liked sailing with me."

"I do. And I plan to. Two ships. A fleet. No one will stop us," she answered, with a slight bow to him, "Commodore Nichols."

Clif glanced up at the other ship, his frown changing into a smile. "Commodore. I think I like that."

Henrietta threaded her arm through his and tugged him forward. "Then come aboard and allow me to show you the second ship in your fleet and we can begin to plan the next adventure."

THE END
(But there's more to come!)

* * *

The series continues in 2024! If you love Clif & Ri, you can find them in *Ghosts, Lore & a House on the Shore*, Book 1 in the Lily & Cassie on the Sea Mysteries.

* * *

Let's keep in touch! Sign up for my newsletter (and get three free books!).

A NOTE FROM THE AUTHOR

Dear Reader,

Thank you for reading this book! *A Pirate's Life for Ri* continues the pirate adventure series I wrote on a whim!

I hope you enjoyed reading this book as much as I did writing it! If you loved it, please consider leaving a review and help get the book into the hands of other interested readers.

Book 3 in this series isn't available yet, but look for it coming in 2024! In the meantime, you can read more about Clif and Henrietta in the series that gave birth to their story. *Ghosts, Lore & a House by the Shore* is available now!

If you'd like to stay up to date with all my news, be the first to find out about new releases first, sales and get free offers, join the Nellie H. Steele's Mystery Readers' Group! Or sign up for my newsletter now!

All the best, Nellie

OTHER SERIES BY NELLIE H. STEELE

Cozy Mystery Series

Cate Kensie Mysteries
Lily & Cassie by the Sea Mysteries
Pearl Party Mysteries
Middle Age is Murder Cozy Mysteries

Supernatural Suspense/Urban Fantasy

Shadow Slayers Stories
Duchess of Blackmoore Mysteries
Shelving Magic

Adventure

Maggie Edwards Adventures
Clif & Ri on the Sea